ELIZABETH KINGSTON

Fair, Bright and Terrible

To Amanda, with eternal
thanks - and a reminder
to always be bold.

xoxo

EKingston

This is a work of fiction. Similarities to real people, places, or
events are entirely coincidental.

FAIR, BRIGHT, AND TERRIBLE

First edition. January 26, 2017.

ISBN: 1542508924
ISBN-13: 978-1542508926

For Tommy

CONTENTS

HISTORICAL NOTE

In the reign of Henry III of England, Simon de Montfort led a rebellion of barons that, for a time, took power away from the crown and gave it to a parliamentary body. In 1265, an alliance of Marcher lords (who were allied with King Henry's son - Edward I) fought to oust Montfort and return power to the king.

During this time of unrest and for many years following, the Welsh, led by Llewellyn, fought against the English for the independent sovereignty of Wales. These struggles culminated in a final Welsh rebellion in 1282, during which Llewellyn lost his life and Edward I conquered Wales definitively.

<u>WELSH WORDS</u>
cariad: darling, love
ab/*ap*: son of
ferch: daughter of

<u>PRONUNCIATIONS</u>
Dafydd: Davith
Eluned: Ell-*in*-id
Gwenllian: Gwen-*lee*-an
Lascaux: Lasko
Rhys: Reese
Ruardean: Roo-ar-*deen*

Who is she that cometh forth as the morning rising,
Fair as the moon, bright as the sun, terrible as an
army set in battle array?

                       - Song of Solomon 6:10

Chapter 1

The Bodies

It all ended in cold flesh. This prince, the war, and every life: it ended in cold flesh, no matter how hot the blood that had once pounded through it. She had always known this, of course. But there is knowing a thing, and then there is feeling the truth of it cut you open and close around your heart.

Eluned had come to London when winter still held, before the thaw rendered the sight more gruesome, to behold the face of her own defeat. She wanted to look upon it before there was nothing but a skull on a spike above the city. But it was too high to see much and the flesh was discolored, his features obscured by his tangled hair. Even still it almost made her wish she could weep, to see this bloodied scrap of Llewellyn, last true Prince of Wales.

It took only a moment to close her eyes in a brief prayer of thanksgiving that God had taken Llewellyn's beloved wife first. King Edward was the kind of man who might have forced that poor girl to look at this ugly trophy. Behold, he would say. This is the end that awaits my enemies.

Eluned pulled her hood closer around her face, staring up at the lifeless eyes. This might have been her own end. It might have been her daughter's.

"Better we are gone from here before any remark how long you look at him, my lady." It was Tegwarad who spoke low, his eyes scanning the half-empty street while his hand rested carefully near his dagger. He was one of her guard. He was Welsh, but smart enough not to speak it here.

"Do any stare at me in wonder?" she asked, still looking up at the face she had come to see. "Do they whisper their suspicion of the lady who seems to pay homage to the rebel?"

"Nay, my lady," came the answer. "Not yet."

"You will tell me when they do, and then shall I be gone from here. Not a minute before."

She kept her voice mild. At least she thought she did. Many times in the month since she had learned of Llewellyn's death, she had found that her perception did not match reality. Always in small ways, like this. It should worry her. Certainly she had not shouted, she reasoned, as she memorized the precise curl of Llewellyn's hair where it fell on his forehead. Had there been anger in her voice? Impatience? She could not say for certain, and Llewellyn did not provide an opinion.

Tomorrow she would be forty, and today she spoke in her head to a dead man, asking if her voice had been too sharp. A frail mind and a hard heart, is that what age did to her? She had thought she might wail at this sight, this evidence that all her hopes were ended. Yet she did not wail or weep, nor even feel despair. She only felt empty, and tired.

"I am told it was the Mortimers who betrayed him, that they did lay a trap."

She heard Tegwarad's grunt of mild interest beside her. He waited, but when she did not speak again he moved from her side to give her privacy. She did not follow to tell him that she believed there was more betrayal in store for those who continued fighting. Now the Welsh nobles would turn on each other. The war went on, with some Welsh still fighting despite the death of their prince, under the banner of Llewellyn's brother Dafydd. She knew they would not succeed, even were there not betrayal in store. It did not need skill in the art of war, nor knowledge of the enemy's plan, to see that without Llewellyn they were lost.

"Truly, I had thought of that," she whispered now. It was not an apology. She was not penitent. She had known that Dafydd would never unite the Welsh. She had known that if Llewellyn fell, there must be another to take his place in command of their hearts. She, and only she, had planned for that. "It was a sound plan. But it failed. I failed."

The only answer was a winter wind that stung her eyes. It didn't matter anymore. There would be more fighting and dying, more cruelty and destruction. She must watch all of it come to ruin despite her foresight, despite a lifetime of effort. Now the only thing to do was to sit very still in the safe place she had fashioned for herself, and wait for it to be over.

For soon it would be over. This was the beginning of the end, and all ended in cold flesh. Be it scattered on the ground after battle, or leering down from a spike high above London, or shivering beneath the cloak of a hopeless Welshwoman, it all ended in cold, cold flesh.

✠ ✠ ✠

Over the next months, the losses came regularly. First came word that Dinwen, the stronghold that in her childhood she had called home, had fallen to the English. Her brother, who had once eaten so many apples that he had been sick all over her best shoes – that impetuous boy had become a man who had ruled the place and died in the assault. His son and heir was taken to Edward, where he would swear fealty and beg the king's pardon. He was a small enough fish that mercy was like to be given, in exchange for all his lands and wealth. Thus would end centuries of her family's rule in Wales, though their bards could sing a history of twenty-two generations in power. The lands they had held when Romans claimed this island as their own – all of it would now be called England.

She sat in her solar and wondered how long until they were forgotten. Her family would be dead history, covered over by time, nothing but a vague and faceless group labelled "savage Welsh" to be dismissed by the English who usurped their place. Long ago she had tried to close her heart to it. By giving her in marriage to a Norman lord, her family made her more Norman than Welsh. It was tradition that a wife take on her husband's nationality.

And so she told herself as she sat, decades after the wedding that had made her a Norman lady, in the room where she had birthed Norman children to a

Norman lord. It was there that word came to her from an abbess, telling her of the burning of the church at St. Anian and the murder of the monks there. Among those slaughtered was Adda, who had served as her father's personal cleric and had fed her wild strawberries and who told her, when her mother died, about the glories of Heaven. The news of it sent a pain through her heart, and she knelt for hours in the chapel to pray for his sweet soul. She prayed too for the many other innocents who were murdered by looting soldiers, only because Edward's forces knew there would be no reprisal. The king would claim the scorched land as his own, build a new castle over the bones of the dead, and call it good.

"Prince Dafydd is captured, my lady," said a voice that came to her sometime in the summer, as she sat in her solar in the keep of Ruardean.

She looked up to see Edmund, physician of the keep and old advisor to her husband's family. It was strange this news should come from him, but when she looked about her she saw others watching her warily. They knew, then, how this mattered to her, and had decided Edmund should be the one to voice it.

Eluned forced herself to inhabit the present fully, to listen to these words that she had known would be spoken. It was almost over. Llewellyn was fallen; his brother Dafydd had carried on but now was captured.

"Then it is done," she said. "Does he live?"

"He lives and is taken to King Edward, my lady," replied Edmund. "There is also word of a bloody skirmish near to us here at Ruardean, just west. Even now they fight."

Now she saw the man next to him – only a boy,

5

really, with a scanty beard on his cheek and so covered in mud and weariness that she wondered he was still upright. She took the cup of wine that one of her ladies held out to her and came forward to thrust it under his nose.

"Drink," she commanded him, and he obeyed. She drew a long and steady breath, feeling the air trickle slow and heavy into her chest, pressing it all out again before she was ready to speak. "What news do you bring me of this fighting so near to us?"

"Only a half-day's ride from this keep, my lady. I am sent to you by Rhys ab Owain, who begs you will send whatever aid you are able."

Rhys ab Owain. Her uncle. He who was more like a father to her than her own father had been. He had danced at her wedding, and pinched her cheek and declared her to possess the keenest wits in the family. She made herself stand still and look at the boy squarely, though all of her wanted to turn her face away.

"Does Rhys know that Dafydd is taken, that the larger host is fallen into English hands?"

The boy nodded. "He has heard rumors of it, but was not certain of their truth."

Of long habit, her mind immediately set to calculating. Whence the news of Dafydd's capture, and what was the likelihood it was true? How much time might they have, how many men might be needed, against whom did Rhys fight and with what numbers?

But in less time than it took to think these thoughts, she had already dismissed them. None of it mattered. All had been lost when Llewellyn's head had been cut from his shoulders, months ago. There was no aid she could send now to change the course of things, and no careful scheming would save them.

Now would come the blood-soaked details that followed decisive victory. She must endure it.

"Tomorrow we will ride out," she announced, "to ask my uncle in God's name to lay down arms and submit himself to the king's mercy. Master Edmund, you will send him this message today and then prepare such remedies as may be needed to tend the wounded tomorrow."

The messenger boy looked caught between a sob and a shout of protest. "In a day there will be no wounded, only dead!"

She sat down to her embroidery again, a cool dismissal. She put in stitches that later she would have to pluck out, so disordered were they, and spoke to the nearest servant. "Bring this boy to the kitchens and give him his fill of meat and drink."

It was as her fingers traced over the green ivy, embroidered at the cloth's edge, that she had a thought that stopped her. Vines and leaves curled at the border and made her think of quiet forests where her daughter had camped with the fighting men of Ruardean. It had ever pleased her, to think of that. To know how safe her child had been under the open sky with faithful companions by her side.

"Stop," she called too loudly. The boy turned to face her again. "Are there other of my kinsmen who fight with my Uncle Rhys?"

"His son," came the answer, and she was standing, the embroidery frame clattering at her feet as she stared at him.

Every person in the room stared back at her as the sound echoed. For a moment she had no command of her tongue. It seemed to her that her skin grew tight, that it could not contain her, that she would split open and everything inside her would spill out before their eyes. And what use would that be? What use was she at all, anymore?

She slid a look to Master Edmund, who seemed a decade older than he had been a moment ago.

"We go now," she said in a voice like a whip, and watched the flurry of activity as they hastened to obey her. Vincent came forward, who commanded the knights of Ruardean. "A mission of mercy only," she told him with a hard edge in her voice. "Any man who would dare to enter the fight, whether for England or for Wales, I will see him hanged ere the next rising of the sun."

"Aye, my lady. But it will go hard, if he calls on them to aid him."

She looked at him, her eyes scanning his face to find signs that he was loyal to her. It was not loyalty that mattered most now, though. He was sworn to Ruardean and so would obey her as far as he was able, she was sure of it. But his heart did not belong to her.

"You will tell them what I tell you now," she said, her voice low and clear. "All that I do in these dark days has but one purpose: to safeguard the lives and fortunes of my children. This course was chosen by my daughter, who commanded you to serve me. If you would honor her command, if you would keep her safe, you will not draw steel for any reason."

He nodded once, his face grim as he went to gather the men.

It was nearing nightfall when they came on the place where the fighting now was ended. From the rise above the valley, they could see how the swarm of English soldiers had won swiftly and decisively over the handful of doomed Welsh. The victors would have cut the throats of many Welsh survivors had Eluned not hastened to stop them. She used the advantage she had as a highborn lady, wife to a Marcher lord, whose vast lands lay but a mile from where these Welshmen lay dying. "I am the lady of Ruardean, and it is my wish," she said in a voice that would cause emperors to hesitate, and soon the priests she had brought with her were permitted to go among them and administer last rites.

She had not even asked her uncle's fate yet, when he was brought to her. Two of her men had found Rhys amid the carnage, and carried him across the field to lay him at her feet. She bade them raise the pavilion around her, a simple structure meant for quick shelter during travel, three sides and a roof. All the while she stood looking down at the chest that did not move with indrawn breath, the killing arrow that lodged behind an ear. Only when the canvas was raised around them did she kneel beside him.

"You lived to be an old man, Uncle Rhys. I am glad of it," she whispered to him. She had last seen him nearly ten years ago. Now every hair was gray, every inch of his face wrinkled. An old lion, who had guarded her in her childhood with a ferocity she had taken for granted. "I am sorry. I am sorry." For staying safe in her fortress while he died in a field. For all her miscalculations. For failing. "I am sorry."

The sun sank low in the sky and she had them bring a torch, and water so that she might wash him. The English commander, whose name she could not keep in her head, made noises about treason and the threat of excommunication until she told him that

9

unless the Pope himself came to prevent it, her uncle would be anointed and buried in consecrated ground. As this English nobody could not boast a personal correspondence with the Holy Father – and she could – the matter was quickly settled.

The blood was barely washed from his face when she heard the men shout, struggling to bring in another body. Eluned did not turn, knowing who they had found and not wanting to see his corpse. Not yet. But then came Master Edmund's voice, calling urgently for mead and light, telling them to be gentle as they carried him under the shelter. It was no corpse.

She turned from his father to him. His chest labored to bring in air, his gray eyes unfocused. "Madog," she said, and clasped his hand to her breast.

His swift look told her everything, the wild hope in it as he rolled his eyes toward her and the keen disappointment when he saw she was not her daughter. Then came the twitch at the corner of his mouth that was almost a smile, to acknowledge that he had been foolish to hope it. She felt her own face mirror the expression. No, she was not her daughter. But they would make do nonetheless.

"Eluned," he rasped in a voice much diminished. "God curse you if you have dared to aid us in battle."

"Nay," she answered, and did not trust her voice to say more. For here was her daughter's greatest friend, ally and companion, who even in this moment thought only of her daughter's survival and not his own. Eluned looked at the pale face and the hard gray eyes above the tangle of beard, but saw an awkward boy on the cusp of manhood who had sworn to her in all his grave solemnity that his life was her daughter's to command. In all the years that had covered his smooth cheek with wiry beard, never had he sworn fealty to any other.

His hand in hers gave a hard squeeze, demanding that she speak.

"Gwenllian is safe, far from here. Nor is there any danger to her from my actions this day or any other day, by Mary do I swear it."

It was true. She would not dishonor him with lies in any case, but in this she would bend all her will to reassuring him. King Edward might once have suspected Ruardean's loyalty to the crown – and the loyalty of Gwenllian's husband, and Gwenllian herself – but the king could not doubt now that the Welsh rebellion had nothing to do with any of them. Eluned's scheme to join the uprising had been thwarted years ago, and she had let it die. After so many months of watching the fight from afar, she would not rush in now at the moment when all was lost.

She broke his gaze to look at Master Edmund. The old man had stopped his examination of Madog, on whose body there was no sign of serious injury. His leg, perhaps – it was at an odd angle. She opened her mouth to ask what remedies they might have need of, only to feel a sick twist in her gut when Edmund gave a faint shake of his head. She knew better than to question the physician's knowledge of unseen wounds.

"Will you take mead, Madog ap Rhys?" Master Edmund asked, and the question left no doubt.

"Aye, and I will hope it is your best brew. I would have that taste in my mouth at my last hour."

They sat him up only a little, resting against

Edmund's knees, so that he could drink it. The men of Ruardean came by, one after another, to clasp his hand and bid him farewell. When they stood lined up beside him he turned his head, Eluned's hand still in his grasp, and saw his father Rhys lying there.

"I came to fight by his side because I knew she would scorn to see me idle. Eluned -" A weak and wheezing cough broke off his words. His hand grasped hers tighter, pulling her face close to his. "I fought where she could not."

"As you ever did," she affirmed.

"It…is a good death," he said, his eyes turning in his father's direction again.

She did not contradict him. There was no use in saying that she had come to believe there was no such thing as a good death. There was only death, and it was always foul, and served no purpose but to clear way for new souls who would die in their turn. She could find no worthy purpose in any of it, until Madog looked at her and spoke again.

"God has blessed me, to send you here in my last hour. Your eyes are her eyes." His voice was fading to almost nothing now. She was sure his pain was great, but he did not break her gaze.

"Would you have me tell her aught, Madog?" she asked him.

A look of amusement passed over his features. "Nay. There is no more to say but that we have been true friends. I only regret my death is not in service to her. For I would -" He drew a sharp breath, swallowed. "Happily would I have died for her."

"I know it. Is certain she knows it too." She felt his eyes searching hers. It was a look so filled with affection that she knew it was not meant for her, and it caused a new thought to come to her. It was so unlikely, but she had learned that it was impossible to predict everything, to see all. So she asked it. "Did you love her, Madog?"

She saw that he knew the kind of love she meant. Amusement came over his face again. He opened his mouth to draw breath and speak. But as she watched, the life left his eyes. He died with his mouth open and half-smiling, gazing into her eyes.

The men did not wail. They did not bemoan his fate or curse his killers, but they wept openly. They embraced each other, a tight knot of grief and friendship at his side, apart from her.

Tomorrow she would bring the bodies to the priory for burial. She would have the monks say a thousand masses for the repose of their souls. But tonight she washed them clean of mud and blood, rubbed them with fragrant oils, and covered them in fresh herbs before laying clean linen over them. When it was done, long past midnight, she sat on the ground between them and called on her bard to sing the history of their house.

Her left hand held her uncle's hand, her right hand held Madog's, as the bard ended with verses devoted to their great heroism. She remembered her uncle's deep voice in song, his roar of laughter. She remembered the first time Madog had lost in a fight with her daughter. The memory of that look he had worn, of mingled dismay and pride and surprise, almost brought her to laughter as she held his still hand in hers. What a life he had lived, and so much of it at her bidding.

"How long does love live on, Madog, when it goes unfed?" she whispered into the empty night air. It was a stupid question, of course. Likely he had loved Gwenllian as a brother, no more. She did not know what he would have answered. She would never know. He would never speak again. "Does it ever die, or is it only hidden and starving in the dark?"

She watched sparks escape from the torch and fly up into the blackness of the night as she sat next to them and waited for dawn, holding their cold flesh next to hers.

✠ ✠ ✠

The letter from King Edward came when summer was ended. It was Walter, her husband, who was named in the message that said a parliament would be held at Shrewsbury. But unlike the king, who had returned from the Holy Land ten years ago, her husband still wandered half-mad among the Hospitaller knights at Acre.

"And so we are sent this message," she observed to her husband's brother, "though Edward knows Ruardean cannot send its lord to speak in this parliament. Why think you he would do such a thing?"

She knew the answer. She thought she did, but her mind was so clouded these days that she had learned not to trust it. Many times she would wonder why her commands were ignored, only to discover she had never said the words out loud. Last week she had sat down to finish the embroidery of an altar cloth but found that it had been done and gifted to the bishop the week before, though she had no memory of it.

"Is certain the king only wishes Ruardean to be informed of such a gathering," said Richard. "It is intended as a courtesy."

Richard was an idiot. Her mind truly was disordered, if she thought he might see something she did not. She must try to make him understand it.

"It is the trial of Prince Dafydd, for the crime of treason. Writs have been sent to many other earls and barons, summoning them to sit judgment." Such was the news that had reached her, and it spoke to the seriousness of Edward's intent. "This is not courtesy. It is a pointed invitation to view the spectacle. I will go to Shrewsbury."

So she did as she was sure the king wanted, though Edward himself stayed a careful distance from the events at Shrewsbury. It was clever in a way that was new in her experience of him, giving the illusion that the outcome of the trial was the will of the people and not his own. It was a smart bit of political maneuvering. At last this king's head seemed fit for its crown.

Dafydd was found guilty of treason and more, in less than a day. She watched as they brought the prisoner up to the hall to hear his sentence proclaimed, and listened as he declared himself Prince of Wales. It was foolish pride that would not save him. But then, nothing would.

His sentence was to first be dragged by a horse through the streets of Shrewsbury. For murder, he would be hanged. But he would be cut down alive so that he may be disemboweled for the crime of sacrilege. For treason, his head would be struck off. And for the benefit of any who would dare such rebellion again, his body would be cut into four pieces and sent to the corners of the realm.

She listened to the people in the hall exclaim and

gasp in horror at the torture that was planned for a prince. It was barbaric. She had never heard of such a punishment, yet it did not shock her so deeply. King Edward had something to say to reluctant subjects, and he had found a way to be certain his message was heard. Oh, how cunning had this king become.

Eluned made sure she was seen in the crowd surrounding the gallows. She kept her face blank while she watched them pull the rope tight about Dafydd's neck. *Wales is no more*, she thought, as the executioner picked up the knife. She was careful never to look away from any part of it, so that any spies for King Edward would be able to tell him she saw it all. She could not stop the look of disgust that crossed her face when they burned his entrails before him, but at least she did not weep at all.

There is no more Wales, she said to herself as they hacked his body into quarters. It was Edward's message, and it resounded through her easily, nothing left to impede its echo. *Wales is no more.*

She repeated it to herself as she made her way back to Ruardean. One day, perhaps, it would feel more real. Right now nothing felt real except for the cold. She was glad that winter would come soon, relieved that finally there was an end to the parade of death and loss that had marched through her life in these last months. It was over. Now she could stop anticipating the worst.

And of course that was when the last blows came.

One day she looked up from where she sat staring out the solar window, pondering where love went when it vacated a heart, to find her son standing there.

"Mother, do you not make yourself ill?" He looked

with concern at the open window, where she sat with the chill air flowing over her face.

He was nearly grown to manhood now. She forced herself to count the years and realized he was sixteen years old. They had last seen each other two years ago, when she had visited him at Lancaster's court. She had given him to Lancaster's household for training, to be reared as a knight and lord in her husband's absence. This had been her husband's command. It had made her son a stranger to her. In exchange for giving her son entirely to the Norman way, she had claimed her daughter's life and destiny. It had seemed a fair enough bargain, until now. Now, when both son and daughter were lost to her.

"William," she said, rousing herself from the numbness she had gratefully sunk into for months. "I am well."

It was not a lie, nor was it truth. Nor was it an answer to the question he had asked, she realized, as he crossed to her with a look of concern on his face. She rose to meet him, and he held her shoulders as he bent to kiss her cheek. He was tall like his father, like his sister. For all the influence of Lancaster's worldly household, William seemed to grope clumsily for words. He must be thinking he should offer her comfort on the loss of her brother, her uncle, her cousin, her country. She spoke quickly to prevent it.

"Why are you come to Ruardean? You should have sent word of your coming."

"I rode to meet Brother Dominic on his journey here." At her uncertain look, he gave her shoulders a gentle squeeze. "I would escort my father home."

She could not ever remember being so paralyzed with amazement. It had been fourteen years since

Walter had taken the cross and left for the Holy Land. The only word she ever had of him came through Brother Dominic, one of the Hospitaller knights who tolerated his ravings. For nearly half her marriage, her husband had wandered through Antioch telling anyone who would listen that he saw angels and devils. Sometimes he was lucid, more often not, and whether he was raving or calm he declared to the patient Hospitallers that he would not come home to England until men of Christ ruled Jerusalem.

She had taken this as assurance she would never suffer his presence again, and blasphemously hoped the Muslims would hold the Holy Land so long as she lived.

And they did. Yet William said he was come home.

Now she remembered the letter she had ignored. She had not wanted to hear again about her husband's madness, preferring to dwell instead on thoughts of those lost things she had loved. So she had told the cleric to leave it unopened. It still waited for her, gathering dust instead of preparing her for her husband's return.

"He is in the chapel," said William, and she went forward, avoiding his offered arm and his sympathetic look. Her son seemed to think she was frail, in body or in mind. Perhaps she would be, soon, if she must play wife to Walter once more.

When they stepped into the chapel there was only her own confessor and an unfamiliar man in a red surcoat with a white cross emblazoned on it. He was Brother Dominic, and he spoke in hushed tones about the long journey and the will of God while her eyes scanned the room. Walter was nowhere to be seen.

Finally, she noticed them all looking toward a jeweled box before the altar, and began to understand.

"Do you tell me he is dead?"

Their confusion and hesitation told her that this too was in the letter she had refused to read. Before she could stop it, a bark of laughter burst from her. "This is Walter? This is my husband come home?"

She threw off their hands and walked to the chest. It was too small for a body, and she turned to them in question.

"His bones," said Brother Dominic. And she laughed again, a reaction that seemed perfectly rational to her, yet clearly alarmed them. She must be careful or they would think his madness had transferred to her. She bit her lips together, trying to stem the hilarity that gripped her as the man explained. "My lady, he did say to lay his heart in the Holy Land, and his bones in England. But when we found him, there were only the bones to bring on the long journey here."

"You are satisfied it is him?" What a merry jest it would be, to think him dead when he was not. "You are sure?"

"The men who found him as he lay dying in the desert knew him. They made a cairn for him, and described the place to us so that we might find him and give him a Christian burial." He held out his hand to William, and she saw Walter's ring in it. "He was well known to many in that land, lady. There is no mistake."

She ran a hand over the garnets that studded the top of the chest.

She said, "You will leave me. All of you. I would

be alone with my husband one more time."

They did, and she felt a twinge of regret at the forlorn look that came over William as the others ushered him out. But he would have time enough with these bones, more than he ever had with his father alive.

She knelt next to the chest and lifted the heavy lid. There was a square of embroidered silk to pull away and then there were his bones, a pile of thick sticks.

"I wonder what killed you in the end," she said to them. "Did you think you would join your angels at last?"

The bones of his hand lay against the rib cage. She remembered the strength of them, clasped hard on her jaw as he shouted that she must guard against Satan, compelling her to beg the Virgin to guide her soul. It was a lifetime ago, but she remembered the strength of him.

"Haps I deserved it, for the sin I committed," she said to his bones. It was so long ago. She could look back now and see the long string of consequences that came from his actions then. Not all were bad. And yet the anger in her was not dulled. The resentment still rose up in her on a great wave of bile.

She let a stream of spittle fall from her lips into the place where his eye would have been. "Forgiveness is for God," she told him. "I am but a woman."

She slid the lid back onto the chest, satisfied at the scraping sound of it, the echo it made as it closed him up alone in a dark little box.

✚ ✚ ✚

Later, William came and found her in her solar

again, where she stared out the window into the frigid air. He spoke and she made herself attend his words. He said he was old enough and would assume his place now, as lord of Ruardean. Lancaster, the king's brother, would counsel him well. Indeed he was to marry Lancaster's little daughter, was that not happy news?

Eluned looked at him, unable to muster any care for her son's ambitions. She only heard that she would no longer rule Ruardean. It was the last thing left to her, and now it too was lost. The cold air wafted her veil as he spoke and she began to accept that she had lived too long.

"I will go and live among the sisters of Saint Anne," she said. It would suit her better than any alternative she could think of.

"Nay, you must marry again," answered her son. And he began to detail the careful plan that would bring them yet more lands and fortune, and secure an even greater place for him among Edward's nobles.

She only looked at him, distantly noting that this was the only time in her life that she did not even want to think of how this might be used to further her own aims. She had no aims to further, anymore.

How unexpected, that this son had inherited from her a talent she had not passed on to her daughter. He could calculate and scheme, see advantages and opportunities where others only saw obstacles. The world was a chess board, and he a budding master of the game. Even now, when she did not respond to these grand plans, he saw her reluctance and shrewdly adjusted his approach to leave room for her refusal. He allowed that endowing an abbey might in time bear fruit almost as plentiful as this marriage scheme, did she not wish to marry again.

"Who do you think to marry me to?" she asked.

"Robert de Lascaux."

The name was nothing to her in the moment she heard it, and then a breath later it was everything. She wanted to laugh again, she wanted to weep. Her whole world taken from her, and Robert de Lascaux offered up in its place. Eighteen years too late.

She did not need count them to know. Eighteen years.

"You will give me tonight to consider which course is best. In the morning, I will tell you my decision."

Her son was not quite yet the lord he meant to be, for he easily obeyed her unspoken command to leave her now. She went back to her chair before the window, where a servant was pulling a tapestry over the casement to block the icy wind that now flowed in.

"Stop. You will leave it open."

"But my lady Eluned," protested one of her ladies with concern. "Night falls. You will be chilled to the bone."

"Leave it," she commanded, and sat there remembering long into the night, calling up the past and examining the future, staring at the stars in the black sky until the cold reached her heart.

Chapter 2

The Lover

"Yes," he said, a word that leaped out of him, loud and eager. Belatedly, he realized that no one had exactly posed a question to him, so he clarified. "I will marry her, and gladly."

He endured the incredulous look of his brother and the slightly stunned look of his friend, simply by avoiding them. Instead he watched his father, whose mouth had fallen open for the briefest of moments before snapping shut. The amazed look was replaced with suspicion.

"Is this mockery?" His father's voice was full of warning. "I have no patience for your jesting in this, Robert."

"It is no jest." He stopped himself from saying more, suddenly conscious he might reveal more than he wanted. Instead he gave his best imitation of a self-deprecating smile. "Can I not obey my father without

I am mistrusted, at least once each decade?"

His brother Simon gave a snort from the corner of the darkened room. "But once in your life would be welcome."

"Then you should rejoice at my assent, and end this frowning." He took a step to reach the door, stuck his head outside and called for a servant to bring more wine. "To celebrate," he said. To soothe the shock for the others, he thought. To steady his own shaking hands.

"The match will bring you land and connections, but none can say if it will bring you an heir," warned his father with a speculative look. "She is old. If your brother is correct in his guess at King Edward's intent, there is fair chance you can gain a title from it, though. I would call that incentive enough for any man, if the man were not you."

Robert drank his wine carefully. He wished he could gulp it down, but that would too easily reveal his agitation. He tried to remember the mind-numbing details his father and brother had given only moments ago, before announcing that the best path forward was for Robert to marry at last. There were some lands that had belonged to a minor Welsh lord, a castle that had fallen, a woman freshly widowed whose inheritance included a large estate that was perfectly located for... well, for some endeavor that was vitally important to his father. But when he heard who this land-holding widow was, he lost the ability to think beyond her name.

Eluned. It sang along his veins, drove out all thought and replaced it with a wash of golden memories. He heard her name and in the next breath there was only the smell of fresh earth and the sound of bright laughter, the white flash of her thigh rising up through the murky depths of his memory to blind him before slipping away again. Eluned. Never had he thought to see her again in this life.

She was widowed at last. She held some lands of strategic importance, his family had some influence with the king, all of Wales was ripe for the taking – and by some wondrous accident of circumstance, Robert was asked to marry her. What care had he for the details of it, much less his likelihood of getting heirs with her? The lands she offered could be the foulest acre of Hell and still he would say yes.

His father watched him steadily, suspicion in every line of his face.

"Why?" His brother Simon asked what their father did not, honest in his bafflement. "Why would you agree to marry at all, at last? And to a woman who is so far out of youth, whose only certain gift to you will be lands and estates that are in England and not France? Mayhap a title, but when have you cared for titles?"

"Can it be I have tired of being predictable?" Robert shrugged. He was careful not to look back at Kit, who sat near but had said not a word. No doubt his friend felt awkward in the midst of this family scene. "I grow weary of France. Edward would reward me for my service to him there, but that service is ended. Why think you I take no interest in expanding our English lands instead?"

Simon scoffed, but it was their father who answered.

"Because you fairly sleep for the entire hour that we speak of land, yet come alive when I ask you to marry. I have struggled in vain to make you follow the least of my wishes, for years. Yet you yield to this one thing without I fight, persuade, or beg." His father fixed a shrewd look on him. "I am not so old that I grow simple. Tell me why I should not believe you lie or jape, that you will consent so readily."

He could not bring himself to say it was because he wanted her. He was too well known for never having wanted anything in his life. Instead of admitting the truth, he looked about this small room where his father now spent most days. He let his eyes roam over the shallow bowl on the table in the corner, used in his father's near-daily bloodletting, then to the bundle of herbs that hung on the bed-post, intended to keep disease at bay, and finally to the heavy blanket that laid across his father's legs. This casual inspection of the evidence of his father's growing weakness was answer enough, but he said it out loud.

"We both grow older, and change with our years." The truth of this bore down on him suddenly. His father would die one day, and all these years of bedeviling him would cease to bring any kind of satisfaction. "It flatters me that you would have Edward give such a rich prize to me."

"What is left of Wales will be carved up and served to the king's favorites. So I ask myself who is owed reward from Edward, and who is free to marry the Ruardean widow and her riches? For that is who is like to be granted one of these new Marcher lordships." He paused to sip his wine and stare into the cup. Probably he saw all the ways Robert was unworthy of so great a favor. "It is fortune, and not your father, who flatters you."

Robert was unsure how to react to this. His usual

way would be to give a reply that answered the sourness in kind. What he wanted was to warn his father against calling her *the Ruardean widow and her riches*, as if she were an object, the spoils of war. But now he only thought how he must not say the wrong thing and push his father into reconsidering the scheme. Maybe honesty was best – to say that he wanted Eluned. It was only a long habit of forced silence that prevented him saying it. There was no harm, yet he could not speak the words.

But while he hesitated, Kit spoke at last, a quiet but firm voice at his shoulder. "Such a lordship would give Robert near as much power as Mortimer has."

Robert turned to see his friend looking steadily at his father, and felt shame that he had not thought of this yet. He had not thought past Eluned's name, but now he saw what Kit must have seen from the first.

"I could use such advantage to speak for Kit," Robert said, as if it was his reason for agreeing all along. "For the return of his son who is held as hostage by Mortimer. With such wealth, and such grand favor given me direct from Edward's hand, Mortimer could not ignore me as he ignores Kit. We might at last make progress on that concern which drew me here."

With a quick look in the direction of Simon, whose countenance had grown suddenly stony, the mistrust began to leave his father's expression. He knew this much of his son, at least. Never had Robert cared for titles or lands or marriage. But he did care for his friend like a brother. Better than his own brother, in fact, by far. He loved Kit's son just as much. It was not hard to believe that Robert would do all this only for the chance of bringing the boy home and safe out of Mortimer's keeping.

"Mortimer is a law unto himself," grumbled his father, easing back on his pillows. "Haps you shall be a fit match for him. Leave me now. We will talk further in the morning."

They were almost out the door before Robert thought to ask. He turned back to see Simon arranging items at their father's bedside. His brother poured more wine, snuffed the candle, placed a fresh handkerchief near. Ever the doting son.

"Has she agreed to the marriage?"

His father did not open his eyes, though Robert was sure he heard. It was Simon who looked up briefly, like it was the most minor detail in all the discussion. He murmured a good night to their father and came to the door where they stood waiting.

"Not yet," he answered, watching Robert closely. "Soon we will have word from her son. Until then you may sleep easy as a bachelor, brother."

✠ ✠ ✠

Robert made haste to be alone, away from his brother and the sharp eyes of servants, and climbed the stairs of the tallest tower. He breathed the frigid air deep into his chest and stared up into the vast black sky and did not even try to think in straight lines.

Kit found him, of course. He set a mug of ale on the wall before Robert. It was satisfyingly large.

"That's Meg's brew, and we won't find stronger."

"We won't," Robert agreed and took a deep drink. "But I wonder will just one be enough."

"As well did I."

Kit proved he was the best of friends when he nodded to a small keg he'd obviously hauled up and set in the corner near the stair. Then he raised his own mug, drank, and rested his elbows against the wall next to Robert. He said nothing for a long and quiet time, only looked out over the wall in the same direction as Robert and drank.

It oriented him, to have his friend at his side, waiting. It gave him something solid and real of the present to hold on to while the past pulled at him. Robert turned his face back up to the sky. There were clouds that obscured the heavens. He wished for them to part, even if only a little. If he could see but two stars, if he could peer into the empty space between the bright points of light, then he would see all the years between then and now – neatly contained, seemingly near enough to touch, infinitely distant.

"Was it her, then?"

It was a question, and not. Kit would not have forgotten, though they had never once spoken of it since Kenilworth. That was another memory, contained in the blackness between stars: an interminable siege and long hours to fill, finding a friend, and confiding his love for a woman he could not have. At the end of it, when they had surrendered at last and the siege ended, it was Kit who had carried Robert out of Kenilworth castle, wasted and half-delirious, endlessly shitting himself and puking. They had laughed at it, and he had been ready to die – had laughed at death, too. He had said her name for the last time that day.

But Kit would remember. So Robert braced himself with more ale in his belly, more cold air in his lungs, and said it again, for the first time in eighteen long years.

"It was Eluned."

Kit gave a slight grimace of confusion. "All these years I have thought her name was Cariad."

"No." Robert gave a huff of amusement and welcomed the little stab pain that came with the word. "That is a word for... is an endearment, *cariad*. A Welsh word." He took another drink from his rapidly emptying mug. "But did I not say her name to you, when I thought I would not live?"

"In truth I thought you delirious and speaking of a bird. A linnet. Eluned." He shrugged. Robert let out a surprised laugh, but Kit only said, "Stranger things have I heard from men in their sickness. Though I did wonder why I should tell a linnet you could not regret nor repent of your love."

Love. Robert turned his face away and looked out into the night again. He contemplated the word, and time. He had lived long enough now to know how much a thing might be changed only by waiting for years to pass over it. So he must ask himself now, a thing he had never thought to question before this. What he had named love in his youth – had it truly been love? And whatever of it remained – was it deep enough, strong enough to still be called love, or was it only the echo of a youthful infatuation?

He had met her in the last year of Montfort's rebellion with the barons against King Henry, just months before Montfort was defeated. Robert's father had declared for the king and gone to fight against Montfort, which meant that of course Robert would not. But neither had he gone to fight with the rebels. He could not understand why everyone seemed so keen to get themselves killed.

Instead he traveled to a place high in the northern hills among lovely placid lakes, far from the fighting that tore at the heart of England. He'd been a happy wastrel, all of twenty years old and following a fair maiden whose name he utterly forgot when Eluned exploded into his heart. She was there, part of Lady Torver's household, keeping herself and her little daughter safe from the civil war that grew bloodier by the day. At first she was only another woman, pleasant-looking enough but married to Walter of Ruardean. And Robert did not care to risk discovery by any husband, much less one as volatile and powerful as Ruardean. There were maids enough without looking to other men's wives.

But one day they rode out with hawks to hunt and as the party rested and ate in the midday sun, he spoke disparagingly of the war. What had he said? Something about the weakness of the king, the zealotry of Montfort, and the foolishness of men who would follow either of them. And she had scoffed at him, called him callow and empty-headed and dangerously close to having no honor at all. It silenced everyone. Everyone but him.

"And for which side would my lady have me lose my head?" he asked, amazed by her self-possession, admiring the way she lifted her chin, already fascinated beyond all reason.

"It matters less which belief you die for, than that you believe in a thing enough to risk your life for it at all."

Her voice was different than any he had ever heard, forceful and melodic, filled with the music of her native Wales. He could not tear his eyes from her as she spoke with fervor on the topic of Montfort's cause. It was not what she said but the sight of her as she said it that captured him. Somehow – and he never could discover how, in all his years of remembering that moment – she managed to deliver an impassioned speech in support of the barons' uprising without ever once claiming that Montfort was right or that old King Henry was wrong. She was surrounded by women whose husbands and brothers and sons were in mortal peril because of Montfort, yet she argued it all so cleverly that they could not rightly object to a single word she uttered in defense of the man's ideals. Indeed her insistence on the rights of all men as bestowed by God and appropriated by the king shamed them all. By the end of it, they all turned their faces downward, cheeks aflame.

But he could not look away from her. Never had he seen anyone burn so bright. She was more alive than anyone he had ever known, in a way he had not dreamed was even possible. Everyone and everything was a cold and lifeless backdrop to her blaze.

The next day she walked out into the bailey and headed for the outer ward alone. He followed, held his cloak up to protect her head from the sparse droplets that had begun to fall, and she laughed at his solicitude.

"I am not spun from sugar that I melt under the rain," she said, and her eyes held a merry smile. "Certes you have seen I am more like to be made of vinegar."

"Nay," he said, glad that she slowed her pace and did not pull from his side. "Not vinegar nor sugar, but of spices that tempt a man's tongue."

And she, oh so bold and alive, widened her smile and called him a pretty rogue with a sideways sweep of her magnificent lashes. He was lost, heart bounding in his chest, everything inside of him leaping toward her.

Wherever she was going, she did not want him to follow. He felt her reluctance to move forward, and dared to take her elbow and steer her to a hidden corner between the stable and the curtain wall. He waited for her to pull away, but she did not. She only looked at him with that lift of her chin, and he felt the excitement in her. When he raised his hand to her face, there was a gentle warning in her look. She did not want his kiss, but let him touch her just barely, the tips of his fingers brushing the soft skin of her cheek.

Her eyes were gray and fixed on his face, her lips parted. *She is hungry*, he thought with a thrill, and then she was slipping away before he could act on the knowledge. He followed her at a distance, to see what destination or task she would hide from him. But it was only a small group of muddy boys who wrestled and fought with sticks and spoke a language not known to him. Just as he realized it must be Welsh, he saw with a shock that her daughter was among them, as loud and unkempt as the others.

The girl saw him, and eyes just like her mother's found his before he could turn away. The child said something to Eluned, who turned and saw him too. He watched her stiffen, her grip tightening on the girl's hand. Like a rabbit caught in a trap – but no, more cunning than a rabbit. Already he could see her thinking, marshalling excuses and explanations for the wildness of her highborn daughter. He forestalled it with a little shake of his head and then a smile of reassurance. What did he care that a child played in the mud?

In the days that followed it was a delightful dance between them, of looks and words, moving closer to one another and then apart again, caught up as in the pull of the ocean tide. Every minute of the day, he knew where she was and managed to exchange a glance, a word. The world around her was thrown into shade, so vivid was she – her words, her quick smile, her eyes alight with intelligence. Every hour of the night he imagined her breath as she slept and longed to feel it against him in the dark. The only thought Robert gave to her husband was to hope he would die in the fighting.

Finally, after a lifetime (or perhaps only days) of anticipation that was by turns delicious and painful, she gave him a look – over the edge of her cup, during a feast, as all around them grew drunk on wine and he on her eyes – and he knew she wanted more than just flirtation. He contrived to be at the door when she exited, waylaying her as she made her way alone to her room, drawing her unresistingly to a shadowed corner. He touched her throat through the veil she wore, felt the mad beating of her heart, and did not dare to kiss her.

It was she who dared. She who had boldness enough to reach for him and put her lips to his, but was so innocent beyond that one act that she gasped when he opened his mouth over hers, delved deep between her lips with his tongue. The hunger he had sensed in her came to life, caused her to hold him tight and pressed their bodies together against the wall. Her hips arched up into him, a sweet sound of pleasure and frustration on her lips. He thought he would perish of desire if he could not have her. Then a drunken reveler passed behind him, and she ducked her head to hide her face.

When the moment had passed he put his forehead to hers and felt the pull of her. Their breaths mingled together, hot and ragged.

"Tomorrow," he whispered. It was a plea, a prayer. "Come to me tomorrow." He told her a servant would wait to guide her to a place where they could meet alone. He tore himself away from her heat, lightheaded with the effort. He spent all night making the arrangements, paying servants for their help and their silence.

In the morning he rode out, his knuckles white on the reins, terrified she would not come. But she was there at the place he had found for them at the foot of the hills. He gave his horse to the waiting servant (Marc, who would serve him well for many years after) and went to her, took her hand, led her up and up until they reached the little clearing. Trees were all around the edge of the space, but on the far side they could look out between the branches and see the lake below. He pulled away the veil that she had worn high to obscure her face, and she said she could not stay above an hour.

There was a shyness in her, a hesitation, as though she had not until this moment considered the gravity of her actions. He too was paralyzed with uncertainty. That she had come, that she was here alone with him, that she could want him at all – it so overwhelmed him that he did not know what to do. It was as if he'd never been with a woman before.

Finally, in desperation, he said, "Will you kiss me,

Eluned?"

And she did. It was a careful flutter at the corner of his mouth, and then her hands were on him, and they could not stop. They established the pattern that would repeat every day that they could manage it throughout that spring and summer: his cloak spread on the ground, her limbs white in the sun, her dark hair unbound and spilling around him as they pleasured each other and he fell deeper and deeper into love. Afterwards, he would rest his head on her bare breast and look up into the sky with her as they talked, and never let himself think of how it could not last.

More than her body, more than her kisses and her sighs, it was the talking that stayed with him in the years to come. She asked him about everything he had ever thought, every place he had ever been, all his loves and hates. He asked her questions until he had a picture of her life outside the patch of grass they shared in those stolen moments. She was raised in a family of Welsh nobility and her marriage to the Norman lord of Ruardean was an alliance to keep peace between their families. She had been thirteen when she went to him as a bride, and had her daughter before she was fourteen. Three years ago she had borne a son but the boy died in his first year, she told him. She said it to the sky and did not turn to him when he asked if it weighed heavy on her heart.

"I give thanks for my daughter every day," was her answer. "She is healthy and strong, and she is mine in a way a son cannot be. But it is a hard thing." She cleared her throat, and he felt the heat that rose up in her chest, her neck. He saw the tear that stood in her eye but did not fall. "When I dwell overmuch on the sadness of it, I pray for those women who have lost many children, and I thank God I have a child who yet lives, and that I live too."

Then she took a deep breath and stuck her chin up at the sky and said, "But I do not wish to be sad with you." She turned her face to him, her hair a heavy fall around her face, a smile touching her lips. "Nor do I wish to talk of God, or sin, or prayers. I would have you kiss me once more before we must go, my Robin."

The lightness in her, the joy, warmed him in the moments they were together and haunted him in their hours apart. Every morning he went to the chapel to look for the carefully placed stone that was her signal she could meet him, and his whole happiness depended on seeing that rough and rose-colored pebble. When it was not there, he lived in fear he would never see it again. He thought he must be nothing more to her than a dalliance, a summer's distraction, while he burned for her, body and soul. She was above him, and though his family's lands in France were not insignificant, it was nothing to the great estate of Ruardean. And in England his family's holdings were even less, a single manor house and a paltry bit of land. He tried to tell her more than once, how the disparity between them troubled him, but she seemed only to hear that he wished to increase his holdings.

"Tell me," she said one day as they huddled together under the extra cloak he had brought to guard against the light drizzle. Rain did not deter them, but only caused them to retreat to a spot where the branches were thick above them. "Have you ready funds enough to purchase a small estate not far from your current lands? It can be had for a good bargain, I think."

Then she told him of Whittington's debts, how he had put this minor estate up as collateral on a loan from a Jew who lived in Lincoln. "By law, Aaron cannot own land, but he can sell the debt to you. The interest has grown until Whittington owes so much that he is more like to kill Aaron than to pay it. So Aaron will gladly sell the debt for much less than its full worth, only to be rid of it."

When asked how she knew of all this, she gave an impish smile and would not answer until he had played his fingers along her ribs, tickling her mercilessly. She shouted with laughter and cried mercy. She lay next to him, girlish giggles fading as she regained her breath, pushing her hair from her smiling face – a sight that he kept in his memory and hoarded like a precious jewel. Then she said that months ago, when a betrothal had been proposed for her daughter with Whittington, she had made some inquiries among the moneylenders. Thus had she met Aaron and learned a great deal about the finances of many local lords. "I learned also how foully the Jews are used, and that they justly live in fear of all debts to them being declared null. So he will sell most gladly, to be rid of that risk."

"And I shall risk Whittington's anger, when I demand repayment."

"Which he cannot repay, for he has not the means, and so you will gladly take possession of the holdings. What is his petty anger to that fine prize, hm?"

Her eyes sparkled with amusement, but there was a satisfaction in her voice too. "And why would you, my sweetest Eluned, wish to see this man so neatly tricked out of his land?"

She scoffed. "Tricked! It is Aaron who is misused, forced into usury because by law he may not earn any other living, and then unable to demand repayment nor take possession of the lands given as collateral. Whittington knew the terms of his loan, and he is a fool did he not see the risk of this."

He watched how her eyes flashed with indignation, and decided to ask her later how exactly she reconciled her admiration for Montfort with that man's poor treatment of these Jews she defended. He did not think she wanted him to buy this debt to aid Aaron, but rather to thwart Whittington.

He said so, and her expression changed subtly. A faint pinch came to her lips, and she said, "I like Aaron very well. And mayhap I have heard that Whittington called my daughter homely, and said he would rather find a bride with more beauty and less Welsh blood."

He laughed and called her fierce, and Whittington an unfortunate fool to have crossed her. She kissed him and with a playful rise of her brows said, "Ah yes, beware to my enemies, who shall be forced to pay their lawful debts. How very vicious I am."

So he sent word to Aaron, who by chance would be in Blackpool on business within the month. Robert met him there and, after agreeing that Eluned of Ruardean was a marvel, they negotiated the sale. It would double the Lascaux English holdings and though it pained Robert to do something that would no doubt bring his father great joy and pride, well – it was a small price to pay to give Eluned her little revenge.

But all the long ride back from Blackpool, he

could only think of how it bought him no more than that. It did not make him her equal and even if it had, still she could not be his. She belonged to another man, and Robert was but a diversion, a lady's brief amour. Then all thought was gone when he saw her again. He had been away for almost two weeks, and half-expected her to have come to her senses in his absence. But when he came to the stables she was nearby, as though she waited for him. She lingered at the edges of the courtyard with a restless and fretful countenance.

He saw the moment when she caught sight of him. Her face became like the sunrise.

Later in their hidden place among the hills, he told her what he had heard on his travels, of the war. Montfort and the king's forces were like to meet in decisive battle any day now. Montfort was the better commander, but would welcome more trained men with mounts.

"I think to fight for him," he said as his fingers stroked over the dark birthmark on her throat, set to the left of center over her pulse and shaped like a teardrop. He loved that mark. He put his lips to it to keep himself from saying that he would enter the fight only for her, because she believed in the ideals for which Montfort fought. Because it might make her love him. It might make her look at him that way again, all of her lighting up at the sight of him, if he went off to war and came riding back to her.

She pulled away to look him in the face, confusion furrowing her brow before it was replaced by something he had not dared to hope for. "You will not," she said fiercely. Her lips began to tremble, tears edging into her voice. "Please, cariad. Say you will not."

She gripped him as though she could keep him there by force, and he stared in wonderment as she pleaded with him to stay far from any battles. He stammered in the face of this outpouring, trying to explain his wish to be worthy of her, to win her respect and love. "Fool," she said softly to him. "Fool. Do not risk death to win a heart that is yours already."

Then she whispered her love between kisses, and he could only bury his face in her hair and hold her hard against him, marveling that they had found each other and were given this time together.

But it must end. Of course it had to end.

In August Montfort was killed in battle, and the royalists were confident in their victory. When next he stole away to meet her, Eluned had a letter from her husband that gave details of the battle and commanded her to come home to Ruardean.

"It is infamous," she said, stunned. "They did not spare any of the barons who fought with Montfort, not even for ransom. They tore their bodies apart. Mortimer sent Montfort's head to his wife as trophy."

"You will go to your husband now?"

"And they call *us* savages." She did not seem to hear him. "Now his cause is collapsed. They all lose heart without him to lead."

That was when he asked her to come away with him. Leave her husband, bring her child. Come to France. She waved off the words. He thought she did not even hear them. She took his hand, pulled him to her, and told him he must come to her at Ruardean. Her husband would be there and then away – he was ever off on either the king's business or else a pilgrimage. Rarely did he stay for more than a month or two. "I will send word," she said, laying her head on his chest. "You will come to me. I will find a way."

He stopped thinking of the future then and kissed her, freed her hair from its golden net, lost himself in her body and her sweet ecstatic sighs. But after, as they held each other and looked up at a perfectly blue sky, he thought of being apart from her for weeks and weeks. He thought of her at Ruardean, and could not hide his outrage that she would lie with her husband.

Of course she must, she said. And of course she was right. He did not want to think of these ugly practicalities, though, and so they argued. He said he could not bear to share her with another man; she said that he had always shared her. He shouted that she was clever enough to devise some reason to stay from her husband's bed, but chose not to. She shouted back that he had less wit than a peahen, if he truly thought she could simply choose to shun her husband's bed for the rest of her life.

A great many things they shouted at one another, none of which he remembered well years later. He only remembered that they argued, and she was breathtaking in her anger, until she said she must get back before she was missed. She would start the journey to Ruardean immediately, she told him, as she twisted her hair and stuffed it back into the golden net. Still he protested that she would make such haste to be with her husband, as she dressed herself and snapped her impatience at him. She searched the grass for a button that had come off her shoe and in the end left without it.

She grasped his face, placed a firm and definitive kiss on his mouth. She said, "You are a great fool, my

Robin. But I love you still. I will love you until I die."
Then she clambered down the path to where her
horse waited, her shoe flapping loose around her foot.

Three weeks later he went to Ruardean, because
her husband had come and gone. But when he
arrived, he learned that Walter had unexpectedly
returned again. So Robert played the part of a
nameless wandering knight begging shelter for an
evening. Through his servant, she bade him stay out
of sight in the room that was his in the knights'
quarters, and she would send word. In the black
before dawn, a young boy came and told him, in a
voice so thick with Welsh accent that Robert barely
understood, that Eluned waited for him in the garden
by the kitchen.

That was where it ended. He remembered little of
it with any clarity, except the smell of rosemary. He
remembered the outline of her, just discernable in the
dark, and how she did not even touch him in greeting.
He remembered his denial when she told him they
could meet no more, and that she said, "It has been a
dream. And now we must wake." She did not explain
why now, why so suddenly. He said again that she
should come away with him, to France. And she
asked him what life there would be for her there, a life
as nothing but a disgraced and corrupted woman who
shared his bed in sin.

She said *my daughter* – and he must have said
something very foolish in return, for her voice grew
hard and warned him that he would not be well
pleased by her answer, did he ask her to put her lover
above her child. He remembered the feeling of
futility, the anguish of comprehending that she had
already made up her mind. She made him swear to

43

come nowhere near her ever again, for her sake and his own. It was over. It was dead.

"It was a stolen season," she said, and then she startled to hear the hushed voice of the Welsh boy who stood guard just outside the arbor. It was a warning. They had only a moment more.

Robert had reached out to touch her one last time, knowing that soon she would be lost to him forever. His hand found her face and when he felt it was wet with tears, the first winds of desolation swept through him. For if she wept – if she, so clever and determined, could not think of a way for them to be together – then truly it was over.

He remembered saying her name, declaring his love, the pain that cut through him at knowing she would pull away soon.

He remembered that she was utterly composed, completely in command of herself until the very last moment. "Oh God," she breathed, and a sob burst from her. "I cannot see your face."

He remembered the feel of her face turning into his hand, pressing a kiss to his palm. And then she was gone.

✠ ✠ ✠

Now he said to his friend, "I prayed for her husband's death and when he did not die, I prayed for my own."

Kit sat slumped against the wall, carefully focusing on Robert's face. They were well and truly drunk now. Robert did not even know how much of it he had spoken aloud. Enough for Kit to understand the most basic facts, at least.

"Then…you came to Kenilworth. Just before winter."

"Came a week later," Robert confirmed. "Or more. Or less." He shrugged. "As soon as my horse could get there. There were a lot of taverns on the way."

He had had some idea of dying for her cause still, the kind of morbid fantasy a rejected young lover would have. Montfort's son was at Kenilworth with the last handful of the anti-royalist forces, so that's where Robert went. He had liked the idea of a last stand against the king's men. He did not anticipate that it would last for months. It was December of the next year when they finally gave up, the whole starving and diseased lot of them.

"Good terms, though, Kenilworth," he said now, apropos of nothing. "Got to keep everything, almost like it never happened."

"That King Henry," said Kit. He blew a raspberry. "Pushover king. Good thing for us, though."

The ale was gone except for a trickle in the bottom of the keg, which Kit poured out. Half went into Robert's mug, half splashed on the floor between them.

"Then you went to France," said Kit.

"Then I went to France," he nodded once. "And fought, and Edward holds Gascony because of me. Well," he waved his hand and swallowed the last of his drink. "More or less. He owes me. Can't give me any more of France, but he'll give me a piece of England."

"That's what they say. Your father. Brother." Kit sat up and clapped a hand on Robert's shoulder. "If you marry the linnet."

It seemed to Robert that it was likely more complicated than that, but he nodded. "The linnet," he agreed.

Then he could not stop the smile that spread across his face. "They want me to marry Eluned. They thought they would have to persuade me."

He burst into laughter, the sound of it cutting through the cold night air, bouncing off the stone walls, greeting the rising sun.

CHAPTER 3

The Choice

Once she had been young, and hope was everywhere. It had lived in every corner of her world. It grew like wildflowers in open meadow and pushed up through rock to reach the sunlight. It was so plentiful and stubborn that it had seemed impossible to kill, once.

Eluned stared at the cold stars and tried to remember that brief moment in time, so long ago, when her world was a song.

For six months, she had lived in that song. Six months, two weeks, and two days.

"And about thirteen hours, I think," she said to the stars. How amusing, that she could remember such a thing. Even more amusing was how she had once fervently believed she would never forget a single moment of those six months, two weeks, and two days. And thirteen hours.

Whenever she thought of him over the years

("Eighteen years," she whispered at the stars), she thought mostly of the end. At first, just after it was over, she could not bear to remember the hours of lying in his arms, knowing he was lost to her forever. Then she spent a fair amount of time forcing herself to remember the bliss, to stare long and hard at every beloved moment until it no longer hurt. After that, she thought of it no more. Except for the end.

No, not the end. The decision itself, to end it – that was what she most often thought of. She recognized the weakness in herself caused by this oversight, this hole in the fabric of memory. If she was to go forward, no matter the path, she must correct this. It was an essential wisdom, to preserve the ugly facts as well as the pleasant ones, to guard against selecting and discarding details on a whim. Now, with the cold seeping into her and a decision to be made by morning – now she would make herself think of all those things that went into the ending.

But to think of the end was to remember the beginning. It was remembering the way he had looked at her with a shining admiration she had never seen from a man. "You are made of spices that tempt a man's tongue," he had said to her, and an unholy thrill had run through her. She could only dimly recall the sensation now, but she did not forget its power. He had looked at her mouth and she was filled with an aching thirst, as though she would die of it as one in a far and scorching desert.

He had seen it, and let her go. That moment, she thought years later. That was when her heart began to slip away from her, escaping her control and landing squarely in his hands. Why? Because he did not reach to take her, but allowed her to reach for him. Because he had not flinched from her vehement political posturing. Because he did not see her as a great lady or an obedient wife or an indulgent mother. He saw only a woman, and desired her. It was a lure she could not, in the end, resist.

"Young Godfrey could not take his eyes from you," Eluned had made a point to say to Mathilda. This was important to remember, lest she fall into a belief that she had been an innocent seduced. Also, it served to remind herself that she had always been cunning, even then.

Robert had come to Torver to woo the young Mathilda and when he abandoned pursuit, the girl seemed likely to make trouble for him. So Eluned had pushed Mathilda into the path of a boy from the household guard. She whispered to the boy that he was not wrong to hope, and she sighed with Mathilda over how handsome and gallant Godfrey was, until Mathilda was ripe for the plucking.

"Wear your red gown," she urged the girl one night, "and leave your throat bare. See if you cannot tempt him!"

And while Mathilda's eyes were thus turned to some utterly forgettable boy, Eluned slipped away from the feast and was kissed. Her first kiss, after nine years of marriage and two children. It was intoxicating. All of it, even that first time with him, naked in a patch of sunlight, when she was so nervous she shook like a leaf through it all – every moment with him had gone to her head like the strongest wine.

That was her great mistake, and her greatest delight: to have lost herself in it so completely. It had required planning and discretion, but it was easy enough to devise a way to see him. She would make the excuse of exercising her mount, sometimes, or her falcon – or she would make no excuse at all. Lady Torver was old, and there were enough other ladies to sit with her and embroider and pray the day away. Two or three times a week, Eluned would contrive to meet him, and leave the signal for him. She would take the little pink stone he had found that first time in their secret place, and put it carefully on the narrow sill under the stained glass Jesse tree.

He would find it tucked into that corner under the bright blues and reds and golds, and then bring it back to her. Every few days, he would see her and slip it into her hand as they kissed. Then her clothes came off, and for the next hour she could stop thinking of planning and hiding and hoping. When she was with him, there was no need to think about anything at all. She could give herself completely to lust.

But it wasn't all lust. This was important to remember, too. Even all these years later, she could easily recall the feel of her heart swelling when he spoke so casually of his father's disdain. Robert had been born a twin, his brother older by only an hour and dead of a fever when they were four. Yet his father had decided, for unfathomable reasons, that the younger could never be what the original heir would have been.

"No son will ever please as well as the dead and sainted one," Robert told her with a heartbreaking shrug. "I have decided it is foolish to try. He will call me wayward and useless in any case. So because wayward and useless is so much more diverting than faithful and industrious," he said with a wicked grin and a kiss to the upper slope of her breast, "and he will despair of me no matter the course I take, I have decided he can curse me while I enjoy life."

"Do you miss your twin?" she had asked. "Do you remember him?"

He directed a small, sad smile at the trees that surrounded them and answered, "I remember little of him except how wrong it felt when he died. It is a strange feeling, like there is a hole in the world that only I can see."

"Do you not think your father sees it too?"

He waited a long time in silence before he answered. "Ah yes, my clever cariad, you have the right of it. It is all he sees when he looks at me. He sees what is missing."

She had wanted to say something then, about fear and emptiness and what it meant when a child was lost. But he had kissed her throat and moved his hand between her bare legs and murmured, "All I see is you." Then she thought of nothing at all. She only felt the sunlight on her skin, the warmth and life spreading through her limbs as his hands touched her everywhere.

There were other things, too, that had naught to do with the forbidden delight of his kisses. She remembered them well. How he was ever mindful of her comfort, always solicitous and attentive to the smallest detail, forever finding new ways to take care of her. Her petty jealousy when he had singled out a shy maiden and danced with her, to still the cruel tongues of the other girls. His instinctive compassion to a scared beggar boy who had stumbled upon their hiding place, which contrasted so sharply with her own impatient reaction to the unwelcome child. Little details that were unimportant now, except that they showed he was a good man. Better than her, she knew. Less selfish, more warmhearted. She remembered him.

And she remembered the feel of those stolen hours, days and days of it, where she lost herself in him. It was never enough. She could not get her fill of it, of him, of who she was with him.

Only her daughter had anchored her to reality every day. Gwenllian was eight years old then, and looked to her mother for how to behave. So Eluned was careful, in the hours she was not hidden among the trees with Robert, to act a proper and chaste woman. Pleasant banter was accepted, courtly gestures and a certain kind of flirtation were allowed. Everything else between them was hidden in their secret meeting place, where she went while Gwenllian played with her cousins and was none the wiser.

"For you, my favorite daughter," she had said one day when she came back from an afternoon in Robert's arms. She handed Gwenllian a handful of little purple flowers.

"I am your *only* daughter, and your hair is different," observed Gwenllian with a small frown. Eluned told her that she preferred this new style because it was so much less fuss. And it was. That was not a lie. She did not say that it was Robert who braided her hair after she had let it down to fan all around them, that it was he who coiled the braid and caught it up in a net before laying the linen veil on it. She wore it like that all summer, because it was so easy to take down and up again.

She told Gwenllian that the flowers were bruisewort, so named because the leaves put in a poultice would help bruises to heal. Gwenllian asked what the flowers did, and the stems.

"I know not," answered Eluned, relieved that her daughter was more interested in the plant than where it came from. "But the roots of it can be given in a tea to cure a sore throat."

Then of course nothing would do but Gwenllian must have the roots. Eluned began to gather some new plant on her way to or from meeting Robert, and soon Gwenllian demanded to see where they all grew. So every day was spent gathering flowers with her daughter, or meeting her lover in their secret place. Was there ever such an enchanted summer?

That had been her life for a season. She had never forgotten it. But it felt more like a story that had been sung to her long ago, so many times that she knew it by rote. He had loved that girl who was so confident it would all turn out well, who was so happy and alive, whose world was, briefly, an enchanted place.

She had been that girl, once. Then it all went wrong.

Forget at your peril. Think back now, she urged herself, unsure if she could. Back to the time when she believed her husband was only a harmless fool to be outwitted. Back to a time when there were only wide-open possibilities in all directions, instead of scraps to be foraged in a small and airless room.

She remembered the argument with Robert, how reality had at last begun to intrude on the space reserved for their love. It should have woken her from the dream, but it did not. Instead as she rode back to Ruardean, she was only fearful he would stop loving her because she must lie with Walter. In the nights away from Robert, she relived their argument obsessively and was mortified that his last sight of her was as she walked away awkwardly, her shoe loose from a missing button and half-falling from her foot.

Then she arrived home and Walter came shortly thereafter, and the little haven in the hills she had shared with a lover seemed impossibly distant. Her husband had always been subject to whimsical moods, sometimes deeply troubled by sadness and other times so filled with a fevered energy that he barely slept. Now he was fevered, agitated with a religious fervor that was sparked by Montfort's defeat.

"God Himself has spoken at last," he told her with shining eyes. "The cause of the king is righteous, and Montfort was naught more than a trick of the Devil that would test men's souls."

She did not debate him when he was like this. But neither could she bring herself to nod meekly and agree, even if it was wiser to play that part. She only waited to see if he would come to her bed, half of her afraid that he did not and the other half relieved. They had been lucky so far, she and Robert. But to depend on luck in the matter of pregnancy was a lethal stupidity, and so she waited for a husband who never came to her bed. She should have gone to him, but somehow she never did.

Within a fortnight he was gone again, setting off on a long pilgrimage to Aix-la-Chapelle where he would see the great relics, and he never touched her. Her fear over what might happen if a babe grew in her belly while he was away was nothing to her joy at knowing he would spend all the winter in the Rhineland.

She sent word to Robert. They would have months and months together, alone. She would contrive to make him part of Ruardean, give him a place as a knight of the garrison. She would find a way to make it work.

Remember this, she told herself now as she sat in the cold darkness of her bower. *Remember how sure you were, and that you schemed even before Walter came back.* It was too easy to fall into the belief that Walter's actions alone had shaped her. And though she might lie to anyone else when it suited her needs, she must not lie to herself.

She had schemed. The ladies who attended her most closely were not her friends or kinswomen. They could not be trusted and so she had begun to gather tidbits about them, prepared to bribe any of them if they saw too much and sought to expose her one day. She had not known these precautions came too late, because one of the servants who traveled with Walter let slip the observation that the lady of Ruardean was uncommonly happy in her time at the Torver estate, that she had been quick to laugh and too often danced with one particular young knight. In all her preoccupation, she had overlooked the crucial detail of which servants had been at Torver with her, which would go with Walter, and what they might reveal. Above all, she had not anticipated Walter's reaction.

Walter returned to Ruardean three days before Robert arrived there. Her husband found her in the tilting yard, where she was watching the men practice while trying to explain to Gwenllian why girls could not, in fact, ever become knights. She had been saying something about the gallantry of noble men when he grasped her gown from behind, pulled her up and dragged her away. This she had remembered vividly over the years: Gwenllian running after them, clinging to her mother's belt as she was dragged along and sending vicious kicks at Walter until young Madog intervened. She could not forget, ever, the look on her daughter's face when Madog said in Welsh that they could do nothing, that they must let this happen.

"You will not tell falsehoods before Our Lord," Walter declared as he thrust her into the chapel.

What a fool he was. Of course she would tell falsehoods. How easy it was to swear innocence. It was even easier as the hours wore on. His suspicion was only sparked by a passing comment; there was no evidence to dispute. But avowals of innocence were just the beginning. He made her kneel for hours before the statue of the Virgin and dwell on wifely virtue.

"For I have seen defiance in your eyes, wife," he said, as though it caused him great anguish, "and I fear for your very soul."

So she knelt until her knees ached. At his command she lay prostrate on the stone floor through the night, her husband stretched next to her because he swore he would not abandon her to the evil spirits that he saw at her shoulder, which sought to steal her soul. He hissed at his visions that they would not take her. She turned her face to the floor and thought, *My husband is mad.*

Mad or holy, it did not matter which. It only mattered that she submit to his visions, and survive.

In the morning she begged him tenderly to let her go and bring them food and drink, but he would not let her interrupt their vigil. She began to feel faint at midday, but when she dared to show it Walter clutched her slumping shoulders and shook her hard, and shouted that she must fight the demons. She began to fear him a little then, because he had never handled her roughly before this. As the second night came on and she knew he would still not relent, hopelessness rose up in her. Her husband's voice was all around her, for hours. It was soft and threatening as distant thunder. It turned her joy to shame.

She thought of Robert. She saw his golden-brown hair in the sun, against her bare breast. She thought of the adoring look he gave her when he spied that same defiance in her eyes. It was sin. All of it was sin, and she felt the weight of it as Walter wanted her too.

As her lips moved to recite the Pater Noster in the small hours of the second night of prayer, she spread her knees apart under her skirt to relieve the pain of kneeling so many hours. And though it was the surest sacrilege to do so, she remembered herself on her knees under the trees with Robert, legs spread wide as he took her from behind – like animals. They were like animals and she had loved it. Her arm had clutched around a tree to steady herself against his glorious pounding as she, panting, had looked out over the lake and smiled to think there were people below, oblivious to their ecstasy. So many people who merely drifted through life's duties, obedient and safe and small. *Never again will I be that*, she had vowed in that moment.

In the chapel, she glanced at her husband and then back to the Virgin, reciting prayers of forgiveness on her knees, remembering that vivid scene, and it all suddenly changed in her mind. The focus shifted away from those imagined people below and moved to the landscape itself – the bright lake, the distant hills, the great wide world. In the midst of it she was but one person, one burning heart. And everywhere there were churches, cathedrals, fortresses, armies. There were men in power here and in Rome and on every inch of soil between. She knew now that all these structures, those she could see and those she could not, wcrc built to confine her, to stop the very thing that brought her joy.

Then she had understood that it was not a world of endless possibility. Some dreams could not be made real. She could not have what she wanted.

It was at that moment that Walter looked hard at her and called on her to renounce Satan, and a great hatred burst inside of her. She screeched. She struck out at him. Her hands clawed at his face while she spewed every vile curse she knew and wished him to Hell.

But Walter was a large and powerful man. He caught her hands away from him with ease, took her throat in his fist, and called on all the saints to aid him in ousting the demon that possessed her. He let her go only when she began to swoon from lack of breath.

"Eluned?" His voice was uncertain. His look was gentle and sane. She nodded, spots swimming before her eyes, and he seemed relieved.

When he asked her to proclaim her innocence again, she only inclined her head. When he told her she must beg forgiveness for all her sins, she made no answer. His fingers tightened hard on her jaw, forcing her face up to look at him, leaving bruises that she felt years after they faded. He was so tall and broad that he filled her vision. Mad or holy, the world was built for men like him. He had all the power over her, because he was her husband and because he could crack her like an egg.

She begged forgiveness for all her sins. Over and over again, until she had no voice left. Until he was pleased.

And then she went about the business of seducing him into her bed.

✠ ✠ ✠

Her fingertips had turned blue with the cold. She stood now, agitated, and blew on her hands as she paced the room. There was no need to remember the details of her marriage bed. Walter was not cruel to her, and she had always done her wifely duties without complaint. But she could not forget that it had made her feel possessed of a demon in truth, to carefully manipulate him into her bed while the bruises of his gripping fingers were still fresh along her jaw. It must be done and quickly, not because she might already carry a child, but because she knew by instinct it would gentle him, tame the wildness in his eyes and kill the suspicion in his breast if she bedded him in this mood. So she did it, because she valued self-preservation more than her scruples.

She had used his guilt and his godliness against him, careful hints and suggestions that his long absence from her bed left room for the Devil to enter. It was easy to make him think it was his idea, that he corrected his own bad behavior by taking her to bed as God intended for man and wife. It only took the rest of that day, between reassuring her daughter she was well and carefully sending a kinsman to intercept Robert before he came to the castle, to steer her husband to her bed that night.

And though she would not pity herself for it, knowing that women the world over must suffer the unwanted touch of their husbands, she could not stop the tears that had fallen silently. They cut a path across her temples and fell into her ears. She told him they were tears born of the overwhelming joy of their reunion in the sight of God, and then she went to Gwenllian's room to watch her daughter's peaceful sleep.

Eighteen years ago, she had sat in the dark with only a candle and the sound of her daughter's breathing, and chose. It was not out of the question to run away with Robert, to live as his lover somewhere far away. If the only cost was her wealth and status, she would have done it. But her marriage was an agreement to keep a rocky peace between the vast estate of Ruardean and the Welsh who lived along this border. Her union with Walter gave wealth and necessary influence to her brother, her uncle, all their children and their people. To abandon this marriage was to abandon them.

"Gwenllian," she whispered to the girl who clutched some leaves in her sleep. There was dirt on her faintly sweaty neck and a scratch across her forehead. "My little warrior child."

Gwenllian might not care if Eluned ran away from this life and forfeited her own future as a Norman lady. But she would care that she could no longer wrestle with her Welsh cousins. She would care if Walter would pull her from her mother's arms, which he would do if he could find them, and almost certainly send his daughter to live out her days in a convent. All the spirit in Gwenllian would be turned to sin and shame, while Eluned would perish of a broken heart without her child. Even Robert could not soothe that ache.

Or maybe Walter would not find them and they would live in a different kind of prison, one of cautious movements and timid action. One day her daughter would understand all that she had lost because of her mother's lust, and hate her for it. And if she were to have another child, Robert's child? And if Robert were to die, or tire of her, and leave her alone and penniless with a bastard or two?

No, the world was not made for lovers to be happy for longer than a season.

Eluned stared at her daughter and almost could not breathe for the pride and fear that surged in her. Such a strong girl, who would too soon be made to quail before a man and do his bidding. Eluned clenched her jaw and felt the soreness left by her husband's hand. If she must choose only one dream to make real, she would choose a fearless daughter over an adoring lover.

"Never will you cringe before a man, beloved," she whispered to her sleeping child. "If it cost me my soul, I swear you shall fear no man."

An hour later it did feel as though it cost her soul, when she told Robert that if he loved her, he must swear never to come to her again. Never to see her, or speak to her, or touch her. When he said in a voice of despair that he would risk anything to be with her, she thought of Walter's fist at her throat. She thought of Gwenllian's sweet sleeping breath, and told Robert not to be a fool. Already she felt dead to herself, standing in the dark before the dawn of the first day without him.

But she was not dead, of course. It did not kill her.

Or at least, it did not kill all of her.

She left him, and in the forecourt as the sun rose she turned to young Madog. "Will you swear to me, cousin, that my daughter will have your loyalty and protection, no matter where she may go? That you will faithfully serve her – not me, not Ruardean, but her and her alone?"

He looked at her with an assessing air, this son of her favorite uncle. She saw his eyes take in the bruises her husband had given her, and the last trace of tears from her parting with her lover. He knelt before her and said, "By the grace of God, by the sword I will carry, and by my love for your daughter, I swear fealty to Gwenllian ferch Eluned, and ne'er will I swear it to any other as long as I may live."

Then she went to the master-at-arms and bribed him to teach her daughter the sword.

✠ ✠ ✠

So it had begun, the long and winding path of eighteen years which led from that day to this one. Now Madog was dead, and the peace her marriage had bought became irrelevant when the Welsh were vanquished. Her daughter had taken up the sword and mastered it, only to put it down again, forever, for love of a man. Walter had gotten a son on her, left on Crusade, and returned to her in a box. She had ruled Ruardean. And now she would not.

In her mind, she went over the lessons she had taken from that time. The first had been that love could make her lose her head as well as anyone, and she dismissed its power at her peril. The second had been that the world was not built for her, that it would try and try again to crush her – and no one would save her from it. She must save herself, or be ground into the dust. The last, and most lasting, lesson was this: that she must choose what she dared to desire with great care, and master the tight corners of the maze in which she was trapped if ever she was to have what she wanted.

All of it was still true.

There was light in the sky now. She must stop contemplating her yesterdays and think instead of the decision that must be made today. It was difficult, with thoughts of the long-dead past swimming in her jumbled mind. She must weigh all options with an uncommon clarity, when all she wanted to do was to take to her bed for a week, or a month or a year, and not think at all.

But despite the recoil of her spirit, her mind churned. She was built this way, or had been made this way by circumstance. She had long ago recognized that every great change was an opportunity, a rare chance to steer the course instead of being caught in the currents. Only the weak hesitate, stumble, or are so cowed by the responsibility that they do not even try.

"Love," she murmured to herself. Begin with that, find where she was vulnerable. "What love is alive in my heart?"

Eluned closed her eyes and thought of her heart, and saw only a smoking ruin.

She stood that way, weary in every bone, eyes still closed, when one of her ladies entered. It was time to start the day. It was time to decide what her life would become next, no matter the state of her heart.

"Joan," she said to the young maiden who emptied

a jug of steaming water into a waiting basin. The girl had come here almost a year ago, to serve Eluned and to find a suitable husband. She was, refreshingly enough, not entirely empty-headed.

"My lady?" Joan turned from the basin and gave the tiniest of courtesies. She held a clean linen square in her hand and was so fresh and young that it was disorienting to think she was ready for marriage.

"You are fifteen, I think?" The girl nodded, then blinked expectantly while Eluned frowned. "Are you disappointed I have not found you a husband yet?"

Poor Joan looked lost, then concerned. "My lady, I am well pleased to serve you and not a husband."

"I have been…" Eluned looked at her, all pink and white and smooth. How would life devour this little morsel? "My mind has been on other matters, but I do not forget your situation. If there is a man worthy of you, I have failed in finding him. But is there any man that you wish to have, Joan?"

She should have asked it before this, of course, because Joan immediately blushed and twisted the linen square in her hands.

"Sir Heward, my lady." Having said the name, she seemed at a loss for further words for a moment. Then she burst out, eager to inform. "His rank is equal to my own and it is his fortune to be vassal to Ruardean which only last year granted him knight's fee and the land is well placed with a very fine house that he plans-"

Eluned waved her hand to stop the girl's breathless catalogue.

"Is this why you would have him? Because he is…appropriate?" Joan seemed to think this was a criticism, so Eluned hastened to assure her. "It is curiosity from me, nothing more. I wish to know how a woman chooses a husband, when she is so fortunate that she is permitted to choose."

The girl bowed her head and spoke, surprisingly, with more than a little confidence.

"It is an attractive thing, that he is not too far below or above me and that he has wealth enough. But there are other such men I might choose, and do not. Sir Heward is kind, my lady. He is not full of vain flattery."

Eluned felt a smile pulling at her lips. "And he is handsome and young. Tell me, though, why marry at all? Why choose marriage to a man and not give your keeping to the Church?"

The girl looked nonplussed. "I would – I think my temperament not suited to a life of devotion. For my family, there is more advantage if I marry well. And I have thought many times how I will strive to be like you, my lady, to ably manage a manor with authority and gain the esteem -"

"Yes, enough. Bring me bread for my breakfast, and the hard cheese." Eluned walked to the basin and dipped her hands in. She did not wish to hear more of how this sweet young girl wished to be like her. "I will wear the deep blue surcoat and have fresh linen. Thank you."

She listened to Joan leave, then wiped the warm water over her face. A temperament not suited to the Church, that was true enough. *But hardly can I say I am suited for marriage.* She could not depend on a new husband to take himself off to Antioch for the next fourteen years, after all. More advantage for her family, yes – that was a good reason. Is this what was left to her, then? Always had her life been defined by how it gave advantage to others.

From the basin her reflection looked back at her, and asked her what she wanted. *Wales*, came the answer, immediately. But Wales was lost. Wales was no more.

Revenge for Wales, came the next thought, and her heart raced.

She thought of Llewellyn in his last hours, when his head was still on his shoulders and not on a spike above London. He had trusted the Mortimers and walked into their trap.

Mortimer. She had cursed that name for half her life. It was a Mortimer who had slaughtered Montfort all those years ago, cut off the great man's head and sent it to his wife. It was that same Mortimer who led the many campaigns against the Welsh, who had claimed so many Welsh lands as his own that you could walk for days and not reach the end of Mortimer territory. And when he died in the midst of fighting only a year ago, Eluned had thought that at last, perhaps, the Welsh might win their war.

But his blood ran true in his sons, who had lured Llewellyn to his death. The older one would inherit a great chunk of Wales and likely be given even more as reward for delivering Llewellyn's head. The younger one, Roger – oh, he was a villain indeed. Depraved and degenerate by reputation, but his sins were even more grave than mere lust and violence. She did not forget that it was Roger Mortimer who had killed two orphaned Welsh boys who were the only heirs to an ancient principality. He claimed innocence of the murders and no doubt made a good show of mourning them even as he happily took ownership of all that had been theirs.

Such an appetite for violence and talent for deception these Mortimer sons had. Naturally they were beloved of King Edward, and so they would only gain more and more. More power, more riches, swollen fat as ticks off the blood of others.

Revenge for Wales. The world would do well with less Mortimers in it.

Joan returned, the blue surcoat folded neatly over her arm, accompanied by a servant with a tray of food and drink. Everything she would need to start the day.

"How useful you are," Eluned murmured almost to herself. "What a laudable aim for a life, to be put to good use."

How lucky, to live long enough to decide what use she would be. To rid the world of a Mortimer or two – what a delicious thought. She could not even be convinced it would condemn her immortal soul. It felt so very right. It filled her with a satisfying sense of purpose she had not felt for years, not since she had given up on aiding the Welsh rebellion.

As she had learned long ago, it must be done within the confines of the maze in which she was trapped. But now she had the power to change the shape of a vital corner of that maze. Shut up in a nunnery, she could only pray for justice. And she had seen how little God listened to her prayers.

"Sweet Joan, I did not say that Sir Heward is worthy of you, and you shall have him if you truly want him. I will see to it." She reached up and pulled her braids free, debating whether she would have her hair washed before she ate. But no, she was suddenly quite hungry. "There are other advantages a married lady has that you have not thought of. You may go to court, and mingle with other noble families. Yes, a great many freedoms."

Joan came forth with a comb, a happy smile on her face as she tended to her lady's hair. Eluned reached for the loaf of bread and tore off a great chunk with her teeth, chewing it with relish and wondering if her son waited impatiently outside her door to hear her answer.

"Do you know," she said as the sunlight grew brighter on her face, "I believe I am more suited to marriage, too."

Chapter 4

The Harsh Light of Day

It was Meg, who brewed the finest ale to be had, who was on Robert's mind on the morning of his wedding. When he had returned from France and seen her again, he had not recognized Meg at all. The sweet-faced seventeen year old girl he easily recalled was vanished and in her place was a sweet-faced old woman with pocked skin and very few teeth. Now he could not escape the thought that Meg was younger than he was, and he was younger than Eluned.

At first, nothing had seemed to matter at all except that Eluned had agreed to marry him. Despite the rather formal language she used in the message she had sent, he had seen her request that they be wed as soon as possible as a sign of her eagerness to be with him again. He had indulged for the last few weeks in fantasies of how joyous their reunion would be. After sobering up – and eventually climbing down from the giddy heights of being able to say her name so freely – it was borne in upon him that eighteen years was a very long time.

Now he found himself dwelling on Meg's few teeth and questioning the reason for Eluned's haste. They were supposed to have time together before saying their vows. A day, at least. But her party had encountered a delay on the road in the form of a washed-out bridge, and now she would arrive directly at the church doors. It must be today, if they were to be wed before the season of Advent prevented it.

The doubt and worries that had crawled into his head were not difficult to silence. All he need do was remind himself that it was her spirit he had loved. He would still want her, no matter if she little resembled the girl he'd known. He would always want her. But he would also like some warning.

For the tenth time this morning, Robert decided that gray was too somber and reached again for the rust-colored tunic. The gray had more embellishment but the rust was a more impressive velvet. And if he put the heavy silk velvet with the belt covered in topaz and emeralds, he thought he would make a fine looking groom. Maybe he would ask Kit which one suited him better. Or at least which one made him look younger. Then again, Kit might tell him he need not bother to expend such effort on impressing his bride.

He picked up the gray tunic and looked at the polished bits of jet at collar, cuffs, and hem. It would match the bits of gray hair that had lately begun to grow at his temples.

"You can always go naked to the church door," came Kit's voice. "But I have seen your bride, and I assure you that you will be sorely underdressed."

Robert looked up at him expectantly.

"You decided to shave the beard, then! Well done, that servant might have wept if you'd called for the razor only to change your mind again. I have not seen your jaw in a year."

Robert resisted the urge to run a hand over his bare face. He was still waiting, and his friend knew it. But when Kit said nothing more, Robert reached for the flagon of ale. Kit's hand stopped him.

"She is handsome."

Robert met his eyes. "How handsome?"

Kit gave a little shrug and a smile. He was clearly enjoying this. "She has all her teeth. Or at least the ones in front. And they are white as pearls."

Robert nodded. He wanted to ask if her hair was still a dark brown, how worn was her face, if she had grown portly and if her eyes still flashed fire. Eighteen years was a very long time. He went ahead and drank some ale.

"You are sure she has a full forty years now?" asked Kit, which lifted Robert's hopes further.

"Forty-one, perhaps, I know not the day of her birth. But I thought she might still be uncommon lovely, if my father seems to think her younger than that."

He had wondered if Eluned put out rumors that she was younger than she was. But he did not think her vain enough for such a ruse. It was more likely that his father, who had spied her at court a few years ago, saw what he wished to see: a bride young enough that there was a chance she might still give Robert a son and heir. Why more grandsons should matter was beyond Robert. His brother Simon had three sons, and they would inherit everything if Robert died without issue. His father should be happy enough with that.

"I did not see her very closely, but she looks younger than that. She has a noble bearing, too. A man could not be faulted for thinking her royalty, such is her elegance."

This assurance from Kit sounded quite genuine, which only compelled Robert to drink more of the ale. He should have written to her. A letter, as expected of a groom, full of praise for her beauty and declarations of his joy at their impending wedding. The household cleric had a great number of examples and suggestions for such a letter, as it was apparently a gesture so standard as to be akin to writing out a bill of sale. But it was unthinkable that he would send such practiced and hollow words to her after all this time.

He had written dozens, even hundreds of letters to her over the years – just never on paper. In his mind he had composed them, page after page filled with the mundane events of his life, thoughts and stories and other tidbits reserved for her, couched in words of love. He had not even realized what a habit it had become, this constant but silent narration of his life to her, until he was presented with the opportunity to make the communication real. And then he found too much to say, impossibly overwhelmed, until she was suddenly arriving in a wedding procession this morning. Now. With a regal bearing and teeth like pearls.

He made to bring the flagon to his lips again, but his hand was suddenly empty.

"Dress, not drink," said Kit, helping himself to the

ale, which he had taken from Robert somewhere along the way. "The procession has begun and there is naught but half an hour until she arrives at the church."

Robert looked at the gray tunic, and the rust. Did it really matter which? It was eighteen years. It was marriage. If she did not like what she saw of him at first glance, it was doubtful she would turn tail and run back to Ruardean.

"I am told the stray branches have been cleared from the path," he said as he pulled the rust-colored tunic over his head. There had been a storm that left debris along the road where the bridal procession would travel. "Tell me it is true."

He reached for the belt covered in topaz and emeralds as Kit answered. "Aye, cleared of every stray leaf, and there's new thatch on the storehouse and the stables are so clean you could serve the feast in them. You can be proud of it, Robin."

Robert fastened the belt, slipped a leather pouch into his pocket, and took a short deep breath before looking up at Kit. He held his arms out slightly, hands up, and gave his friend a doubtful look.

"Well? Will I please this regal bride?"

Kit frowned in consideration a moment, then shrugged. "Even were she not regal, she is still a woman. No man can predict what will please a woman."

Robert dropped his hands and headed for the door. "By Mary, what kind words from my bosom friend."

"Kind words or honest words, Robin. A bosom friend can offer both, but not always at the same time."

✠ ✠ ✠

She was only a green and gold shimmer in the distance, and he almost could not bear the anticipation of seeing her. He found himself fixing his eyes on the place where her hands held the reins.

There was music, and the chattering of a thousand voices. There were banners flying, ribbons fluttering, and colorful petals falling, flung over her and strewn in her path on her slow ride toward him. But all he could hear was the beat of hooves that had galloped toward her a lifetime ago. All he could see was the memory of his own hands gripped tight on the reins, knuckles white and aching, as he rode to meet her that first time and chanted to her in his head, *Please be there, please be there.*

She was close now, sunlight flashing off of emeralds and cloth-of-gold around her perfectly serene and familiar face. The years had barely touched it. It was a white, smooth mask that showed nothing. *Please be there*, he thought.

He might have stood there for hours, just looking at her, if Kit had not cleared his throat rather too loudly. Then Robert was in motion, striding toward her, reaching up to lift her from the horse, and the feel of her weight, her body – how she so naturally leaned down and put herself into his waiting hands – caused all the color and sound to burst forth on his consciousness. It was Eluned. Eluned in his arms. Here and now.

"My lord de Lascaux," she murmured with downcast eyes, and it looked as though she meant to bow her head to him, to pull away and bend her knee in some sort of courtesy, but he would not allow that. He could never allow that.

"Cariad," he said.

Her eyes were on him then, a flash of gray intelligence under a still luxuriant sweep of lashes. She looked startled. But she did not smile even a little, and her chin stayed stubbornly level as a little pinch formed in her lips. He remembered that pinch, though it had not used to be so severe. It meant she was suppressing unwise words.

Without thinking, he did what he would have done years ago in a secret sunlit patch of grass, far from prying eyes. He kissed her, pressed his lips to that endearing pinch. The crowd was pleased. He could faintly hear them over the pounding of his heart. She was warm, a sudden heat rising from her face accompanied a sharp intake of breath. He ended it quickly, fearing she would stiffen or pull away.

Amid the cheering the priest beckoned them forward, and holding her hand high in his, Robert led his bride forward to the church doors so that they may say their vows. It was strange and yet perfectly right, he thought, that these would be the first words spoken between them after so many years. As he waited for the cheers to subside, she looked full at him, her eyes roving over his face. He could not read her expression except to say that he saw no chagrin or regret. He thought he looked much as she did, with more lines around his eyes and less tautness to his face, but still recognizable for all that.

"I pledge to you the faith of my body, that I will keep you in health and in sickness, and in any condition it pleases the Lord to place you." He repeated the words after the priest, watching Eluned closely for any emotion. Her composure was absolute, a stark and unnerving contrast to the tumult in him. "And that I shall not abandon you for better or worse, until death parts us."

She said her own vows steadily, easily. Even when the priest enjoined her to promise obedience and compliance to her husband, she repeated the words without hesitation – without even a sideways glance at him – and Robert began to fear that he had dreamed everything about her, and all that had been between them.

Once they had entered the church to celebrate the mass, he let himself look at her in quick glances and secretive gazes. There were furrows etched into her brow and her hair was a darker brown now, with strands of silver running through it. It was coiled in heavy braids inside a golden net that glittered with emeralds. He imagined anyone looking at her would see what they were meant to see: wealth in great abundance, power and status that set her apart. But he looked at her and saw her hair unbound, sliding over her bare shoulders. He knew the feel of it in his hands as he braided it, softness between his fingers as she sang a Welsh melody to him.

She wore a bliaut of deep green, touched with gold embroidery all over. The inner lining of the wide sleeves, the laces along the sides, and a border at the hem – all were made from cloth-of-gold, and he had an idea what such extravagance cost. It was her veil that made him smile to himself. Made of some wondrous sheer golden fabric, light and shimmering, it hung from the net that bound her braids. It draped across her throat and framed her face. Any other woman who was no longer a fresh girl would use the veil to conceal the few threads of silver in her hair and draw attention away from her face. But she did the opposite. This was the Eluned he knew, bold in her declarations and daring the world to see her as she was.

His Eluned was in there, beneath all the riches and all the years. He was sure of it.

But his conviction was tested as the day wore into the evening. He expected her eyes to come alive with keen assessment when he presented her to his father, but she only uttered commonplace greetings and calmly assured him that she was honored to join herself to his family. Others came to embrace her and congratulate them and, whether well-known acquaintance or stranger, high-born or humble, family or not, she was polite and distant.

She was a perfectly agreeable bride, pleasant and bland. In his direst imaginings, he could not have envisioned this.

Even when she introduced him to her son, she did not betray any extra warmth or animation. He could never forget how well she adored her daughter, which made such a striking contrast to her indifference toward her son. Robert began to feel the first trickle of real dread as he looked at the boy who had been born more than a year after he and Eluned had parted, and who looked so like his dead father.

What had these years been like for her, how had they so changed her that she would be like a stranger to her son? She almost seemed to embrace the distance, to pull it close and shove it between herself and her son even as the boy – so obviously, to Robert's eyes – wished to close it.

"I have hoped to meet you in France, my lord, but

am full glad that you are come to England instead."
William smiled at him, and it caused Robert to catch
his breath. It was Eluned's smile, that he had last seen
before this boy was born, shining forth from her
son's face.

"Wherever your fair lady mother is, there I am glad
to go." He watched William slide a tentative look
toward Eluned, and endeavored to find a topic less
awkward for the boy. "But tell me, do you travel to
France soon?"

"First I will go to court and make my oath to the
king, but after some time attending my affairs at
Ruardean it would please me to see Gascony, I
think."

"May it please you to taste Gascony first." Robert
waylaid a passing servant and, taking a goblet filled
with wine, offered it to William. "It is from our own
vineyards."

He smiled at William's fervent compliments on the
wine while closely scanning the crowd. There was no
one, in the Ruardean party or anywhere else in the
hall, whom he thought could be Gwenllian.

When he took his place in the middle of the high
board with Eluned seated beside him, he could think
of nothing to say to this quiet woman who did not
look at him. He watched as she stirred her spoon in
the pottage of beef and wine, the silence growing
between them until he decided he must say
something. Like a blind man feeling his way, he
carefully touched on something he knew to be close
to her heart.

"My lady, I am sorry I do not find your daughter
among our guests."

She looked out over the noisy hall as though to

verify this before answering him. "I would not have her travel such a distance when her child will soon be born. It is best for Gwenllian to stay at her home in Morency."

"It is not her first child, though?"

"Nay, her son was born two years ago and by the grace of God both child and mother came through it in good health."

He wanted to ask if she was happy her daughter had married so much later in life than she had. *I had not even an hour between being a child and becoming a mother*, she had once said to him, with furrows in her brow that echoed the ones etched there so many years later. But he could not mention such regrets now, in this place and with this company. He did not know if she had even told anyone that they had known one another years ago.

"Morency," he said instead, and watched her mouth pull taut. "You have married your daughter to a formidable man. I have seen him fight at tourney, and think I have never seen a man better at the sword."

Her chin thrust outwards, a gesture that said everything to him. The glittering veil at her throat fluttered, almost distracting him from the matching spark in her eye. He felt warmth spreading through him at the sight, like a burst of summer had visited him in the chill.

"She is more than a match for him." There was the hint of a triumphant smile at her lips.

"If your spirit runs true in her, I would expect no less."

She seemed for a moment as though she might contradict him, but said nothing. Instead she gave him a startled glance, as though she had forgotten and then been reminded he was there. Her mouth pinched shut again, holding in words he was sure she might have spoken if not for the many listeners nearby.

"Yes, her spirit." She took a sip of spiced wine.

"Even in France we have heard many rumors concerning Ranulf of Morency over the years. I trust he is not so bloodthirsty as the gossips would have us believe?"

"I have had little acquaintance of him. But it has been enough to know that only the most foolish would trifle with him, even were he not great friends with the king."

There was a bitterness in her voice at the last word, and a tension that radiated from her. So she did not like King Edward. Maybe she even hated him. He opened his mouth to ask but a flourish from the musicians, heralding the entrance of the next course, interrupted him. He felt a stab of annoyance. There was so much to ask her, so much he wanted to know. He wanted to hear about every minute of her life for the last eighteen years, and what she had felt when his name had been spoken and she was asked to marry him, and if she remembered the time it had been so wet and cold that they had huddled together beneath their cloaks and only talked for the whole afternoon.

But this was not the place for that. Later, after they finished the feasting and revelry, they could talk freely.

Three roasted swans, so elegantly reconstructed that onlookers could be forgiven if they thought the birds quite alive and swimming on the dais, were followed by two equally impressive peacocks and one magnificent crane whose gray feathers were painted silver. There were enough sounds of appreciation as the servants carried the dishes through the hall that Robert thought it must be a sufficiently splendid display, but he could not help looking to her to see if she took any delight in the festivities. She smiled at it all – at the dishes sailing toward them, at the merry music playing, the chattering guests – but there was no mistaking the emptiness behind the smile. It worried at him, that hollow pleasantness she wore. It caused something like despair to rise up in him to see her wear it so consistently.

As she held her hands under a stream of fragrant water that a servant poured forth from a golden ewer, he watched her closely. There was a wistful look that floated across her features as she looked at the ewer that was shaped like a dragon, water pouring forth from its mouth, and he remembered a brooch of a similar shape that she used to wear all those years ago. *A bit of my old home,* she had called it, because dragons were a symbol of Wales.

In a flash of insight he suddenly understood, and felt like the callow young fool she had named him on their first meeting. He waited until the servant retreated before speaking.

"Eluned. I am sorry we could not meet before our wedding feast, for I would offer you comfort in a less festive company for the loss of your brother. And Dinwen, that was your home before Ruardean." She paused in drying her hands. "I have remembered well how you spoke of its beauty, the bluebells in spring."

Her gray eyes turned to him again and knew he had not imagined the sadness in her. She did not speak for a long moment, and he began to worry he should not have said it. But then she nodded in acknowledgement, and spoke.

"I would petition the king to grant us those lands, if my lord husband wishes it."

There was no doubt his father had communicated his ambitions to her, of the lands and titles he hoped this union would bring. But he did not want to speak of such arrangements just yet. Lands, titles, political ambitions, all the things her wealth and connections might accomplish in the future – all of these seemed like the smallest, easiest prizes. Far greater was the challenge of finding her again beneath this stilted speech, this empty expression.

"Hardly can I even believe I am your lord husband. But knowing that it is so, I am content to let you tell me which lands will merit the effort. Your talent for such things can only have grown since you recommended this estate to me."

There was a moment of startled confusion in her eyes again, and then it was as though his words had woken her from a deep and troubling sleep. She looked at him directly at last, in recognition, a tiny smile playing at the corner of her mouth as she spoke.

"You have done well with it. This manor house is tripled in size from the days when Whittington held it, and the land and villages so much improved they are near unrecognizable." She leaned a little closer. "Did my lord Whittington's curses follow you to France?"

"Curses were the only thing he had in abundance, and I invited him to spend as many as he liked."

Her response was a look of such fondness that it dazed him, made him a green boy again. Then turned to wave away the servant who offered her the swan in mustard sauce, taking instead the woodcock baked in pastry. With a little puff of steam, she broke open the hard pastry, and as she spoke the fragrance of the bacon that was wrapped around the tender meat made him reach for his own plate.

"I have thought often of the good it may have done for Aaron of Lincoln, to sell it to you," she said. "But we can no longer name him Aaron of Lincoln since he has quit that place. I fear Whittington may have done him harm out of spite."

"Let your mind be at peace. Aaron came to me in France for a short time before moving on to Basel." He spooned the mustard sauce over his meat, his appetite fully recovered now that she spoke so naturally. "It was not the anger of Whittington he fled, but the mood of England toward the Jews here."

There was a short pause as she sipped the wine. "You told him to come to you." She did not ask it, but he knew it was a question nonetheless.

"I did. He was so burdened with worry for the fate of his sons, and what protection I could offer was trifling. I am sorry France was no better for him than was England, but he has had great success in Basel. If he had known of your concern, is sure he would have sent word to ease your mind."

This admission did not alter the arrested look on her face. It seemed to trouble her, though he could not imagine why. She only murmured, "Your kindness would shame the saints," but she said it so softly that he was glad to pretend he hadn't heard it.

He watched her fingers playing with a bit of pastry crust. Her earlier indifference was now replaced by an air of distraction, as though she were thinking very hard and only sometimes remembered to take interest in the celebration around her. From the corner of his eye he saw his brother approaching, only to be intercepted by Kit before he could reach the place where Robert and Eluned sat. Kit drew him into conversation, and Robert smiled his thanks at his friend before turning to Eluned again.

"Only last week I wrote to Aaron, and gave him news of our wedding." He took his cup in hand and gestured at a servant to fill it with the plain wine, unspiced because it was a finer vintage. "He is a merchant now, and we deal together in wine. Taste and you will see why it is in high demand, and why he is so glad to know I will always keep a portion aside for him."

He held the cup to her lips and she drank a swallow. Her lashes lifted, an expression of pleasure at the taste, her eyes meeting his over the brim of the cup. In an instant they were back in that moment a lifetime ago, when she had looked at him over the edge of her cup and he had known they would become lovers. For only a breath, the thrill of deep awareness connected them – and then she looked away and said something about the wine as he watched her skin go pink and then white.

All through the rest of the meal, he reveled in the memory of that moment. He told her of his estate in France, how he had assumed its management and led the seemingly endless efforts to keep King Edward's French lands safe from Spanish aggression. She had great interest in it and asked many questions, as he expected she would. There was still such confidence and competence in her, magnified and polished by the years.

She was changed; she was wary. But she was still Eluned, curious and discerning, and to talk to her like this again gave him hope as nothing else had.

A troupe of acrobats tumbled through the hall to the great delight of the guests, and she allowed a polite smile at their antics. He thought of telling her how Kit's son had been taken as surety against an imagined aggression and what might be done about it. But this was the wonder that he still could not comprehend – that he need not hurry to tell her everything now. They would have tomorrow, and the next day and the next. He would not have to surrender her after an hour and wonder when he might see her again. Now the dessert came, and they would soon end the feasting and be alone together, to talk and lie together all the night through. It seemed an impossible wealth.

"My son will go to Edward's court, and I would have us follow him there," she said as she was served a dish of spiced pears, painted in gold leaf and set in almond cream. "There we may hope the king remembers you if he truly will make a new lordship in the marches."

"Christmas with the king, then? We will meet with many others who think that prize should be theirs."

Her lips pursed. "None have done such a great service for Edward as you have, in preserving his duchy. You will remind him of this, and I will add our petition for Dinwen which lies close to the lands which are my marriage portion. I have experience of ruling in the marches, you have experience of maintaining his power in border lands. He is beholden to you, and will be happy for such an obvious choice. He values expediency, this king."

As she methodically laid out the points in their favor, she cut the gold skin away from the pear to get at the flesh. Careful and exact movements, careful and exact plans. There was no hint of a woman who was given to passionate outbursts. There was no relish in her voice, nor even interest as she spoke words that in another age would have been imbued with fire.

"If it pleases you," he said.

"If my lord has no care for the lands or title, or if there be other plans for achieving this ambition, I am content to do as I am bidden."

He stared at the discarded golden peel beside her plate, glittering and empty, and thought he had not felt such despair since the moment she had said he must never see her again.

"I would speak of anything else now, Eluned. There is time enough to plan such things." He took care to say it without rebuke. Then he lowered his voice to a conspiratorial whisper, desperate to see that hint of a real smile in her face again. "Instead let me entertain you with tales of my father's visit to me at Christmas four years ago, when he thought to gift me with a bride from Scotland. She was so amusing and he was so appalled at her brashness that I admit I was almost tempted."

She gave a delicate snort. "Not Atholl's youngest girl?"

"That was her," he replied. "She was barely out of swaddling and her first words to me were to ask how much older than Methuselah I was."

He was gratified to see her pause in bringing the spoon full of almond cream to her smiling lips. "And how did you reward this impudence?"

"With laughter, of course. She looked conscious of the insult and then assured my father he looked quite hale for all that he'd fathered a son so old."

She did not laugh, but he could tell by the way she

pressed her lips together that she very much wanted to. It heartened him. It was enough, for now.

✚ ✚ ✚

When it was time to withdraw to their bedchamber, the ceremony was less boisterous and more private than it might have been if they had been young. This was the first thing about the day to make Robert glad he was not in fact twenty years younger. Before leaving the celebration in the hall he danced with Eluned. It overwhelmed him. It brought up vivid memories of how they had danced so long ago, all the effort they had put into hiding their feelings in public, the many furtive and freighted glances exchanged, and the thrill they had taken in every slight but sanctioned touch. For all he could see, though, it was only a dance to her. She looked as if it held no meaning for her at all.

He was still reeling from both the memories and her detached demeanor, when his brother and Kit brought him to where she waited in the room they would share. She had gone ahead of him by only a few minutes, and stood waiting for him in her full dress. The priest spent an inordinate amount of time blessing the marriage bed, a sure sign of his father's influence. Eluned was unnaturally still throughout the prayers, a resplendent statue in the shadows of the room.

The small party of well-wishers took their leave, with only Kit and one of her ladies lingering behind the rest. Kit gave him a look that was commiseration and encouragement before clapping a hand to his shoulder and quitting the room.

"I need no more help, Joan." Eluned was removing pins from her hair and waving the girl away. "Go you and find Sir Heward. Better you learn now what he is like in his cups, before you are wed."

The girl blushed a little, made her courtesy to them both, and was gone. The embers glowed in the hearth and the music of the minstrels could be heard faintly, drifting from the hall. Her cloth-of-gold sleeves flashed dimly as she moved her hands over her hair, and the laces at the sides of her bliaut had been loosened. It was such a perfect picture of intimacy, this quiet moment in this room with her as she prepared for bed, that he could almost believe they had never lived apart.

"Let me," he said, and came forward to where she struggled to free the pin that held her golden veil.

She went still as a statue again, unmoving beneath his hands while he worked at the cloth pinned behind her ear. For a moment he thought he could smell fresh grass and wild primroses, so vivid was the memory of their first time together. He was as uncertain as that now, as tentative – while she stood calm and expressionless. He thought of her few scant smiles, and of her eyes meeting his over the cup. How she had flushed so prettily a few hours ago, this woman who pretended to be made of cool marble.

He finally freed the veil at one side. Then he brushed his fingers along the shadowed place beneath her jaw, and felt the frantic beat of her pulse. He bent and kissed her there, where the state of her heart was not hidden from him.

"Eluned," he said, and took her lips. She was not a cold statue anymore, but a soft and fragile thing. He felt her trembling, felt her warm lips open beneath his, and it was like no time had passed at all. It felt so comfortable and so very right that he could almost believe it was just another dream of her, even down to the taste of anticipation, the promise of deeper passion.

He rested his forehead against hers, heard her quick breathing, felt her hand touching his. It was just like before, like all the countless reunions they had had in their secret place. A kiss in greeting, the relief in finding her there, then the little stone given from his hand to hers before they would lie down together under the shade of the trees.

He did not have that little stone, now. It was long lost. But in the silence he reached into his pocket to close his fingers around a familiar shape, and slipped it into her waiting hand. He opened his eyes to watch her pull slightly away from him, open her hand, and stare down at it. She wore a look of wonder.

"I found it." He spoke just above a whisper, fearful of breaking the spell. "I searched until I found it. I kept it to give to you on our next meeting."

Her fingertips traced over the silver button as his had done for years, following the design of a griffin under a band of lent-lilies. These were symbols from the arms of Ruardean, and he had hated the design even as he had loved it, all these years, because it had been hers.

"You thought…" Her voice trailed off as she looked at it. The wonder in her face was gradually replaced with something else, something between disbelief and confusion. And then her voice changed, too. "You thought we would meet again?"

She moved a step away from him, and it broke the perfect, still circle of enchantment that had held them.

The little distance suited the coolness in her tone. Still she gazed down at the button that had held her shoe – that had failed to hold it closed – all those years ago when they had believed they would only be separated for a few weeks.

"I hoped. I never stopped hoping for it." He admitted it easily, so sure was he that it would reach into her and find the woman who had been his lover. "I never stopped loving you."

Her body moved in shadows beneath her loosened gown as she lowered herself onto a bench near the fire. She held her hand open, palm flat, the button staring up at her. He waited in the silence that stretched between them, as he had waited for years and years.

"I told you to stop. I told you not to hope."

"You did." He smiled. "I have defied you."

She turned her face up at last and looked full at him, stern gray eyes in a pale face. There was no answering fondness there, no happiness. It dispelled whatever was left of warmth in the room.

"You have loved a dead memory," she said, not unkindly. "I am no longer that girl."

He shook his head even as a feeling of dread began to grow in him. "You are Eluned, who I loved. Naught can change that."

But there was something in the way she held herself, or the tilt of her head – something was not right. His Eluned was there, he was sure of it. He had tasted it in her kiss. But there was something in her that told him he was wrong in some essential way.

"We think memories are truth," she went on, calm and relentless, "but they deceive us even as we cherish them. The truth is that many years ago, we were foolish and arrogant. We lusted and we sinned. We called it love. But that summer ended long ago."

"Do you tell me your love ended with it?"

"Love," she said, and moved her head in a little gesture of dismissal. The golden veil still hung at one side of her face, because he had only freed one pin. It shimmered with her movement, trailing down the side of her neck to her shoulder, reflecting the little light from the fire.

That was when he saw what was wrong. The birthmark on her throat was there. It was everything he remembered – the size and color, the height from her collar bone, the teardrop shape – except that it was on the right side of her throat. Not the left. Yet he remembered it vividly, exactly. He closed his eyes and saw it, a bright image preserved over the years. In his memories he ran his finger across that mark and opened his mouth over it and looked for it every time she threw her head back to laugh as they sat in dappled sunlight. He had thought of it a thousand times over the years. He remembered that mark on the left side of her throat as well as he remembered her saying *I will love you until I die*.

He opened his eyes and looked at her, his breath coming too fast. He had remembered it wrong. It was as simple as that. As damning, as awful as that: he had remembered it wrong.

His Eluned burned hot and bright as the sun. She was the cleverest person he had ever known. She loved him and called him her Robin. She had a mark on her throat just to the left of center.

This empty woman before him now was made of cold stone and spoke to him in a reasoned voice about the deceptiveness of memory. She waved away the notion of love, and called it the dead past.

"You have held that summer as a treasure," she said, her gray eyes fixed on the hearth and the button forgotten in her open palm. "You have hidden it away for safekeeping, to be taken out only rarely, to savor or to venerate. But I have laid the days of it before me like playing cards upon a table, one after the other. I took them out and examined them over and over again, until there was no mystery to them. Until the shine wore off them and I could see them clearly."

It was like standing on the sand as the tide came in, sure footing lost in a swirl of water that threatened to pull him under. It was all the more terrible because she was entirely right. He had held those memories as his greatest treasure. He had built his life around them, protected them, believed they were the most real and important part of himself.

Yet the mark was on the wrong side of her throat. Her voice held no fire; it was only a little sad.

"What was it to you?" He asked it though he feared the answer. He had always feared it. A dalliance, a distraction, an amusement for a bored lady.

"It was a dream," she said.

She had said it before, in the dark and with the smell of rosemary all around. *It was a dream, and now we must wake.* But he had not woken. His waking was eighteen years late. *You are a great fool, my Robin,* said the Eluned of his memory, and he knew he must leave this room now, immediately.

But he paused as he passed her where she still sat unmoving, looking at the glowing embers. The silver button he had thought to carry to his grave sat in the palm of her hand. He stepped toward her to take it back, but her fingers curled over it in the same instant. He was sure it was a reflex, an impulse. She did not look to him, nor even did she seem to blink.

He looked for a moment at where his token was hidden in her hand, the white beneath her nails where her fingertips pressed her fist closed. Her expression was not changed. She did not even glance at him as he left her alone and walked out into the bright colors and gay music he had arranged to celebrate their joyous reunion.

Chapter 5

The Work to be Done

Christopher Manton seemed to her to be entirely too observant. It was an intelligent attentiveness, one in which he often noticed important things that others missed entirely. While virtually every member of their party stole quick, assessing glances at her as they traveled, Manton had saved his scrutiny for his friend, her husband. He was ever at Robert's side, whispering in his ear, watching him carefully, showing a concern so discreet that Eluned thought she was the only one who saw the extent of it. She did not have much personal experience of friends – none at all of deep friendship over many years – so she reserved her judgment of this behavior, of this friend.

"Kit," Robert said to him now as they all sat together in a private room just a day before they would reach Edward's court at Rhuddlan. "My lady wife would ask for Dinwen from the king."

He went on, naming the other lands that could be added to theirs if the king would grant them, but Eluned heard only the echo of him saying *my lady wife*. There was a hint of gravel in his voice that had not been in his younger self. It was not the voice that had lived in her memory, but it was a perfect accompaniment to the twist of irony in his words. He named her his lady wife as though it were a trick played on him, and he invited his friend to share in the humor.

Lands and wealth and worldly aspirations, on and on he spoke. She let his words float past, utterly uninterested in these things that had dictated her whole life. Instead she thought of the contents of her baggage, items packed with care and forethought of the task ahead. Her finest gowns, the gifts for Edward and his queen, bundles of medicinal herbs from Master Edmund; and alongside these necessities were her uncle's psalter, Madog's knife, a silver button from a forgotten shoe.

In her mind's eye she saw those objects, the metallic glint of them in the dark corners of her baggage, their real worth known only to her. *How long does love live on, Madog, starving in the dark.*

"Mortimer."

The name woke her, pulled her out of her reverie with a jerk that drew Kit Manton's eye. Robert was speaking now of the Mortimers, which pieces of Wales might be claimed by that family and how likely was Edward to favor the younger brother.

"I will wager the lady of Ruardean can tell us many things about the Mortimers," said Robert, who raised expectant brows at her. It put crooked furrows in his forehead, which mesmerized her for a moment. She had never thought of how his face might age. If she had, she would not have guessed at these rumpled good looks, this appealing ruggedness.

"If my lady Eluned has any insight, I will be grateful for it," said Kit. His look was just as expectant as Robert's, but without the edge of hostility lurking at the back of his eyes. She was fully awake to the conversation now.

"Insight?" she asked in a mild tone, watching him closely. "Into the Mortimers?"

Kit nodded. "The new Lord Mortimer, or his younger brother Roger who will be at Edward's court."

"But do you not have long acquaintance of them both? Can you not see their stronghold from your own estate?"

He blinked in obvious surprise, as though he had never expected her to know such a thing. And indeed she had not known, until she had decided she should learn something about this friend to her husband. Manton was a minor lord, his father granted the small estate by old King Henry, only a speck on the map next to such a vast and mighty force as Mortimer. He had been at Kenilworth, where he had probably met Robert. He had returned from France two years ago with a wife and some number of children. And he was like a brother to Robert de Lascaux.

"You see?" Robert reached for his cup with a sidelong glance at his friend. "I told you."

"Told him what?" she asked.

Kit Manton looked back and forth between Robert and Eluned for a moment before answering her himself. "That you believe there is no such thing as a small detail, nor is any person unimportant."

A small silence settled over them and she looked down at the table. It held a plate heaped with a variety of wastel bread, some stuffed with dried berries and some with bits of apple. Of course Robert would remember more than just the words of love they had exchanged. Of course he would. Just as she remembered which of these breads he would prefer, how he would tear the small loaf in half and then half again, before biting into it.

"Only a fool overlooks a thing because he thinks it beneath his notice, you said to me once." She could feel him looking at her, and she shifted her eyes away from the bread. "Anything might matter, and so it all matters."

She pushed away the memory of the servant who had told Walter that his wife had smiled too much at a young man. Yes. It all mattered.

So his friend knew, then. In his face, in the way he held himself, she could see that this man knew Robert had been her lover. She could also see that Manton reserved his judgment of her, as much as she reserved her judgment of him. Yet why would a friend who was like a brother bother to reserve his judgment?

"Ah. You need me," she said to Kit Manton, dispensing of the delicate dance she might have indulged in, had she more time or inclination. "Is it some scheme against Mortimer, or must you simply get by him to achieve some other end?"

From the corner of her eye she watched a wry smile curl Robert's mouth. "I wonder if my lady can deal with a man without she schemes or looks to gain the advantage of him."

She would have scoffed at this critical tone and asked him if he had ever dealt with any men who did

97

not scheme for advantage with every breath, but Kit Manton cast a silencing look at his friend and then looked directly at her.

"Mortimer holds my son as hostage, my lady, and I would have him back. Call it what you will, only help deliver him home."

There was an urgency to him, an intensity that suggested he felt danger breathing on his son's neck at this very moment. All her senses focused on him, everything in her alert and attentive.

"Which Mortimer?"

"It was their father who demanded a hostage, the old lord before he died. My son has dwelled in the household of Isabella Mortimer for more than a year."

Of all the Mortimers, Isabella was the least likely to instill fear. And to demand hostage was no strange or cruel practice in itself. She waited for him to say more, but he did not. It must be a tangled tale indeed.

"Come, tell me." She could hear that imperious ring in her voice, which had no place in this small room with these men. She took a deep breath and strove to control her tone. She did not like being in these close quarters with them, this intimate talk. She missed her cold and empty bower. "I can only advise you if I know the full circumstance. How came you to be compelled to give your son as hostage, and what are the conditions of his release?"

He nodded once, firm and decided. It made her like him, that he did not bristle at her impatience or take a condescending air, nor show an overweening deference. It was a rare thing to be accepted as an equal, from a man. Indeed it was a rare thing to be called to counsel her husband at all.

"My estate is small next to Mortimer, and to the great abbey that bounds us to the north, but its value is not small. There is silver in the ground at the western edge, and we are given permission of the king to mine it."

He went on to tell how thieves would come and come again, as frequent and unstoppable as rats to a granary, harrying the guards at the mine and stealing what they could. They slipped onto the property from the west – from Mortimer land – "Though I do not accuse Mortimers of profiting from it," he was quick to say. It was only that they did nothing to prevent the thieves. Finally one day, they had learned where the thieves were camped in the wilds just across the river on Mortimer lands. Word was sent to Mortimer's castellan, but Manton did not wait for his powerful neighbor before acting.

"The castellan gave no reply, and Mortimer himself would be at least a week in answer. And I knew he would only say that they could spare no men from their…Welsh campaign." Here he cast an apologetic look to her, then shrugged. "So I sent my own men. But when they arrived in the place, they found no thieves. They found only some of Mortimer's garrison men, who accused us of sending armed soldiers west without permission of the king."

He did not have to say more for her to know the accusations against him: Mortimer would have thought Manton had sent an armed party to Wales last summer, at the height of the fighting.

"Had you any dealings with the Welsh princes, that your allegiance to the crown might be questioned?" But she knew the answer. If Manton had ever inclined toward helping the Welsh, she would have known of him long ago.

"Nay, my lady, nor did my father ever have any such dealings. And so did I say to Mortimer, but still he saw aggression where there was none. He demanded proof that we did not conspire to lay claim to that corner of his lands. It was his true fear from the start." Here he waved a hand in irritated dismissal. "There was an old dispute over that border between our estates, but it is long dead."

"It would not matter," she said. "He would see only that you sent armed men onto his land without his permission, and he would seek to explain it as greed and ambition. As a show of good faith, you offered your son as hostage?"

"Aye, on the condition that he be returned to me when I renounced any claim to that land. And so I did, but old Mortimer died just days before the quitclaim reached his hands. Now his son pretends ignorance of the terms and keeps my boy as surety against future aggression."

No doubt there was some reason, something that motivated Mortimer to keep a hostage of seemingly little value. With time and ample consideration, she might guess at it. But she had stopped caring why cruel men were cruel, and what their cruelties revealed. All that mattered was that the Mortimers did as they pleased, and took whatever they wanted only because they wanted it.

"How old is the boy?"

"Robin has had his eleventh birthday last week."

She could not help but give a little flinch at the name, but resisted looking toward Robert. "I do not say it is right, but still you must see that he is in as fine a household as you could hope for, at an age where he would be sent as squire anyway. Many would be glad to have their child in the charge of a lady such as Isabella Mortimer."

"He is not there as squire."

"Nay, but I do not doubt he is tutored as one and treated well." It made her tired, these cares of his. She did not want more cares, not even for a moment, not even borrowed from this man who could not simply be glad that his son was whole and healthy. "I have said it is not just, but there is no harm and much good that may come of it until you learn a way to gain Mortimer's trust. Wherefore this urgency to have him out of her hands?"

"But that's just it, my lady. Isabella will soon deliver my son to the safekeeping of her brother Roger Mortimer."

At this, the fatigue in her fell away and a flare of rage rose up to steal her breath. It was so swift and fierce that she felt dizzy with it. She was saved from voicing her outrage only because words were impossible to marshal, so she simply stared at him with eyes wide and her mouth falling slightly open. Kit Manton spared a glance toward Robert, and she saw some kind of understanding between them. It was Robert who spoke, and now his voice was gentle again, devoid of irony but still a low rumble that reminded her he was no longer a boy.

"The Welsh princes of Powys," he said. "I did not doubt you would know of their fate."

"They were kin to me," she said, the fury pulling her voice tight. "Through my mother's side, they were kin. I petitioned the king for their keeping when they were orphaned, but he gave them to Mortimer."

She had fumed about it for months. Two

orphaned boys, last in a royal Welsh bloodline, and Roger Mortimer had been made their guardian. When their little dead bodies washed up on the shores of the River Dee two years ago, with no one left to inherit their vast lands and wealth, it was Roger Mortimer who was granted everything. The vicissitudes of fortune, said the Mortimers. Murder by design, believed Eluned and many others.

For a moment, she imagined Robert's reaction, and Kit's, if she told them she was already planning to kill Roger Mortimer and so they need not worry. They would laugh and think it a jest. Even she almost laughed at it, the idea of someone like her – a slight, aging woman of diminishing worth and importance – somehow killing a professional soldier as formidable as Roger Mortimer. That was why she could do it, of course. There was sometimes great value in being dismissed as unimportant. There was an advantage to absurdity.

But these men before her did not think her unimportant, nor dismiss her worth. Kit Manton looked at her, honest and grave, concern for his son written on every feature. She could see how, in this one aim, he was like her: Whatever it took, no matter who must be made ally and what must be sacrificed, they would do it all and gladly, to win against Mortimer.

"I lived away from England too long," he was saying. "I tell you plainly, lady, that I understand little about the Marcher lords save that they are known to have more power than other lords of equal rank."

"More autonomy, I would say," she corrected him. "And more of a taste for brutality, among other things. They answer to no one but the king and even he cannot control them entirely, as I presume you will have discovered when you appealed to Edward."

It was Robert who answered her. "He said it is not a matter to be settled by the crown, and dismissed it."

"As is to be expected. It is a dispute between two lords, and the more powerful man wins." She paused as Kit's features hardened with a bitterness she understood more than he could ever know. "It is a harsh truth, better accepted than denied. Might wins in the Marches as it does in all the world."

"You do not think I can win against so strong a house as Mortimer, then?"

He had the look of a plain-dealing man forced out of his element. Her eyes roamed over his fair hair, ears that stuck out straight from the sides of his head, the lines around his eyes and mouth that showed he had lived a life of laughter. She felt a sudden pity for him, so clearly was he a good man whose only concern was his son's safety.

"I think force will not win your son back. Cunning is a more sure way, but first you must have something the Mortimers need badly enough to give up this advantage they have over you. And that will likely require too much time – years, even. Since force and cunning are not available to you…" A faint smile tugged at her lips. "You can wrestle with a trained bear or dance with it, my uncle used to say. You may risk looking foolish to dance with a bear, but are a little less likely to be torn to pieces. That was always the strategy he employed when he must deal with Mortimer."

Kit's eyes lit with curiosity. "You have an uncle who has won against Mortimer?"

"Against old Mortimer, and only in small

confrontations." She looked at her hands, white fingers against the dark wood of the table, and prepared herself to speak the words. She had not needed to say it aloud, before now. It would hurt. "He is dead. In the fighting this summer past."

"Not your Uncle Rhys?" Robert held his cup suspended halfway to his lips.

At her nod, such a look came over him that she had to turn away. She tried to swallow through the terrible burning in her throat. She had only to endure it until it passed. From the corner of her eye she saw that he reached toward her as though to take her hand. But he stopped the movement short, and that hurt too.

"He called you the keenest wits in your family."

She gazed at him for a long moment, enduring the pinpricks to her heart, the unexpected flood of gratitude that left no room for anything else. She was suddenly a starving child who is given a crumb and would beg for more. Who else was left to her, that knew this about her uncle? Who else understood what he had meant to her? If she thought there was a chance she could do it without losing command of herself, she would ask him to repeat to her everything he remembered of what she'd said. She would beg for every word and every story about her uncle that she had told Robert, that he had kept fresh and pristine in his memory, locked in the same place as his foolish love for her all these years.

Now he raised his cup and said, "A good man, and a life well lived. May his soul be at peace."

Kit murmured something similar, and they drank to her uncle's memory. She nodded, pressed her trembling fingers to the table and fought for composure in the lengthening silence. It came only when she recalled they had been speaking of Mortimer and how best to win against him. She could help this man.

"Edmund, the older brother, will be like his father. Concern yourself with his judgment," she said when she was sure her voice was steady. There, that was better. Easier to talk about these mundane plans, soothing even. "To play friend to Roger Mortimer is wise as well, but by law it is Edmund who holds your son. Roger has nearly as much power as Edmund, and from rumor he will soon be equal in wealth too. Is certain he will be given a piece of Wales to call his own. But it is too much to hope the brothers will be rivals. They have too often acted as one in common interest."

"You say I am to play friend to the Mortimers? While they falsely hold my son?" It was gratifying to see that Manton did not seem offended by the suggestion, merely skeptical.

"At least you must not play at being their enemy, which is what they will expect from you. You have sought my experience of dealing with Marcher lords and what I know is that without fail, they hold tight what power they have and seek to increase their lands at every opportunity. Where opportunity does not exist, they create it. This is even more true of a Mortimer, by far."

The weariness had crept into her again. Endless hours spent in consideration of how best to kill Roger Mortimer only energized her, yet these few minutes of focusing on someone else's problems exhausted her. It left her undisposed toward diplomacy, yet she must think of a kind way to tell Kit Manton that he was weak, that he must be like the dog who bares his belly to show submission. "You must discover why he thinks you are a threat to him, and then show him you are not. You must make him believe that you do not share these ambitions."

"That will be easy enough. I do not share them." Kit eased back in his chair, his features relaxing. "I am not an ambitious man. I leave it to my son to strive for more one day, if he is so inclined."

"Nor will he be inclined, if he is anything like his namesake," said Robert. Then he slanted a crooked smile in her direction, a careless little thing. It caused warmth to bloom in a region of her heart.

She found herself on her feet, the sound of her chair scraping against the floor filling the room. Both men looked at her with slightly widened eyes, as startled as she was by her sudden move.

"I would rest before the evening meal."

They both hastened to rise even as she made her way to the door. Manton opened the door for her and made a brief bow, thanking her for her counsel. She looked at his gleaming gold hair flop over his forehead as he straightened, and watched as he pushed it away in what was surely a habitual gesture. She decided that she liked him. In the usual way, a man like him – easygoing, no great ambitions, artless in every way – would only rouse her contempt. But the world looked very different to her of late, as did the men who moved in it. If more were like Kit Manton, perhaps she would have been quite different, too.

"I will speak to Isabella Mortimer. She holds Edmund's trust. We can hope that she will give some indication of why they contrive to hold your son, but she is no fool," Eluned cautioned. "And she is a Mortimer through and through."

Kit smiled at her. "If I could choose any wit to match against hers, lady, I would choose yours."

She could think of no reply to this, so she merely nodded in what she hoped was a graceful acknowledgement. As she left, she caught sight of Robert choosing a round of wastel bread. He picked one that was stuffed with apple, as she had known he would, and he tore it in half and in half again. What useless bits of knowledge her famed wit held onto.

✠ ✠ ✠

They sat together at the high board in this little manor house a half-day's ride from the place where Edward held court. They were joined by other highborn guests, as was usual, but there were few in this place. She watched as Robert laughed with Kit Manton until that man said he would find the scribe and send a letter to his wife before they reached court. Now the guests next to her spoke to one another, leaving Robert and her alone in an expectant silence. He drank, and she watched his throat move as he swallowed, and was made dizzy with a lust that was no longer only a memory, no longer theoretical.

She had miscalculated, or had failed to calculate at all, the effect he would have on her.

How careless she had been, to think that she was past the age for such feelings. In all the memories she had forced herself to stare in the eye, she had somehow forgotten the physical reality of him. He was only an inch taller than she was and did not tower over her as her husband had done. Though he had thickened with muscle, his youthful litheness was not entirely lost. The result was a presence that was not intimidating or dominating in the least, but still imbued with a very comfortable masculinity. It infiltrated her senses until she could taste him on the air she breathed.

She did not know where he slept at night, but it was not at her side. The young girl in their party with the copper curls and inviting smile often drew his eye, but if he bedded her he was uncommonly discreet about it. Eluned looked now for the girl among the diners and found her in a cluster of other maids, her bright laughter at a finely calibrated volume designed to draw male attention without grating on the ear. The girl was clearly vexed at Robert's failure to look in her direction and surreptitiously shifted her glance to Eluned, who was poised to meet it.

It was an unexpected pleasure to watch the flush on the girl's face grow deeper until it was almost purple. It was exceptionally unbecoming, Eluned thought, clashing as it did with her red hair. The poor thing looked mottled and mortified. Ah, youth.

Robert's inquiring voice interrupted her thoughts. "It is more than a decade, is it not, that you ruled Ruardean in your late husband's absence?"

"Fourteen years." Her breath quickened uncontrollably, though she told herself it was witless to grow nervous because he spoke to her. It was only that he had not spoken to her alone like this since their wedding night. She was unused to it, to him.

Poison, she thought. *The blade. An accident.* These were her options for ending Roger Mortimer, and repeating them had become as soothing as prayer. But she felt Robert's eyes on her and was not soothed.

"I have not offered you sympathy for his death." He gave her a frank look, assessing but not unkind. "Should I?"

They had never spoken of Walter. She had never said she loved him, or hated him, or felt anything at all toward him – and except for that long-ago argument they had had, Robert had never asked. He had never wanted to know. Yet now, he did.

"I spat on his bones," she heard herself say.

He took a moment to consider this. "No sympathy, then," he said blandly. Then he gave that roguish half-smile. "But I shall save a drop of it for his bones, little though they need it."

She looked away sharply. He had lost none of his charm at all. From the moment he had lifted her down from her horse in front of the church where they were wed, she had seen her mistake. There always was some flaw, in all her plans, born of impatience or blindness or her own arrogance. In this case, it was all three: impatient to get at Mortimer, blind to what Robert might still feel for her, arrogant enough to think her own feelings could be easily controlled. There were other men she might have made her husband, and gotten the advantages of marriage without this constant flood of feeling, these uncomfortable twinges of conscience. Other men who would not be hurt by her indifference.

"I make no claim to be the best of wives," she said. And then her tongue defied the iron rule of her reason once more and said, "I never was, as you have certain cause to know."

He opened his mouth but before he could answer, servants came to fill their cups and offer fragrant plum tarts. It did not break the atmosphere that she had conjured with her words. She thought of the little pink stone, of how often she had plucked it from her pocket and set it in the precise spot where he would look for it. How she had hugged the secret to herself until he came and pulled the clothes from her, as a starving man peels an orange. She was sure he must think of it too, so heavy did the memory of their sin hang in the air between them.

When the servants left them, she watched him as he slowly twirled a spoon in his fingers.

"How many others have there been since me?" He tried for a careless curiosity, but she heard the bitterness in it even before she understood his meaning. "I was the first, I think, but I wonder now how many came after me. Fourteen years, fourteen men?"

He might have stricken her and called her whore before all the king's court, and she would not have felt so insulted. She sat frozen in the face of it, trembling with an outrage so sudden and complete that she could not think past it. She was the lady of Ruardean, daughter of a noble line that stretched back to antiquity, mother to a warrior and a mighty Marcher baron, and she would not suffer such offense. She sucked in her breath to answer, but bit her tongue when she realized the only words she had were inadequate and overly defensive.

His spoon was digging at a plum, reducing it to paste, his mouth in a sullen curve. She had hurt him. He had lain himself bare to her, confessed his love without reservation, and she had called it a dream. Now he believed what had been between them was so trivial to her that she would repeat it with another – with a great many others.

Let him think it, she commanded herself. It would be easier for them both, and kinder to him. Hope had no place in her plans.

"Eighteen years," she corrected him, despite her intentions. "Never think I forget that number any more than do you." Then she slowed her quickening breath and returned to a more brisk tone. "But it was fourteen years that I had the sole rule of Ruardean, because my husband did not honor his duty as its lord. If you are so fortunate as to be granted a lordship the equal of Ruardean, I will offer you what experience and knowledge I gained in that time. Then I think you will not malign me, but have cause to be glad of my many years without a man by my side."

He looked as if he would say many things, but kept himself from it. After a moment's pause and another idle stir of his spoon in the wrecked tart, he said, "These Welsh places that Edward would call England and rule as his own – think you it can be done without more blood is spilled?"

"Do you weary of fighting?"

"Do not all men weary of fighting, in time?"

"Edward does not," she answered. "Nor will he stop until his dying breath, to call the whole of this island his. But he has spilt the blood of the last Welsh princes who would resist him. There is little need to spill more, so well did he break the spirit of those who followed them."

A grim look overcame Robert's face. "I have heard Dafydd was tortured and torn in pieces as his punishment."

"You have heard it and I have seen it." She looked away from the pulpy mess of plum tart, the blood-red wine in her cup. "I went to Shrewsbury. He was hacked, not torn."

She knew he watched her, but she did not turn her face to him. Instead her eyes found the girl whom Robert had flirted with so often, and she stared the copper curls. They shone in the firelight and bounced gaily about her fresh young face. It was a lovely sight. Truly it was.

"Eluned," he said, and his voice was full of feeling.

She wanted nothing more than to lay her head against him and rest. It was not her lust and longing that threatened to undo her, but the warmth that came from him in these small moments. With just one word, he could reach inside her and speak to her innermost sorrows. No one else even guessed that she felt such things.

But he thought she had many lovers. She had hurt him. And she had other work to do. *Poison, the blade, an accident.* It was better this way. If she succeeded and was found out, she could not say what punishment there might be for a murderess, even one as highborn as she was. Until recently she would have assumed she would be imprisoned for the rest of her life, or banished to exile. But after the torture and execution of Dafydd, none could say what punishment might be called reasonable. Every day the rules were made anew for Edward's kingdom.

She blinked, swallowed hard, and spoke before Robert did.

"You need not fear that any grand battles must be fought to hold what land the king may give you," she assured him. It was easier, and soothing, to talk of these more commonplace worries. "There is no troublesome viscount who will lay claim to it, such as you dealt with in Gascony."

"Nor a Castilian king to ally with such a rival. But if the Welsh wish to resist, there are as many mountains for them to hide in."

"Let them hide there, and they will starve with only their pride to fill their bellies."

He furrowed his brow. "Would they not steal out in the night to help themselves to my cattle and crops?"

"Some may try, but only if they are not treated fairly under English law. Any resistance will die quickly if they are assured they can prosper without a fight." She allowed herself a small smile, but made sure she did not look directly into the warmth of his eyes as she did so. "Your French vassals gave you no such resistance, I think, or your wine would not taste half so sweet."

Even if she had never known him well, there would be no mistaking the pride in him. She was glad to see it, in spite of herself. He had built something to be proud of, in spite of his claims that he had no ambition.

"Gascons may quarrel among themselves, but put all quarrels aside in the face of outside threat," he said.

"Certes you were an outsider when you came to them, and they had known only the rule of a steward since your father was a boy. Yet you won their love, and defended Edward's lands too, and all the while your land increases its yield. Few estates are so esteemed for their wines." She thought of how different from Wales was that fertile, sunny place he had lived so long. "By whatever means you achieved it there, you may do so here as well."

"It only wanted patience," he shrugged with a

modesty that she could not imagine any other man would show, "and common cause in peace time as well as in strife. And in France I had me no clever wife to smooth the way."

She wanted to ask why he had not married in all these years. She wanted to ask about Kenilworth, and why he had stayed so long from England, and if he had never made peace with his father. Instead, she said, "Wife or no, the lessons you learned there will serve you well here."

He was looking intently at her, so she reached for her cup and drank to prevent herself from saying more. The girl with the copper hair laughed again, throwing back her head, glancing toward the high board to see if Robert noticed.

"Patience and common cause," he said, still studying Eluned. "A clever wife indeed."

Probably he thought they had common cause as man and wife. There was a great prize to be had from Edward in the form of lands and power, and she should care about that. Probably he thought it only wanted patience, and they would grow together again, build a life in common. Probably he thought she cared about his friend's son, and would work to see him brought safe out of the arms of the Mortimers.

But she did not care. She did not want to build anything, not a fortune or a dynasty or a marriage. She had no care for Manton's boy, but was glad to know another detail about her enemy that might prove useful one day. She had only one cause, and it had naught in common with her husband's aims.

"You would do well to rely on virtues more constant than my cleverness," she warned him. It was spoken with a tartness, but meant as an honest bit of counsel.

"And what else about you can I rely upon, Eluned?" He sat back in his chair and looked her over. The ironic twist was back in his words. "It seems you offer me little more than your wits and your wealth."

An ache was forming between her shoulder blades, so stiff and straight did she hold herself. In truth, what had she to offer him? Only bitterness, and a hatred that ate at her. A few tables away, the copper-headed girl fended off the attentions of a knight.

"I will not deny my lord his right to our marriage bed," she said.

She thought of the cold stars, of quick poisons and sharp blades, while she awaited his reply. Finally he let loose a scornful breath, a sound that scoffed at her as he stood up from the table with cup in hand.

"Is no wonder your last husband wandered in the desert for half your marriage." He gave her an elegant bow. "We all thought him mad, but I think he was only seeking some warmth."

Chapter 6

The Longing

Amid a small crowd of advisors and bosom friends, King Edward was describing the effort over the years to hold his duchy in France. It was a tale in which Robert featured prominently, and by the end of it he was so covered over in royal appreciation that he could almost believe the last two decades of his life were not wasted.

"By the saints," he said to the king with a smile, "I think I have pleased my king almost as much as I have pleased my father. It is he who should be heaping thanks upon you, for he will tell you that my desire to serve you well is all that commends me."

This effectively turned the conversation, with amusement, toward Robert's father. Happily, his brother Simon was present and prevented Robert from being too dismissive of his own accomplishments, which might convince the king he was not worth elevating. Simon was right hand to Edward's most trusted advisor Burnell, who assured him the king looked to reward Robert in some significant way. It seemed all that was required at this point was a show of desire on Robert's part – and he must avoid displeasing the king, of course.

Surprisingly, it was hinted that Eluned, of all people, caused the king to hesitate. "Your cause is strengthened by your marriage," Simon had said to him when they had arrived at court, "but there is something in your wife that gives Edward and Burnell pause. I cannot imagine what it may be, nor do they ever say it outright. Yet do I feel certain she is under scrutiny."

His wife would soon be joining them here in these lavish royal apartments, for a not quite private audience with the king. Simon had urged Robert to speak with Eluned first, to warn her of these vague suspicions and tell her that all their hopes hung on her performance. He had not done it, because he was sure she would need no reminder to step carefully with a king. That anyone would think she could need counsel on her conduct was laughable. She would scoff at him, or be insulted. He found he did not wish either of those things, and so he stayed silent as she had gone to closet herself with the queen.

Yet when she entered the room and faced the king, Robert tensed in fear of what she might do. Perhaps she would misstep. She did not love him, nor seem to have any great care for his ambitions. To his own astonishment he found that he suddenly *did* care. Lands, a title, a fair amount of power – he had not cared even a week ago, yet now he inexplicably hoped for all of it.

"My dread lord," she said to the king, and sank so low in a courtesy that she might be kneeling. She stayed there, waiting for Edward to bid her rise.

It was only a moment of calculated silence, three slow heartbeats at most. In it, Robert saw that his brother had been right. The king's advisors watched her closely, and her bowed head had all Edward's considerable attention.

"How glad we are to see you again, lady." Edward gestured and she rose. He waited until she looked at him before continuing. "It is how long since you have visited at court? Three years, I think."

"At Windsor, my lord," she replied with a nod. Robert saw now that she did not look directly at the king, but kept her eyes slightly lowered.

"On that occasion, you came too late to see your daughter wed. Now you too are freshly married, yet how different is your greeting. You are a full minute in our presence without questioning our royal authority."

Robert felt his brother's startled look of question, but he would not meet it. He was too transfixed by Eluned. He did not know what he expected – for her chin to come up in defiance of Edward's stern tone or a challenging flash in her eyes, perhaps – but what he saw defied everything he had known of her. Never would he think to see her sink slowly to her knees, her eyes never rising, her color unchanged as she spoke into the hush.

"I pray so great and merciful a king may find it in his heart to forgive the foolish words of a foolish woman. A mother's love oft overwhelms her reason, and in such times she may speak rashly. In faith, I do sorely regret it. There can be no one better than the king to choose a husband for my daughter. It has been well proven in the years since they were wed, and I have thanked God every day that my own will could not prevail over your good wisdom."

This little speech seemed far more than a mere apology for words spoken years ago. Edward observed her in an uncomfortable silence while a tension gathered in the room. Robert held his breath, wondering if the king's famous temper would burst over them. After a moment of studying the king's inscrutable countenance, though, he rather thought it was surprise and not anger that silenced Edward.

In the end, whatever the king saw in Eluned pleased him. The mere ghost of a satisfied smile curled his lips before it disappeared as completely as though it had never been.

"Come, there is no need for this humility," said Edward with a frown of kindly concern. He stepped forward to take her arm and pull her up to her feet. She was no taller than his shoulder. "Had we taken insult, we would not have granted consent for your marriage to a subject we love so well."

Robert came forward to stand beside Eluned, not in answer to the king's mention of him, but because Eluned seemed almost to shrink in the face of Edward's solicitude. In the moment he reached her side, he thought he must have dreamt it. There was no fear in her. She appeared empty of all feeling.

"As my king has loved him," she murmured, "so shall I love him."

She put her hand on Robert's arm and when he laid his hand atop hers, he nearly flinched at the feel of her icy fingers. The king looked to Robert with an approving smile.

"Married less than a fortnight and you have wrought such a change that I would not know her." He clapped Robert on the shoulder. "It is a lesson I shall remember, that a good and proper husband will constrain unseemly pride. If I could have married you to that Castilian upstart we might have secured my duchy a decade sooner."

The other men laughed. Eluned wore a wooden smile. Robert tried to think beyond the way her fingers curled around his wrist, and how she seemed to drift closer to him even though he could plainly see she did not move at all. There was no time to puzzle over it. Now was the moment that he must, as his brother had forewarned him, make his ambitions known to the king.

It was easy enough. Everyone in the room naturally expected that he would want as large a slice of Wales as he could get, so he merely agreed with the general mood. His brother was more than happy to suggest exact boundaries, and most of the hour was spent listening to them speak of places that were unpronounceable to him. The only place he was careful to single out by name was Dinwen, not trusting Simon to remember it. Even at the mention of her ancestral home, Eluned showed no great interest in the proceedings. She only nodded when it was said that the keep had suffered no great injury, and its new lord's first task must be to strengthen the fortifications.

There were no promises made, of course. There were only subtle insinuations and careful hints among all the very general talk of what to do with all these conquered lands. "We will consider and make our mind known soon after the Epiphany," said Edward, but it was obvious he would not have allowed this discussion among his favorites if he did not plan a handsome reward for Robert.

He waited until the king had praised the wine in his cup, which was from the de Lascaux vineyards, and then he said there were eighty barrels brought as gift to the king and his court. There was a very fine little book, shining with gold leaf and tiny gems on its cover, containing a history of King Arthur. This was Eluned's gift, and it pleased Edward even more than did the wine.

They took their leave amid smiles of satisfaction and reaffirmations of great esteem. A lady-in-waiting showed them to their rooms, which were so large and well-appointed that they were the greatest sign of royal favor yet. Eluned walked through the outer room to peer into the bedroom. In the main room, she looked at the small refreshment set out for them, asked him if he required aught else, and when he indicated that he did not, dismissed the servants.

They were alone, or as alone as anyone could be at court. He watched her as she went slowly about the room, looking closely at the tapestries on the walls, a casual inspection to find any obvious spy-holes. He saw none, and did not think any would be discovered. This was not Windsor, and there was no need for trickery to learn secrets when there were so many servants and courtiers happy to listen and gossip.

She touched the fur-lined blanket that had been placed on the long, cushioned seat beneath the window, and ran a finger across a velvet-covered pillow. "How highly Edward values you. I do not like to think what his wrath might have been, had his duchy been lost."

Robert shrugged. "Even were it not the last piece of his French inheritance, he would not be best pleased to lose it. Any man would be loath to lose the Aquitaine."

"Nor would his grandmother have been best pleased by it. Haps he fought so hard for fear the great Eleanor would chastise him from the grave."

He was sure she pictured it, the ghost of the famed Eleanor terrorizing the king. Her face was almost alive with it, amusement softening her eyes and satisfaction in the set of her mouth. These glimpses of her true feelings came when he least expected them. He knew that he was a fool to look for them, to wish for them. He was fool to think they were any kind of truth.

"How much of it was real," he asked, "and how much was put on for show?"

She looked at him squarely, amusement gone from her eyes. She did not ask what he meant. "With this king, all is for show. But that does not mean it is not also real."

"You fear him?"

"I should," she said. "I am sure I should feel fear." She sat under the curving casement. There was a little carved ivory box on the seat, which she smoothed over with one hand, like a talisman. "To go on my knees before him, to give him the book of King Arthur's history… Know you that Arthur was a Welsh king?"

"Aye," he said. She had told him that, long ago.

"Wales is Edward's now. Everyone in it, and everything it will be."

She fell silent, looking at the box under her hand. For the first time, she looked almost old to him. The lines on her forehead were more pronounced, her eyes tired.

"There is the piece of it which may be given to me," he reminded her. "Though it seems you have little care whether it will be mine or no."

The pinch formed in her lips. "Wherefore did I abase myself before Edward if not to ensure that he does not withhold your prize because of me?"

"I do not say you are against it. I say you have little care." He waited, but she did not deny it. He wanted to go to her, tip her face up to his, and kiss the tightness out of her lips. But it would change nothing. She would only bear it, and he would only hate her for bearing it. "Why did you consent to marry me? I was fool enough to think it was for love, but you make it plain you have none. Nor do you share any of the ambitions of this alliance, or the fortune and power that it may bring. Verily, I have thought until my head aches and cannot guess the truth of it."

She hesitated before speaking, and he recognized the look on her that plainly said she could find no reason he should not know the truth. "My son wished it." she said, and lifted a shoulder in a helpless little shrug. "I do not want to live closeted away in a nunnery, nor as a widow who must defend my land alone and be forever rejecting suitors who lust for my wealth. What else is left for a woman, but to marry?"

"But why me?" he persisted. "You would have no lack of suitors, as you have said. Is it because my offer came first?"

She shook her head faintly. "Because I knew you would not..." Her hand smoothed over the ivory box again, as though it held the words she wished to speak. "Because you would never be cruel, or dishonor me. I knew you were good."

She made him think of it, of what her life with Walter might have been. He had known she did not love her husband, that she was unhappy, but he had never heard – from her or from rumor – that Walter of Ruardean was anything worse than overly zealous. Pious to the point of madness, but not a monster. Yet she would let kindness and honor be her chief concern when choosing a new husband. What woman held such things in high regard, unless her last husband had none of it?

"You think I will give you no reason to spit on my bones."

She let out a little sound, the ghost of laughter. "Aye, I think that." She looked full at him. "Nor did Walter give me good reason for that profanity. Was only my foul temper. In faith, I have thought me many times that he deserved a more pious and obedient wife."

He looked her over, this seemingly demure and dutiful woman, and felt a keen stab of resentment for the way she had stamped out all signs of the girl he had cherished. She wanted him for his lack of cruelty, and not because she had missed him for eighteen long years. How improbable it was that such a careful lady had once been his most passionate lover. He allowed himself to remember her younger, impudent tongue and how it had used to glide over his cock while her husband was away at war.

Thinking of that was a mistake. Now the image was with him, and instead of making it easier to hate the woman before him, it set his blood on fire. She would never be that way again. He knew it. He had only to look at her in all her disinterested detachment, to know she was absolutely and irrevocably changed.

"I do not want piety from you," he said, and all the things he did want from her flashed through his mind.

She could not have guessed his thoughts, or else there would not be that little relief that crossed her features.

"I am full glad to hear it." She smoothed her hands over her skirt and rose with a polite smile and an air of decision. "I would sup here and not in the hall tonight. The morning is soon enough to face the curiosity of the full court. Will my lord join me?"

He was caught between laughing and recoiling at the image of sitting through a meal alone with her, the hours of stilted conversation. "Nay," he shook his head. "I go to find Kit, and see if he has discovered when Mortimer arrives."

"Soon," she said. "Isabella is expected tomorrow, and Roger Mortimer but two days behind her."

He did not ask her how she knew, but wondered at the awkwardness that seemed to creep over her after she had spoken. When she said no more he turned to the door to leave her.

"Robert."

The urgency in it caught his attention nearly as much as the fact that she had spoken his name. He turned back to her, breath held in anticipation of what she might say. Her back was stiff, her face expressionless.

"I do not ask where you have passed your nights, and gladly will I continue in my ignorance. But now we are here, it is better that the king and his court think you are not displeased to keep company with your wife." She looked toward the bedroom, and then to the wide seat beneath the window that might easily serve as a bed. "I do not say that you must constrain your conduct in any other ways. It wants only a little pretense, to avoid unseemly gossip."

He wanted to laugh with her about it. He wanted to say that they had vast experience of this pretense, but in reverse – months spent pretending *not* to share a bed, pretending they did not want each other. But he stood in the silence and ignored that irony, because she said she would gladly continue in ignorance. The permission she granted him was as plain as the limitations on it. It was another kind of irony entirely that he could not help but observe aloud.

"The first time in eighteen years my name is on your lips," he said, "and it is to tell me you will not constrain my conduct."

She flushed, and he did not know if it was embarrassment or anger that caused it.

"I have no doubt there are beds more inviting than mine where you will prefer to lay your head. But it is only in mine that you may find a lordship."

"Then to be sure, my lady," he said with his cockiest smile and a slight bow as he gestured to himself, "you will find this lordship there tonight."

He turned away and left with haste, trying to ignore the way she jutted her chin out, the momentary blaze of spirit that might only be his imagination.

✠✠✠

"I think your brother is closer to Burnell than you thought him," murmured Kit from behind his cup. He nodded toward the front of the hall, where Simon sat with a clutch of Edward's advisors. "See how they speak in each other's ears while their eyes never cease looking over the crowd. Like a pair of gossiping grandmothers."

It was true. For once there was no derision in Robert when faced with the sight of Simon diligently seeking to curry favor. Instead he felt something like admiration.

"How much does he hate me, I wonder?" Kit looked at him as though surprised by the question. Robert shrugged. "Think but a moment on it. I went to Kenilworth in defiance of our father and the crown, then to France where I refused to wed or do anything that it did not please me to do. Simon is the good son who has done everything our father wanted of him and more. But I will be rewarded, not he – though it is he who works tirelessly at gaining this fortune."

Kit looked at Simon, assessing him from their position at the far end of the hall, and scoffed. "Do you say he gains nothing from all this?"

Robert smiled. "Haps he has lived these many years in hope of my death, and has so accustomed himself to disappointment that he is happy to call Burnell's whispers his reward."

They were leaning against a wall in a quiet corner, where they had some hope of privacy as long as they kept their voices low. Kit turned to him now, resting his shoulder on the thick tapestry that hung behind them. He was suddenly serious.

"Do not say it even in jest, Robin."

"Jest? Nay, is no jest that he loves the position he has gained here."

"Do not say he has wished for your death. If he has lived in hope of anything, I think it has been your approval." When Robert snorted at this, Kit shrugged. "He looks at you as a hound does, waiting for some sign of favor."

"Simon barely knows me well enough to call me brother. Is our father he means to please."

"You do not see it."

There was a sigh in Kit's voice, as though he knew his words would be disregarded. It was unusual for his friend to disagree with him when assessing someone's character, and Robert valued his opinion especially when it came to his family.

"What do I not see? Tell me."

"Think you that your father has ever let Simon feel as worthy as you? But if there were envy in your brother, he would have not have wanted you in England. See how fully he is embraced by Edward's favorite advisor." He nodded to where Simon leaned in to listen to Burnell. "He could urge the king to keep you in France forever, and ask to be given greater holdings of his own here. Instead he uses his influence to give you power and contents himself with whatever he might gain from your advancement."

Even as Robert considered this, his brother's eyes found him. In them, he saw the eagerness, the hope that Kit spoke of. How had he not seen it before? Robert had felt their father's disappointment so persistently that he had given little consideration at all for what his father might feel toward Simon. But it was likely that he was not the only one to be compared to a brother, and found wanting.

He let out a short, rueful laugh. "I am glad to have a friend so shrewd. You save me from my own blindness."

"Not blind," countered Kit, turning to face forward again. "Though you would have it otherwise, you care for them both. Your judgment is overcome by your heart."

His friend was looking over the crowd now, probably searching for that red-headed flirt. But they had known each other so long that Robert was very aware that Kit was refraining from voicing certain thoughts. He knew as well that they were not thoughts about Robert's family or fortunes. He took a fresh swallow of ale before asking.

"And what of my judgment as concerns my wife?"

Kit was shaking his head almost before Robert had finished speaking. "*There* lies a trap I am not eager to step into. Let us speak of anything else."

"A trap! You can only call it that because you would speak ill of her, or of me." Robert smiled in disbelief, more amused than annoyed.

"Nay, I call it that because I have me a wife. Do you give me your opinion of her, or of my marriage, in all the time you have known me?"

"I have not, but I will give it now in exchange for yours."

Kit narrowed his eyes at him, considering. They were both half-smiling and serious at the same time, as was the usual way when one of them issued a dare. Finally, Kit raised his brows, let his grin widen, and said, "Very well. I will not let you forget it was your idea. Let us move closer to the door so the cold will keep others away, and I would have our cups filled."

They moved to do it, and when they had drink enough and were sufficiently isolated from the courtiers and servants, Kit pulled his cloak tight against the draft and raised his cup as a gesture that

Robert could begin.

"Your wife is a fine woman," he started. Kit looked at him in patient expectation until Robert continued, "But she acts so like a mother toward you that I wonder you can lie with her."

Kit tipped his head, conceding the point "Is rare enough I have done so."

"Rare? Enough to sire seven children."

"Ah but how many have I sired on women more welcoming?" Kit's broad smile faded as he looked into his cup. There was little accounting for his serious turn, except that he had likely sensed some of Robert's disapproval. "Now you must give an honest opinion, as you want one in turn. Tell me what you think of my wife's husband, that you have not said before now."

"I think," said Robert carefully, "that she is merry and full of kindness. And I think her husband is too glad that her wits are not sharp and her heart inclined to trust. I think she depends on her husband to act with discretion, and would only suffer if her husband made her seem a fool."

"If her husband fucks his way through England, you mean."

"Aye, that is my meaning."

They drank a moment in silence while Robert tried to gauge how his words had been received. All he could see was that Kit was preparing to offer his own insights. Robert was beginning to regret entering this conversation. But then at least half of the time they dared each other, one of them regretted accepting the challenge.

"*Your* wife," said Kit finally, "is more comely than you deserve, more clever than either of us can guess at, and as cold as the frozen sea."

Some jongleurs were drawing the attention of everyone else in the hall, beating a drum and singing a song about some battle or another. Robert looked toward them, and tried to imagine Eluned laughing, or dancing, or reaching for him – for anything – with hunger. All he could see was her on her knees before the king.

"She used to be filled with fire."

"And I used to have more hair on my head," said Kit, and there was impatience in his tone. "You are both far from your youth. You have married a woman, not a memory."

"I never dreamed the woman could be so far from the memory," he confessed. He had not told Kit what she had said on their wedding night. In his mortification, he could not describe any of it to his friend. He had only been glad to have someone to pass the nights with, talking of nothing important while Eluned slept alone.

"Eighteen years is a long time," said Kit. It was hard to know why he was so thoughtful, as they had both expressed this sentiment a hundred times in the last month. "Her brother died, you said, and her uncle."

Robert nodded. "Both dead this year, when Edward took Wales."

"You have said she had more pride for being Welsh-born than ever she had for her Norman marriage. Now she has lost her Welsh family, the Welsh home where she was born, the Welsh prince Llewellyn."

"She was there to see the judgment and punishment of the last Welsh rebel, Dafydd," Robert added.

Kit's eyes widened a little at that. "And she is freshly widowed and freshly married. All this in the last twelvemonth."

All this was true, and Robert had thought it many times since his wedding night. There was reason for her to be so changed. The jongleurs struck up a new melody, a gay and carefree air that could not have been a starker contrast to their conversation. He waited for Kit to say more, but his friend stayed stubbornly silent. Finally Robert braced himself with a deep breath and spoke.

"Now you have said what you think of my wife, tell me what think you of her husband."

"I think he loves her." Kit turned his head and looked him in the eye. "I think he is better than a brother to me, but he is a fool who has lived these eighteen years as slave to a memory."

Robert looked away from this accusation. Kit had likely seen this in him for all the years of their friendship. But Robert himself had not seen it until she sat before him and declared that she did not hold those days as a treasure. Cards on a table, she had said, as though it were an afternoon's amusement for a bored lady. He saw her cold white fingers idly shuffling through the only hours he had felt fully alive, his deepest desires laid out before her in little painted squares.

"Take heart," Kit was saying. "In time her sorrow will pass and she will return to herself."

"What if she does not?" asked Robert. "What if I tell you that I have misremembered her, that I was wrong about everything?"

To say it aloud made it real. It gave a name to the

formless fear that had been born when he glimpsed her bare neck in the firelight. From the smallest, most beloved detail to the most defining feature of her character, he had been wrong about her. It felt like catastrophe, yet he had said it so coolly that Kit only shrugged.

"What does it matter? She will always hold your heart, Robin, whatever her true nature."

"Nay. I cannot love her as she is."

"Oh?" Kit did not look at him, but he fairly reeked of skepticism as he turned back to look over the crowd in the hall. "As you say. Then you will not mind if that little Polly keeps me company tonight."

"Polly?"

"Red hair. Sweet mouth. Blue eyes that are rarely off you." Kit drank down the rest of his ale in a long gulp. "If you're to sleep in your own bed, I have a mind to offer myself as consolation to the poor lass."

"Go," said Robert with a smile. He tried not to think of the cold bed that awaited him. "I will avoid any red-headed maidens I see on my quest to refill my cup."

"My thanks. And I will lend my counsel, Robin, from my years of experience: marriage requires a fair amount of ale in a man's belly, but not this much, and not this soon."

Robert pushed off the wall and looked steadily at his friend. "If you will act with discretion with your Polly, I will drink my ale with moderation."

But he was drunk within the hour and stayed that way long into the night. By a grave miscalculation, he was beginning to sober as he stumbled into the room where Eluned slept behind the bed curtains. The fires were banked, the air was crisp, and he was tired and hazy enough to succumb to the promise of warmth inside. His hand found the split in the heavy curtains, warm air flowing over his fingers. She lay on the far side of the bed, a lump beneath the blankets. He climbed in and said her name, but the only answer was her even breathing.

He could not forget that he had dreamed of this. Of sharing a bed with her, all through the night. Of waking to her warm body next to his. He held himself very still as he lay on his side facing her, trying to calculate the distance between their bodies as his head slowly stopped its drunken spinning. His hand rested between them and he realized his fingers were touching her braid, a thick rope that ended in a soft tail of hair.

It, at least, felt the same as he remembered. He rubbed it between his fingers and thought again of the darkness between stars. It was the same darkness that held her apart from him now, filled with all the empty and broken years since last they had lain by each other's side.

Do not risk death to win a heart that is yours, she had said to him with tears in her eyes. But maybe he had remembered that wrong, too.

He might never know how much of what he remembered was invented or imagined. There was no single, verifiable truth. There was only memory. He could choose his own truth, decide whether she had stopped loving him or had never loved him at all.

In the dark, with the brush of her hair between his fingers, he knew he had not been wrong about her. She had been filled with fire. She had wanted to be with him.

Eighteen years. Never think I forget any more than do you.

She had said that, too.

In the black of their first night together, he decided to believe she had truly loved him, as deeply and as truly as he had loved her. Because he could not bear for it to be an illusion, he decided it was not. She had loved him, even if she denied it. Even if that love was now gone.

The pain was no less, but somehow it was more bearable. His longing for her was a familiar and comfortable ache. It curled in his belly again, radiating up to his heart and spreading down his arm to his fingers, which pressed the curl of her hair to his lips as he fell into sleep.

Chapter 7

The Mirror

She woke to find his face inches from hers. It should have alarmed her, but instead it felt like the continuation of a dream. Not that she ever dreamt.

It was dim, the light from the fire filtering through the yellow bed curtains. A servant must have come and gone, lighting the fire and withdrawing discreetly. Robert seemed to be deep in sleep and she was only half awake, which she sleepily decided was a very agreeable state of affairs.

"Robert."

She meant to say it sharply, to see if he was close to waking, but her voice was husky with sleep. He did not stir in the least, so she allowed her eyes roam over his face and take in all the tiny details she had determinedly ignored. His lips were full – like a woman's, she used to tease him – and his nose a perfectly straight line. Those features were exactly the same, but the rest of him had changed with the years. A spray of lines radiated from the corners of his eyes, carved deep by smiles and sun. There were flecks of silver in the hair at his temples, and his skin was a little darker, the flesh not as tight across his cheekbones. She had thought it impossible that the beauty of his youth could have faded into something even more attractive, but the truth was undeniable: he was one of those men who was more handsome with age.

"Robert!" She managed it louder this time.

He answered her with a loud snore. It pulled a smile from her, because it made her world unrecognizable in the most laughable way. There was a man in her bed, for the first time in more than a decade, snoring. And it was Robert, who above all men was never supposed to be there. She found herself leaning into the smell of stale drink that hung around him, breathing deep. She let herself imagine what it would feel like to wrap her legs around him, to press the heat that grew between her legs against him, how he would awaken and respond.

The rising lust woke her fully. Her mind was dizzy with the sudden welter of feelings. It was too much all at once, the heat and the hunger and the nearness of him. She must have reason, or she would drown in it. She closed her eyes against the sight of him and forced herself to think. Clarity was key. Think. She must not hide from herself, not if she wanted to succeed. She wanted him, yes. She wanted him even in the foulness of his morning breath and his drunken snoring, which meant that her old infatuation was not as dead as she had thought. It was not dead at all. It coursed through her, a terrible longing in every beat of her heart. Simple lust was nothing next to that.

Poison, she reminded herself, *the blade, an accident.* She had a purpose, and old infatuations would only hinder her. She dwelt on the thought of Roger Mortimer's many offenses. She imagined him dead until her mind was calm and clear again.

Then she opened her eyes and saw the tip of her braid clutched between Robert's fingers, and all calm and clarity was lost. There was only an unbearable sweetness, a giddiness that swirled through her, an impossible hope leaping up in her. She remembered this feeling. God save her, she had missed it.

She pressed the tip of her finger gently to the slight cleft in his chin. She looked at his mouth, remembered the sight of it kissing her belly as the sunlight filtered through the trees above them.

"Robin," she whispered, "my Robin." All the transgressions she had committed in her life, all the things that might send her soul to Hell, flitted through her mind. She had confessed them all, except for him. "You were my favorite sin."

She might have kissed him then, because the little scratch of his morning beard was so tempting against her finger, but she looked up to find he had woken.

His eyes hadn't changed either, brown and liquid, fixed on her. For a moment, she saw only the sleepy surprise in them. But a look of comprehension came into his face, and she did not know if it was because he had heard her words or because she was touching him. She looked away from his eyes, to her finger at his chin. Slowly, she pulled her hand away. When his lips parted as though to speak, she turned away and sat up, pushing the bed curtains apart and bringing her feet to the floor, and started to walk away.

But he still held her braid. She felt the pull of it, of him, as she stood on the floor with her back to their bed. The air she stood in was cold, all the warmth behind her.

"Let me go, Robert," she said softly.

He did not. She resisted a shiver, holding herself rigid against the tension in her braid as she listened to his breathing and waited. *Let go let go,* she thought, praying that he would not say anything. She feared she might be cruel, if he did – and she did not want to be cruel to him. But finally, after a long moment, she felt the braid swing free and come to rest against her back.

She pushed away the thought of him and stepped further into the cold chamber, considering how vulnerable was a man in bed, and how that might be the surest way to murder Mortimer.

✠ ✠ ✠

Isabella Mortimer was tall and stately, easy to find in the small crowd of ladies despite her subdued dress. She wore very little jewelry and seemed nearly as indifferent to the talk of the ladies as she was to the needlework in her hand. Eluned could not help being reminded of her own daughter. Save that Isabella was much older, it might be Gwenllian sitting there bored, a head taller than all the other women. Except that Gwenllian would not be able to hide her irritation, and would never look so at ease in a dress.

Or perhaps Eluned was wrong. It struck her again, with force, that her daughter was no longer the girl of her memories. Even now, Gwenllian undoubtedly sat among her own ladies, heavy with child and quite happy to wear a dress. The fierce warrior was gone, replaced with a docile wife. One more loss.

"How happy I am to find you here, Isabella," she said pleasantly when the moment was right. "And grown so much since last I saw you."

Eluned watched a crease of confusion appear between Isabella's eyes, but she did not say more. She preferred to let Isabella feel a moment's disadvantage.

"I fear I must confess I do not know you, my lady."

There was something in Isabella's expression – or perhaps a lack of something. Eluned could not identify it, though it felt familiar.

"It would be a wonder, did you remember me. I was barely more than a child myself, when I came to your wedding. I am Eluned de Lascaux, who was the lady of Ruardean."

"Oh. Oh yes." Isabella reached out her hands as though to embrace her, then remembered herself. "How glad I am to meet you."

Eluned schooled her face to show none of the immediate suspicion she felt. There was no reason for Isabella Mortimer to be eager to meet her. Yet there was an absolute sincerity in her. If it was an act, then Isabella was a very great actor. Considering the family she came from, it was more than possible that she was unusually deceptive. But Eluned decided it would be most expedient to respond in kind with warmth and eagerness.

They took a place near the fire together and talked, while the other women of lesser rank gave them space and privacy. No doubt they were all desperately trying to hear every word, but it only took a wave of the hand and a meaningful look at the musician, who repositioned himself strategically and interfered with any attempts to overhear them. They exchanged the obvious pleasantries, and it was plain Isabella was not inclined to the kind of empty chatter that was so common to court ladies. Eluned was glad to move straight to a more interesting subject.

"You will know that Christopher Manton is like a brother to my husband, and so must I count him as my friend," she began. "Will you tell me, then, how fares his son in your care?"

"He does very well, and so he has told his father and mother in his letters to them." She was polite, but a hardness crept into her voice. "The boy is treated with honor."

"To be sure, and never would I doubt it from a house as great as Mortimer." It was marvelous, how perfectly she said it. She almost convinced herself. "Yet his father fears the boy is away from his own family too long. You know that my son was sent to foster with Lancaster when he was even younger?"

"I know it."

"And he did not forget me, or his father. So I have said to Manton and he has heard me. Still I think he fears the boy will be gone so long that he will grow to manhood in isolation."

"His fate is not in my hands. That responsibility belongs to my brother."

Now Eluned knew what she had seen in Isabella's face, so plainly did it show when she spoke of her brother's authority. Bitterness. Resentment. The gall of it, of having the reins wrested from her hands.

"Your father put the boy in your charge, I was told," she murmured, and watched the telltale flex of a tiny muscle in Isabella's face that told her the other woman was gritting her teeth.

"He did. For years he gave our stronghold at Wigmore into my keeping, and everything in it, including what hostages we held. But on his death last summer, my brother Edmund took control of all. Decisions about such matters as hostages were never mine to make. Now I am not even consulted."

She clearly regretted that last admission, so Eluned was content to pretend she had not heard it. Eluned flicked a glance toward where the other ladies sat, all of them watching Isabella's tense face.

"It is a rare man who will gladly let a woman rule in his stead." Eluned let a smile curl her lips as she spoke. "Or a mad one."

She was rewarded with quick huff of amusement, and an answering wry smile. She had not given much thought to Isabella Mortimer at all over the years, except to consider her one more in this clan of cutthroats. But their castle at Wigmore had been of critical importance in the campaign to conquer Wales, sending food and weapons to the English as they fought for years. If Isabella had truly ruled there, then she should be Eluned's enemy.

She did not feel like an enemy.

"You had the keeping of Ruardean for many more years than I held Wigmore."

Eluned nodded. "To any other I would say it was God's will, who commanded my husband to serve elsewhere. But to you I will say it was the will of men. A weak man left it in my care, and his strong son now comes to take it back." She shrugged. "But it is men who are meant to defend fortresses, not women."

"Do you say that is God's will too?"

"I say it is what men call God's will, and so long as

men rule on earth and God in Heaven, then what you
or I think matters very little to either of them. I also
say a woman is wise to step gracefully out of their way
as they lurch along the paths to power."

That gained her a real smile, and the first twinge of
shame in her breast. Would she befriend this woman,
only to slay her brother? In her mind she tried to
weigh the possibilities and outcomes in her usual way,
but no clear answer came. Befriend Isabella, gain
valuable information about the Mortimers, insights
that would help her in her plan – maybe even help
Kit, a good and worthy man. But also: befriend
Isabella, deceive her daily, hide lethal intentions
behind a friendly face, and then perhaps one day
watch her learn of Eluned's betrayal.

She watched as Isabella changed the subject,
talking at ease now about her falcon and wondering if
the weather would be temperate enough to fly it
tomorrow. It struck her that they were not so very
different. Isabella was but a few years younger. She
too had been widowed, though it was many years ago
– a decade or more without a husband. She had also
held a great stronghold for years, only to have that
power taken from her. The fighting between England
and Wales killed her father, just as it had killed Uncle
Rhys.

*She is loyal to Edward; she aided in the fight against the
Welsh*, Eluned reminded herself. But how could she
condemn her for being loyal to her family? For
performing the duties that fell to her, which were
given into her hands by the men who held her fate in
theirs? It was no more than Eluned had done. And
she saw, now, that Isabella too held herself at a
careful distance, the hint of calculation in nearly

everything she said.

This was why she felt so familiar: they had both been shaped in the same way, by the same forces. And at the end of it all, here they both sat, discarded, among the ladies embroidering at Edward's court.

"Come," Eluned said. "Let us walk out to the hawk house now and I will see your falcon. It is not too cold outside, and I grow weary of these walls."

She would be careful. She would acquaint herself enough with Isabella to learn a little of her thoughts on her brother Roger, but not so friendly that it would feel like a betrayal. Perhaps she would be lucky, and find that Isabella had no love for her brothers after all.

It was as they walked through the brisk air past the stables that she saw a flush come up in Isabella's face. She was quickening her step, her face turned down to the ground, but Eluned saw the flick of her eyes toward a man who stood with a horse before the stables. He was transfixed, staring at Isabella's rapidly retreating form.

Eluned waited until they had entered the hawk house and she had said a few admiring words about the bird before asking.

"Who was that man who caused your step to hurry?" Isabella was no green girl, and yet she twisted her hands together in agitation. Eluned shook her head lightly. "I would not pry, Isabella, nor would I ask confidences of you. I only saw that you were not best pleased to see him, and would be sure you have no cause to fear him."

"No," she answered. "I do not fear him. He is no one of importance, and hardly a villain. He was friend to my father for many years. I only did not wish to speak to him now."

The blush was returned to her face, making her quite pretty despite the haughty look of indifference she wore. So it was love, then.

"Will you walk with me again tomorrow?" Eluned asked her. "If the weather holds, we can fly this lovely bird."

"Yes," said Isabella, visibly relaxing. "Yes, that is much more agreeable to me than any other entertainment the court can offer, I think." She paused a moment, burrowing her hands into the thick wool of the cloak she wore. "I would have my nephew come with us. He has a passion for falcons."

Eluned caught her breath, then hid the tiny sound of surprise by bringing her cold hands to her lips and blowing on them. She spoke lightly, taking care not to seem too curious. "Nephew? I did not know your brothers had children."

"As they are neither of them married yet, you may say they should *not* have them." Isabella smiled and turned to watch an austringer return a goshawk to its perch. "Three nephews, all baseborn, one of Edmund and two of Roger. Edmund's boy has traveled with me."

"It is good of them, to admit to their bastards and bring them up as Mortimers."

"Their care, too, has been entrusted to me." Isabella slipped her arm through Eluned's as they left the hawk house, a gesture of familiarity that might be sincere fondness or pure manipulation. "Roger is especially fond of his sons, and it has put him in a temper that I allowed his boys to stay at Wigmore to pass the season with Robin Manton. My nephews are great friends with him."

Eluned's smile was automatic, but it took her a few moments to formulate a response. "His father will be happy to learn his son has companions. And he will know of your kind solicitude as well. He has heard a rumor that the boy would be given into Roger's care."

"It is my intention to ask Roger to allow him to remain in my care, for there is no lady of equal rank in his household. By Mary, there are no ladies at all – nor even a household, if truth is told. Better he waits until he has made one before he takes on the education of children."

She said no more, and Eluned bit her tongue against enquiring further. So many questions, so many possibilities – but there was time enough to learn it all. For now, it was enough to know Roger Mortimer's sister did not want him to take custody of the boy. It was a great deal more than enough to know he had children he loved. That was a great gift indeed.

✠ ✠ ✠

In the hall, she caught sight of Robert immediately. It was chance that every time she stepped into a place where he was, no matter how crowded, her eyes found him. It must be chance. Or maybe her eyes had learned the trick all those years ago, and had never unlearned it. When he noticed her, she quickly looked to Kit Manton who stood next to him, and then her gaze moved restlessly over the scattering people around the hall.

It was late in the afternoon, and servants were setting up tables in preparation for the evening meal. Robert and Kit were near one of the hearths, each holding two cups of wine. She made her way to them.

"Do my lords have such a great thirst?" she asked.

Kit held a cup out to her. "We make a study of all the wines on offer in England's finest household. Will you give us your opinion? I say there are none that match the quality of Robert's wine."

She took the cup and looked into the deep red liquid as she addressed Robert. "But what think you, my lord de Lascaux? Surely it is your opinion that carries most weight in this matter."

When he did not answer, she looked up at him with raised brows. There was that soft look there, as though she had said something he found endearing. She could feel herself grow warm in response, thinking of how they had parted this morning. The edge of hostility that had been in him since their wedding night was gone entirely.

"It is your opinion we seek," said Robert easily, holding one of his cups out to her. She took it, and was glad of the excuse it gave her to look down at her hands once more. "You hold what we have deemed the two finest wines in Edward's stores."

"Excepting your own," Kit interjected.

"Excepting the de Lascaux wine, yes, which my lady has already tasted." He inclined his head to her. "So you will make an excellent judge. In your left hand is a wine whose cost is only a little less than ours."

She took a swallow of it and found it too tart for her liking. "It is unfair to serve it without spices," she told them. "The taste suffers for the lack of them."

The men looked at each other a moment, and then back to her. Robert gave an impatient wave, urging her to sample the other wine. She brought it to her lips to sip, and found herself taking another, deeper swallow. It was delicious.

"You see, she may try to spare my pride, but her face tells the truth." Robert was grinning now, a boyish satisfaction in his face.

"Do you say it is better than Robert's wine, lady?" Kit asked her, a challenge in his voice.

It was clear her opinion would settle a dispute between them. She thought Kit Manton was more proud of the de Lascaux wines than even Robert was. Clearly she must endeavor to be both honest and careful with her words, for such a very grave question.

"I will not say that it is better, but I will say that if you told me it came from Robert's vineyards, I would believe you. The flavor is different, though." They both still looked at her, expecting more. She wanted to laugh at them, they were so like boys who waited to be told which of them had won a great prize. But she had no prize, nor had she ready words to describe the difference between wines. She shrugged. "It is so rich. It is heavy on the tongue, but not too strong."

Robert nodded. "It is a better flavor."

"It is not," Kit was insistent.

"It is from Spain," Robert was saying to Eluned, ignoring Kit. "Not far across the mountains from -"

"It is not better!" Kit's words overrode whatever Robert would say, and they began to talk over each other, quarrelling about it. She was put in mind of her cousins when they were young boys, and almost thought the men would resort to a wrestle in the dirt until one cried mercy. She watched them a while, and was considering asking them how much of the wine they had drunk to have reached such a state of absurdity when a laugh escaped her. She bit her lips against it, but it was too late. They had stopped their arguing to look at her.

She turned to Kit. "Verily, sir, my lord husband has the right of it." She was unable to stop the smile that unfurled across her face at his dismayed look. "The first you gave me is a wine whose flavor is so tart it needs a wealth of spices to make it agreeable. It is inferior to Robert's wine, which needs no such correction. But this Spanish wine is so rich it overwhelms the senses." She turned back to Robert, pleased in spite of herself at understanding where his friend did not. "You have done it a-purpose. By Mary, I did not think you to have a mind so given to commerce, my lord."

He gave a little bow of acknowledgement, delight in his eyes. "I did not think to see the dimple in your cheek again in this life, lady."

She turned her face down, flustered, glad she held a cup in each hand and so could not twist them together as Isabella had done. If it would cool her cheeks, she might drink down more of the wine only to cover the confusion in her. "There will be no lack of buyers for Robert's wine," she said quickly to Kit, explaining.

"Yet you say the Spanish is better?" he asked, still confused.

"A better flavor," corrected Eluned. "It is a wine to savor on the tongue, in slow and small mouthfuls, for very important occasions or guests. But Robert's wine is the better to sell in great quantities to wealthy households, because the taste is far superior to other common wines yet it can be drunk as easily as any ale and served with any food. I would gladly stock the buttery with it, and not the Spanish wine."

Robert gave her that crooked little smile again, lines creasing the corners of his eyes. "And I will gladly give my lady wife a very good price on it. Haps I might even give it at no cost, if she will smile so again."

He was trying to flirt with her. She pressed her lips together, unsure if it was a laugh or a sob she was suppressing. Robert de Lascaux was flirting with her.

It took only a moment, one quick breath, until she could turn to Kit again and say, "But I agree with you. If I must say one wine is better, I will say it is the de Lascaux wine. Flavor is but one consideration, and not the most important. I am more mercenary than that."

Kit Manton was scrutinizing her as closely as she felt sure Robert was. Whatever might be said next was lost in the appearance of Robert's brother Simon, who indicated he wished to speak to Robert alone. When they had walked off a little way, leaving Eluned alone with Kit, she set both cups of wine down on a bench nearby and spent a moment looking down into the ruby liquid.

It would make Robert very wealthy, this wine he had produced. Likely he would never admit to it, but she was sure he had spent years in the planning of it: cultivating the crops, finding the perfect blend of grapes, improving the yields until he could be sure of adequate quantities to import here. And now it would be served at the king's own Christmas court, where half the noble households of England would taste it. She wondered if his friend even knew the extent of his hopes.

But she did not ask his friend about wine. Instead, she said, "I have spoken with Isabella Mortimer about your son."

Then she told him everything she had learned of how the boy was cared for, how Edmund Mortimer would make any decisions about his release, how Isabella wished the boy to stay in her care. The urge to question Kit more closely about his dealings with the Mortimers pulled at her, but she resisted it. It seemed to her an ill omen, how very often in her life the ambitions of that family had thwarted her own. It was better that Kit Manton try his luck against them without her interference.

Even as she thought it, Kit asked, "Will you not ask her why I am still so suspect they will hold my son? If I could but know the reason -"

"She will give you the truth of it sooner than she gives it to me," she said, not sorry for the brusqueness of her tone. "Nor do I think she knows any truth, but only guesses at her brother's aims. This is men's work, all of it. Taking him, holding him, releasing him – it is all done by the hands of the men, not the sister."

He did not take offense. He only looked at her, thoughtful, until she saw him decide she was not lying or hiding anything. In the same moment, she realized she was in fact hiding something from him. Not by intent, but by instinct. If she were honest with herself and with him, the simplest way to gain the advantage was to have Robert confront Roger Mortimer about all this in the presence of the king, where a straightforward answer must be given. It would force the Mortimers' hand, deprive them of whatever game they were playing.

But it would anger them, and their spite would fall on Robert. The thought of it chilled her blood.

"It is better you deal directly with the Mortimer brothers," she said to Kit now, forcing her lips to form the words through the dread that had clenched her jaw tight. "Assure them they have naught to fear of you, that you act only in good faith with them. I can give you no better counsel than you waste no time at this."

Kit's gaze shifted to just over her shoulder, something catching his interest behind her.

"Let us call it a fair sign, then, that Roger is arrived even as you say the words, and earlier than expected."

She turned, the sound of greetings filling the air around her. At the entrance to the hall stood Roger Mortimer, tall and barrel-chested.

She had thought the sight of him would fill her with emotion. With fear or hatred, or perhaps even doubt. Instead she felt only a strange calm as he raised a hand to hail someone across the hall, as he reached for the ale brought to him by a serving girl. She only wondered distantly, even as he leered at the girl, if he had entered this same way more than a year ago, with Llewellyn's head in his arms. Did he gloat of his treachery? Did he present it with ceremony to his king, or did he let it dangle from one hand as he reached, laughing, for his cup?

Now he was putting out an arm, grasping at the serving girl. A spike of alarm pierced the numb as she watched the girl twist to avoid his hands. She was too young to see what Eluned saw: that running would only make him determined to catch her. But then some men approached, calling his name, drawing his attention and allowing the girl to slip away. She was a smart little mouse, darting into the shadows and putting a fair distance between herself and his hands.

The blade, Eluned decided. Poison if she could not get close. An accident would be her last choice. But she hoped, watching the girl scurry away, that it could be the blade.

The thought, as ever, soothed her. She turned to the bench where she had set the wine, trying to remember which was which, choosing one at random.

"I think Simon has been too modest," Kit was saying, his eyes still on the group of men surrounding Roger Mortimer. "Of course he would know Mortimer, but they look to me like near companions. He never said so."

Eluned turned to see Mortimer's hand out, grasping Robert's in greeting, both of them smiling, talking. Beside them stood William, her son. The venom rose up in her, quick and sharp. She would rend him to pieces with her own hands here and now, with hate choking her and the foul breath of fear hot on her neck.

"My lady."

Kit's hand was on her wrist, a sudden move to hold her hand steady as he tried to pull the cup away from her tight fist. The wine had spilled, splashing onto her skirt. She made her fingers loosen the grip, made herself mumble an apology for her clumsiness. She looked across the hall to watch the men speaking pleasantly to each other, and was reminded in a flash of who they were.

They were Norman. Robert and William were Norman lords, favorites of the king. She need not fear for them. Mortimer was not their rival nor their enemy.

Even as the realization flooded her with relief, she felt an urgent need to be away from them, alone. It had come over her so quickly, the murderous intent. Her mind was now filled with images of Roger Mortimer laid out before a jeering crowd, his face as the axe fell, hacking him into quarters. It was not horror that she felt at the image, but a keen hunger.

I am become vile, she thought, with a sinking in the pit of her stomach.

"I must find a fresh gown," she said to Kit, turning away. "And so must you find dry shoes." For the wine had soaked his feet, she now saw.

He gave a warm smile, so kind and alive. He had probably never thirsted for blood in his life.

"Aye, I would be more presentable before I meet this man I must make friend," Kit agreed. He gave a little frown of concern and asked, "Are you well, lady?"

She could not pretend she was, so she did not try. "My stomach is unsettled. I will… I should rest."

He steered her around the small puddle of wine she had made, leading her out of the hall. They passed a small knot of courtiers who lingered near the stairs to the minstrels' gallery. The man that Isabella had blushed at was there, asking a boy with a lute if he knew any love songs from Andalusia. She waited until they were well past him, then paused in her step.

"Do you know that man?" she asked Kit.

"In the green cloak? Aye, he has some little land to the east of mine. He is Robert de Hastang."

She thought of Isabella, hands twisting, her mouth tight as she hurried away from this handsome man.

"She has a Robert too," she murmured.

She became aware of Kit's scrutiny as she stood there, rooted to the spot. Finally, she looked to him and said, "You would do well to make a friend of him, I think." Then she swept past him and made her way to her rooms.

In the wide seat below the window casing, she curled with her uncle's psalter. She did not eat the meat or bread her ladies brought to her, nor drink the wine. She had them pour out some mead, which she sipped slowly to ease the sickness that had settled in her belly. Though the night was mild and the wind low, she did not pull the tapestry away from the window so that she may have a glimpse of the stars.

Instead she looked down at the prayer book, occasionally opening it to scan the words written there. *The way of the wicked will perish*, it read. There was no comfort for her in the painted pages. It was left to her to contemplate what she was becoming, what stain the sorrow was leaving on her soul and how helpless she was in the face of its spread. She thought of her uncle's hands holding this book in prayer. She remembered Madog's face, the light in his eyes and the smile on his lips when she had asked him about his love.

It was late when Robert came into the room. She had changed into her warmest night robe and pulled the heavy, fur-lined blanket up to her shoulders as she sat in the window seat, intending to make it her bed. He said nothing, only crossed the room to pause at her side. She did not look up.

After a silent moment he put out a hand and picked up the end of her braid, brushing the hairs against his thumb. He waited like that, a light and questioning hold that she answered with her stillness, her refusal to look up. Then he walked into the bedroom, leaving her alone. She heard him climb into the bed.

This is how it would be, she knew. He would wait patiently for her. He had seen her desire for him, the places where her resistance began to erode away, but he would not take her. As he had done once before, he would wait for her to reach for him. He thought she was emerging from a darkness, that she would turn naturally from it. He would wait for her heart to slip into his hands again, because he still believed that her heart was whole and uncorrupted.

Chapter 8

The Ashes

"De Vere was a close friend to my father," William said, "and my father's brother has said he gives good counsel."

Robert and William were in the gallery above the hall where a knot of men were gathered around a large and rough map of England spread out on a large table. These many lords were advising their king where it would be best to build fortifications around Wales. It had been William's suggestion that he and Robert observe it from a distance, not hiding but not participating unless they were asked. So they stood above and assessed the great lords and advisors assembled below. Robert tried not to think of it as gossip. It was useful, if he was to become one of them, to know who may be trusted. Having been raised in Lancaster's household, William was well acquainted with all of them, and was glad to share his opinions.

But it was no great insight to observe a fair amount of doubt in the boy when he spoke of de Vere, so Robert lowered his voice and asked the obvious question. "Think you that your uncle tells you wrong?"

"I do not think it malicious. In faith, I would be surprised if my uncle is capable of malicious intent." William gave a smile. His mother's smile, with a twist of mischief. "Richard is a fool."

"So you disbelieve him on principle."

"Nay, I have reason to think de Vere cannot be entirely trusted. My sister has told me he cares more for his own fortunes than he does his alliance with Ruardean." William nodded toward another of the men who stood around Edward in the hall below. "She has said Bohun, though, is a man who cannot conceal a thing, and I agree with her. Gwenllian likes him for it, even when what he fails to conceal is a contempt for her."

"Why would Bohun have contempt for your sister?"

William shrugged. "Whatever the reason, it is a personal mislike and not animosity for Ruardean."

Robert turned from the view of the hall, resting his back to the wall as he looked at William. "Your sister comes so regularly to court, then, that she has developed a distaste for the man?"

There was a little silence, and Robert had to resist a smile when he saw William's mouth go tight. Just like his mother.

"Gwenllian lived much removed at Ruardean until her marriage. She has only ever come to court once, in those few weeks when she was wed."

"And when she learned not to trust de Vere?" Robert asked. "And ran afoul of Bohun. A very busy few weeks."

William took a few moments before speaking, his eyes trained on the men below. He seemed to choose his words carefully.

"It was where she learned not to trust de Vere, because he did not warn her of the king's intent to arrange her marriage. Nor do I think she ran afoul of Bohun, whether at court or anywhere else." He looked up, his expression of uncertainty reminding Robert how young the boy was. "What has my mother told you of Gwenllian?"

"That she is married to Ranulf of Morency and has one son by him, another child to be born any minute." He shrugged. "That she loves her dearly."

"She has said that to you, that she loved Gwenllian dearly? Now, or long ago?"

It took every ounce of Robert's will not to widen his eyes in shock. "Long ago?"

"At Torver. In the year Montfort died at Evesham. Were you not there?" William was watching him closely. "My mother was there, and my sister. And you."

Robert nodded carefully. "Your mother told you we met there?"

The little tension dissolved with William's easy smile.

"Nay, I had it from one of Lancaster's men that you were there that summer. She has never spoken of you to me." His smile dimmed. "She does not speak of much to me at all. It is Gwenllian whom she held close to her heart, because my sister was kept at Ruardean to be reared while I have been in

Lancaster's care almost as long as I can remember."

Robert was still recovering from the shock of hearing Torver mentioned, so he was less observant than he should have been. But he did not think there was envy in William's voice. Some disappointment, perhaps, and resignation. He wondered if the boy sensed what he did – that Eluned purposely held herself apart from him.

"Yet you seem to know your sister well, for all that you did not dwell at Ruardean," he remarked.

"She was faithful in sending word to me all the years I was with Lancaster, and when I would visit Ruardean she taught me…" Here his voice faltered, and he glanced back down to where Edward's counselors gestured over the map. "She understood better than I what it would mean to rule there, and she wished me to learn all I could of it. It is because of her I speak a ragged Welsh, and know all the men of the garrison, what skill in fighting each one has."

There was something he was not saying, and Robert could not guess at it. But as long as William was in a mood to speak of his sister, he could try to satisfy his curiosity on one point.

"When we arrived here and met with the king, your mother spoke an apology to him as greeting. Why?"

"She has a sharp tongue," said William with the ghost of a grin. "Or so I have heard. Nor was I there when she came to court to protest the betrothal and found Gwenllian already married, but they say she was in a temper that matched Edward's in his worst moments. I cannot imagine it."

"Can you not?" asked Robert in mild surprise. It was no strain on his imagination at all to picture it. It was almost a delight.

"I have ever seen her composed and controlled. But then, that is all she has ever shown me." William looked at him closely again, the assessing look that was uncomfortably reminiscent of his mother. "And now my sister tells me this composure is all she is shown as well, lately. It strikes a fear into Gwenllian, and hear me well: fear does not easily find a home in Gwenllian's breast. Dread is not in her nature, and it is a terrible wonder to me that she has admitted to it."

Robert thought of what Kit had said, that so much had changed for Eluned in the last twelvemonth. Three years ago she had stood before the king and railed at him, yet three weeks ago she had abased herself before him, not a flicker of spirit in her. Hers were the movements and words of one who accepted an absolute defeat. He had seen it in men before, when they suffered definitive loss in battle. It was rare enough in his experience, and he had never seen it in a woman. But then, he had never known a woman who had had such fire as Eluned.

William's eyes were on him, and uneasiness came off the boy in waves. Robert thought of telling him that Eluned was not always so composed, that there were moments when she smiled even though he knew she did not intend to, moments where he saw her breath catch. Most often it was when he came to their rooms in the evenings. For weeks now, he would enter to find her sitting among the velvet-covered cushions where she would stay all night. There was no cool composure in the way her breath sped up when he stood near her, in the way she studiously avoided his eyes. It was the same ebb and flow of attraction and resistance between them as it had been at Torver, the same delicate dance but without the playfulness.

Every night he lay in bed, wondering if she would come to him, and wondering why she did not. *My favorite sin*, she had said, when she thought him asleep. And then she told him to let her go.

He looked at her son and knew he was not alone in thinking it was more than an icy self-control. There was something she hid, something that even her son could not uncover.

"There was more to her anger than a marriage contract," he said to William, whose mind was so like his mother's, yet whose openness was anything but. "You think there is more that happened between my wife, her daughter, and the king. That is what you hint at?"

"Aye, I think there is more. If it will affect Ruardean and my rule there, then I would know it."

"If it would affect your rule and Ruardean, your mother would tell you." There was no question in Robert's mind. Even if she did not adore William in the way she had Gwenllian, she would never let harm come to her son. He believed in that more than he believed in her long-dead love for him, more than he believed in his own ill-advised love for her. "She is loyal to you, William. She married me only because you asked it of her."

"You think she married you for me?" William looked at him for a long moment, his brows raised in a gentle incredulity. The idea seemed to amuse him, but he did not dispute it. Instead he turned back to look at the assembly of men below, directing his attention there. "Anyone can conceal their true feelings when they feel they must. It would amaze you, the enormity of the secrets that can be hidden at this court. It is too easy to trust a man who plots in secret against you."

Robert looked down to see who William was watching now. It was Mortimer, moving a block of wood that was meant to represent a fortress, pushing it further westward on the map.

"Mortimer does not have my trust, I assure you," he told William, who shook his head in reply.

"Roger Mortimer should not be your concern. This hostage he holds – is the boy so dear to you?"

Robert nodded warily. Though it was no secret, he had never spoken to William of his concern for Kit's son and did not know where he could have learned of it. Court gossips had better things to whisper about, surely. "He is as close to a son as I have ever had."

"As am I, through your marriage, though I cannot call you father." William gave him a happy smile again. He looked back down at Mortimer and said, "Have you never wondered why the Mortimers came to mistrust your friend Manton?"

There was a suggestion under his words that Robert did not like. "If you think to set a suspicion in me against Kit -"

"Not him. That is not my intent, I am clumsy in my words." His grimace of embarrassment reminded Robert that he was still a boy, if only just barely. "I mean only that there was no reason for them to demand a hostage, nor less to keep him. If a neighboring lord, a man whose holdings and strength were not one tenth of mine, came armed and unannounced onto my lands I would not do as Mortimer did. Very well, you will say, I am not like a Mortimer. But I have known a great many of the most powerful barons and have been taught the ways of a great many more, and I tell you that none would ask for an heir as surety unless there was reason to fear the worst."

"They have said they act out of caution. Too much of it, to be sure -"

"They are guided by reason, and I ask myself who would tell them they have reason to suspect Christopher Manton."

Though his immediate reaction was skepticism, Robert did not say that it seemed unlikely. In William's face was a seriousness and intelligence that told him he would be a fool to dismiss this. And after all, the boy knew more than he about the people surrounding Mortimer, and their likeliest schemes.

"Why do you tell me this?" Robert asked him, curious. "I think you do not often share such private suspicions, and it can mean little to you what Mortimer thinks of Kit Manton."

William gave a slight shrug. "I am a Marcher lord and you will become one. The others, these men," he gestured to the tableau of lords gathered around the king, "They are a pack of starving dogs, loyal to their own hunger above all else. But your marriage to my mother unites our lands, our fortunes, our strength. And so I mean to help you as I would expect you to aid me if ever I am in need. I will rely on it." He looked at Robert, serious. "Look you to learn who would warn Mortimer against your friend, and why. Someone has whispered poison in his ear."

"To what end?"

"That is for you to discover." William turned to leave, then paused after a step. "Your brother is the kind of man who might know such a thing."

✠ ✠ ✠

Two days later, they watched as William made his oath to the king after the Christmas mass. Robert said a prayer they could soon leave this court. He was not made for the whispers and the shadows, as Simon was. Even William, young as he was, managed to strike a perfect balance between artful and guileless. It was a skill that Robert had no interest in mastering.

But he did want the reward Edward would give him. And he could see this was the best place to learn why the Mortimers kept Kit's son as surety. He had not told Kit of his conversation with William, preferring to keep his own counsel until he discovered something more concrete than suspicions. The days passed and he watched as Kit became more friendly with Roger Mortimer, the two of them comparing the charms of every passing serving girl while Robert crawled into his bed alone.

He missed France. He missed days long gone, when he would spend his time laughing with Kit and his son, riding out into the vineyard where he knew every inch of the land, and telling himself that somewhere Eluned was thinking of him. What a flattering illusion he had created for himself. He felt the loss of it keenly.

"Isabella has said her brother reconsiders the conditions under which they took the hostage," Eluned told him the day after Christmas. "Is clear to me they begin to feel shame for it, now they see Kit Manton means them no ill."

"Have you wondered why they ever thought him an enemy?"

He was careful to ask it in an offhanded way. He

had not confided in her about this yet, for reasons he could not name. It was partly that she did not confide in him, over anything, and partly that he did not wish to tell her all the things her son had said. Mostly it was that he was afraid his eagerness to be close to her would push her further away again. In some moments, they were almost like old friends. But she seemed to him as a wild and wary animal – one step wrong, one noise too loud, and she would retreat to a place he could not follow.

"I have asked her," she said, folding a square of golden cloth carefully and handing it to one of her ladies with instructions to take it to the queen. "But she says only that they knew little of him when he brought an armed party onto their land, so it was natural to call him enemy."

"And they did not think it out of proportion to demand a hostage."

Her mouth grew tight and he heard contempt in her words. "They are capable of such malice and deceit that they expect it of others in kind."

That was all. It might be enlightening to see her speak to her son on the subject. If ever he found the two of them together for more than a bare instant, perhaps he would steer the conversation that way. Maybe even tonight, when Eluned would join in the holiday celebration and William was sure to be there too.

But when they arrived in the hall, the wine was already flowing and William was dancing with the king's daughter. Robert heard his name called, bellowing and boisterous, and saw it was Kit.

"Is a joyous start to this Twelvetide season," Kit proclaimed as he thrust his cup into Robert's hand

and swept Eluned into his embrace.

He watched as his friend swung her around, laughing, and dropped her to her feet before him. She stepped back, flustered, her mouth open in surprise at this extravagant gesture, her eyes flicking to Robert in alarm. Kit's face was flushed but he seemed steady on his feet as he put his hands to Eluned's shoulders and said, "I shall have my son home, and it is all your doing, lady. I would kiss you, were your husband not a jealous man."

"They have sent him home?" she asked, her eyes wide in disbelief.

"They will. Roger Mortimer has told me only minutes ago, that his brother will see Robin home to my wife in time to celebrate the Epiphany. I will go myself tomorrow so that I may see him safe delivered with my own eyes." He smiled broadly at Robert, who saw the relief in him at this news. "Praise God I believed you when you said we must listen to your wife."

"Nay, it is none of my doing," said Eluned, a warm smile spreading across her face. "Anyone may give advice, but few could turn an enemy to friend so quickly."

Robert found himself laughing, his heart light for the first time since he had left France. They sat at a table laden with food, music in the air, the wine from his own estate in every cup, and joined in the celebration. To prove Kit wrong about his jealous nature, he urged his friend and his wife to dance together while he sat and watched and was mad with jealousy. Tonight she wore her hair in the fashion popular at court, abandoning the veil for a simple barbette and fillet with her braid pinned in a coil at her nape. The dance was lively, though, and the braid came half-free to trail down her back and swing with her movements.

He prepared to abandon his drink and his place at the table so that he could go to them, cut in and take her hand, touch her and laugh with her as easily as his friend did. But he turned to find Roger Mortimer there, waylaying him with praise for the wine. They sat together, and were joined by Kit and Eluned in time.

"This one," said Mortimer, nodding at Kit, "tells me he will send his son to squire with you in another year or two. But I have told him the boy has a rare talent with the sword, enough that he may be better served at Morency."

All eyes fell to Eluned, who wore a pleasant but guarded smile.

"Gladly will I ask my daughter if her husband would take the boy as squire." She looked to Kit. "I cannot say if there will be a place for him there, though, as I am sure there will ever be in my husband's household." At these last words she put her hand to Robert's arm, and he was reminded of how her fingers had curled around his wrist when she stood before the king.

"I had not thought to send him so far," began Kit thoughtfully.

"You know little of Morency if you think the distance should be your only concern," said Mortimer, who smiled into his cup. He flicked a glance at Eluned before saying. "Your boy is like to come back with all the skill you could want and more arrogance than you can stomach, with Ranulf of Morency to teach him."

Eluned raised a hand lightly to her mouth, turning her head aside, hiding her smile. After a moment, though, she nodded her head as her shoulders shook with laughter.

Roger Mortimer gave a booming laugh when he saw her agreement. "I like the man well enough, but his head is so swelled it is a wonder he can find a helm to cover it."

While the men laughed, Robert looked to see she had grown suddenly sober. All her mirth was gone, replaced with unease. He put his hand over hers where it rested on his arm, felt her fingers flex in reaction, and wished he knew even one thing that was in her mind.

The night went on with her quiet reserve back in place while the rest of them laughed and sang and danced. She was too obviously troubled, and he was not surprised when she excused herself from the revels.

He made his excuses and followed her within the hour. It seemed likely the merriment in the hall would go on long through the night, and though he shared Kit's happiness at the good news, he did not share his friend's growing fondness for Roger Mortimer. Loud and brash and boastful, it was rich indeed that Mortimer dared to call another man too arrogant.

Robert had come to anticipate with pleasure the first moment of entering their rooms at night. It was always quiet, with a tension that was not anger, and he could pretend to himself for a moment that this was the night she would be waiting for him in the bed. She never was, though. Tonight, like all the other nights, she sat among the pillows in her heavy night robe. She had pulled the tapestry aside a little, so that she could see a sliver of night sky through the window.

This time, for the first time, she looked up at him as he entered. There was not an invitation in her face as she gazed at him. He did not know what it was, but he thought she did not want him to leave her alone as he usually did. Careful of the lamp on the nearby table, he came to where she sat and eased himself down on the seat next to her. She moved herself slightly to make room for him, her hand on the psalter she held open on her lap.

"Do I interrupt your prayer?" he asked her.

She shook her head slightly, running a finger along the edge of the page.

"I was not praying. I looked for a verse I heard once, but I think it is not here. It is scripture, though I cannot say where I heard it."

"What is it? None would call me an overly pious man, but haps I have heard it too."

She closed the little book and rested her palm on it, and spoke to the jeweled cover. "I was poured out like milk, and then curdled like cheese." The words in her mouth sounded almost wistful, though her lips were set in a grim line. Then she shrugged her shoulders, a little gesture that tried to say it was unimportant. "The words were like that."

He put his hand over hers where it rested on the book, careful to move slowly, giving her time to pull away. When she did not, he felt hope leap up in him. "What lays so heavy on your mind, cariad?"

This is where she would turn cold and distant. He waited for it, cursing himself in the little silence for calling her his love. But she did not turn cold. She pressed her lips together in something between a grimace and a smile, and she laid her other hand over his.

"Cariad," she said, her eyes large in her face as she looked at him. "No one has called me that since you. I cannot remember…" She faltered, looking down at her hands on his, and spoke in a whisper. "In some moments I can scarce believe I was ever that person you loved."

Only her mood stopped him from the wry remark that his mind threw up like a spiked defense. He would not be angry at her, not when the word *cariad* was in her mouth and she held his hand. Not when she spoke of the past without scorn.

"You were that person," he told her, turning his palm up against hers, curving his fingers around her hand. "You are. I see her in you still."

"Do you?" Her mouth lifted in a sad semblance of a smile. "I do not see her at all."

He waited a long moment, remembering her laughter and dancing earlier tonight, remembering all the little moments in the last weeks when she had let down her guard and he had glimpsed the Eluned of old. He did not speak until she looked up at him.

"When you are not sure of the answer to a question of great importance, do you still look into the sky?" It startled a little laugh from her, and she nodded. He pulled the cloth away from the window next to them, letting in the light from a full moon. "As do I. I learned it from you. You said it was good to remember how vast is the universe, and how many possibilities there are that we can only guess at."

She looked up at the night sky, and her face in the moonlight deprived him of words for a long minute. He had seen many women whose comeliness could stop his breath, many who were more beautiful by far, but no woman he had ever known could match the sight of Eluned as she turned her eyes up to the stars.

"Will you tell me more?" The Welsh lilt was more pronounced, turning her voice to music, her words drifting to him like a sweet sad song. "Tell me what I was. I cannot remember."

He spoke slowly, twining his fingers with hers. "The girl I knew was daring and bold. At times her temper ran ahead of her reason, but her wits would always save her. She could charm anyone at all if she remembered to try, but she had no talent for hiding her impatience with fools – and so she rarely tried to charm a fool." He watched a smile dimple her cheek. "She looked very much like you, her face was the same despite the many years. Except that every last hair of your head was dark – and your skin was more pale, I think, or else your mouth more red."

She let out a breath of a laugh, wrinkling her nose in amusement. "Neither. I used to hold crushed berries to my lips to color them, when I knew I would see you."

"Did you really?" he laughed.

"Yes, and I would bathe my face in milk, and brush my hair for hours on end." She pushed the psalter off her lap and, one hand still entwined with his, pulled her feet up onto the seat between them. She tucked her legs beneath the heavy robe, relaxed and natural. "I remember your kindness. Do you remember when that boy saw us, and you ran after him? I thought it was to frighten him into silence, because that was my instinct. But you gave him all the food you had, and some coins, and you asked him to forget he had seen me at all." She looked up at him, all trace of amusement gone. "My artifice and your kindness. Haps we have not changed so very much."

He shook his head. "Nay, I will not let you say you were all cunning and calculation, though I loved that part of you as well as any other. It was that part of you which left the little stone for me, to tell me you would slip away to be with me. I would never have had you otherwise."

His words put heat in the air between them, the reminder of those naked afternoons together. It flared up amid the comfortable warmth, turning the reminiscence of friends into the awareness of lovers.

Her eyes stayed fixed on their clasped hands. "What if that is the only part of me that lives still?"

If he had not wondered the same thing, he would not have a ready answer. "Never could your fire give way entirely to cold calculation. And there was such a fire in you, Eluned, that I have never seen its like." He leaned closer, pulled their joined hands to his heart. "I would swear on my life it burns still."

She looked at her fingers in his, pressed lightly to his chest. "Aye, it has burned and burned. Until I am left with naught but ashes."

She gave the barest shake of her head, silencing whatever he might say. Her hand rose to his face, fingertips stroking the hair from his temple and drifting down to touch his mouth. He could not think how to answer her. He could hardly breathe when she was this near, when she touched him and he was aware of her body beneath the robe every instant.

"Robin," she said, so soft that he strained to hear it. She leaned forward and rested her forehead against his. "It was only with you that she lived, that girl. These many years, she has been a dream no one else remembered."

He slid his hand up beneath her heavy braid, holding her to him. "I remember. You are no dream."

Her skin glowed with moonlight, yet he could almost feel the sun of a lost summer on his shoulders. He was a nervous boy again, amazed that she had come to him, terrified she would pull away. "Will you kiss me, Eluned?"

She made a mournful sound, a choking laugh of recognition as her fingers spread into his hair. "I will." And her lips were a tentative flutter on his for only a breath, before her tongue was hot in his mouth.

The effect was instant. He had forgotten. That was the only coherent thought as he kissed her. He had forgotten the wildness, the melting, the utter obliteration of everything that was not her. He drank her in and she went to his head, the strongest wine he had ever tasted. How could he have forgotten? It was a blaze that would consume him, and he wanted nothing more. He wanted nothing else. There was nothing else in the world but her mouth, her arms around him to pull herself nearer, her hands low on his back, urging him.

He found his feet, his mouth still on hers, pulling her up with him to stand. The tie that held her robe closed – could it be so simple? One little pull on it, and the heavy cloth came open and fell to the floor at a push. There was only a thin shift beneath, so thin he could see the outline of her breasts beneath the loose fabric. Her mouth was at his throat, hungry and hot, her breath against his skin. He wanted all of her, all at once – every inch of her body and every sigh, every scent, every taste. He went to his knees, sliding down her body to open his mouth over her breast. She inhaled sharply, cradling his head against her, as he tasted her through the linen. It slid over her skin, wet and dragging against the hardened nipple beneath his tongue.

"Robin." It was a gasp, high-pitched and sweet, a voice he remembered. He took his mouth away and looked up at her face in the flickering lamplight. Her lips swollen with kisses, her hair coming free, desire in every feature. This was Eluned. This. Not a cold, untouchable statue of a woman dressed in rich clothes, but a reckless and greedy wanton who gasped his name.

He rose, carrying her shift up with him to bare her legs to his touch. Her hands came to his belt, resting on the stiff leather for a bare instant before pulling it through the buckle and dropping it to the floor. She took his tunic in her hands, gathering it in bunches to pull over his head and he said, "The bed. I would have you in a bed." He had used to dream of it, when they lay together on the grass.

He carried her there now, at last, finally. His only regret was the darkness, no way to see her away from the lamplight. But there would be time, he told himself as he hastily removed the last of his clothes and bent over her. She was his now. There would be no more hiding away, no stolen hours. In darkness, daylight, and firelight, she was his and he was free to find the tender skin of her inner thigh, to rake his teeth along the softness and hear the keening sound she made. He thrust his tongue into her heat, his hands sliding under to grip her and hold her up to his mouth like a ripe fruit.

The taste of her, the sounds she made and the feel

of her under his tongue reminded him. He knew her, what she liked and how she wanted it. He came up, stretching himself over her, pulling her leg up high over his hip. There was a moment, suspended above her, when he was unsure. There was only blackness, he could see nothing of her at all. She was all sensation, and he could only feel her absolute stillness beneath him. But then her hands were on his belly, moving downward until she found him and guided him into her.

He moved in her, his mouth open on hers, both of them panting, reaching. He forced himself to focus on her, exerting a ruthless self-control, following her every reaction, every cue. He could feel her struggling, fighting against release or fighting for it, he could not be sure. He gripped her leg, pulled her knee up and held it as he shoved himself deep. "There," she gasped, a harsh inhalation at his ear. "There, don't stop." He drove on, her breath hot on his neck as she clenched around him, her voice rising higher while he lost all thought, all control, her body arching up to his as he let go, let everything flow into her.

He was only dimly aware, as he sank down onto her, that she was still moving. His arms came up, dead weight obeying his slow brain, but they did not close around her. She was slipping away, sliding from beneath him. It was only later – minutes that felt like hours – that he realized she was gone. Gone from the bed, gone from the room, not a sign of her in the blackness that surrounded him.

Delight and dismay pulsed through him as he gradually comprehended it. For a moment he thought he heard her in the outer room, but then he was sure she was gone. He gulped air, felt his sweat turn cold in the frigid night air.

His hand closed around her discarded shift, the only outward sign she had been in his bed. He pulled it to him, knowing himself a pathetic, lovesick fool but unable to stop himself. She had been here, with him. She had called him Robin and took him inside her, all flame and passion, every inch of her alive.

And then she left him.

He gripped the fabric of her abandoned shift, a bellow of rage and confusion strangling him. He would have loosed it into the night, but his fingers found a hard little lump among the cloth. If he had not run his fingertips across it every day for eighteen years, he would not have known it in the dark. It was the button from her shoe. The button he had handed to her on their wedding night. She had sewn it into her shift. Just below the collar on the inside, where it would rest against her heart.

He curled himself around it in the blackness, a tangle of hope and despair twisting inside him through the long hours of the night. Alone. Clinging to the evidence that he meant something to her, even if it was something she fled from, and abandoned.

Chapter 9

The Opening

She could not stop it. She could only command her legs to move, move quickly, do not make a sound, do not let him hear the awful racking sobs that had begun in the first breath after she had convulsed in release beneath him.

It was appalling. She stopped at the seat beside the window and shoved a pillow hard against her mouth and was stunned to find she could not control it. It was outside all her experience of herself. She was no stranger to weeping, had known tears enough for a lifetime – but this was something more, something that terrified her. Frantic, she pulled her heavy robe over nakedness, biting her lips together in an attempt to contain the sounds that leapt from her throat. If he heard her sobbing, he would come to her. He would comfort her and ask why she wept and she had no answer. She only had her mortification and horrible, uncontrollable, inexplicable sobs.

In the lamplight she saw her thick slippers and did not pause to put them on. She only picked them up, transferred them into the fist that still held the cushion pressed to her mouth. With her other hand, she took up the lamp and left their rooms, desperate to be somewhere he would not follow. She must not see him until she had some control, or until she could understand why the sobs would not stop.

She stumbled down the hall, down the stairs, no idea where she might find any corner where she could be alone until she was outside a little chapel. It was the queen's small chapel, where she and her ladies said their prayers when they did not wish to trudge through the cold air to the larger church. It looked at a glance to be empty.

Eluned left the lamp just inside the door and retreated to the darkest corner, her arm braced against the wall. There she hunched over herself, a curl of misery around some wound that left her weak and gasping. There was no stopping the sobs, so she no longer tried. She wept and wept, muffling the grief in the pillow, a storm of anger and sadness that ripped through her and left her confused and helpless and humiliated.

It was like any other storm; she must wait for it to pass. But it lasted so long that after a while she sat herself down on the floor and pulled the slippers over her numb toes, buried her face against her knees and soaked the heavy robe with her tears. At last, when her face was swollen and her throat parched with thirst, the tears slowed to a trickle and she tried to make sense of it.

Robin, she thought, *my Robin*. There was no reason

for her to weep. It had felt like a miracle, his skin hot against hers, the feel of him moving in her, every inch of her awake and exulting. He touched her, and she felt like a song being sung. Impossible as it was, it had truly been her – *her* body, *her* heart – transformed into something sublime. He could make her into that. How stupid she was, that she had believed it would only be a comfort. A little tenderness, perhaps a little excitement. Not the same wild, pagan pleasure of their youth. She would never have suspected it could be that. She wanted it again, now – his mouth on hers, his arms around her. But even as she thought it, the hot tears slipped down her face anew.

It softened everything in her, to think of him. Better to think of something with no soft edges.

Poison, she told herself. *An accident. The blade.* But that pulled a fresh sob from her, so she pressed her hand to her mouth and drew slow and steadying breaths. She no longer knew herself.

Full of fire, he had said. Cold and calculating, daring and bold. Alive. He remembered her. He knew her. And still he looked at her with love. Still he wanted to lie next to her in the night.

The tears had stopped. She put her hand to the wall and found a niche there, a statue of some saint inside. She levered herself up by its toes, then retrieved the lamp. There was oil enough inside it for a few hours, at least. There were woven rush mats on the floor of the chapel, a beautifully embroidered cushion meant for kneeling, and little else. She picked up the cushion, taking it back to her dark corner. In the quiet here, now that the tears had subsided, she would calm herself. Lamp in hand, she saw that the statue in the niche was of the Madonna. It was carved from wood and looked at her with sweet, forgiving eyes.

For a moment, she was back in the chapel at Ruardean, laying prostrate on the stone floor through the night while her husband described the evil spirits that tried to steal her soul and drag her to Hell. She could hear his voice even now, promising he would save her from them.

"Too late," she said softly to the Madonna, to Walter's memory. "They have got me, in the end."

Spots of pain appeared along her jawline, the size and shape of his fingertips pressing into her flesh. The old anger was a distant throb, as familiar and unremarkable as breathing. Years of her life, the shape of her soul, all formed by those few hours. Deception and trickery, heartless strategizing, hard choices that had made her hard. She did not think Robert could fool himself into admiring her still, if he could have seen her through those years.

But he did love her, and she felt it like a pain all through her. Within a fortnight, she could be assured that Mortimer had returned the hostage safe home. Ten days, say. At the Epiphany, the boy would be safe home and she could act against Mortimer. She could have those ten days with Robert, loving him as freely as she had always wanted. But it would be ten days spent hiding the ruinous hatred that lived in her, and hiding what she planned to do. She contemplated it for the barest instant.

No. She could not do it. It would be too much like that time with Walter, manipulating him into her bed, giving her body while hiding her heart. She wrapped her arms around herself and rubbed at the tickle of phantom tears that had once dripped into her ears.

Even the memory of it made her feel foul and loathsome. That had been done out of necessity, because she must do it to survive. There was no such need with Robert.

And more than that: she loved him too well to let him bed a lying murderess.

She sat under the watchful eyes of the Madonna until the dim light of sunrise began to filter in. Her tears were spent. Her fingers ached with cold. She pressed her hands to her body beneath the robe for warmth and when they were thawed, she could feel the brush of Robert's hair against her palms. It was silky, soft as a baby's – a detail she had forgotten.

But she could also feel cold flesh. She could feel her uncle's lifeless hand in hers, and Madog's. She wished she could forget the feel of them. She wished it. But she could not.

✠ ✠ ✠

If she did not need to dress, she would have delayed returning to their rooms. But she was too acutely aware of her nakedness beneath the robe, the unrelenting chill in the air, and the sounds of the household waking. She was relieved, upon entering, to see that the servants were already stoking the fire and setting out food and drink. She was not ready to face him alone.

Robert stood at the window, holding open the tapestry to look outside and letting in a flow of frigid air. He did not turn, even when he heard the servants greet her.

"Nay, leave the water on the fire," Eluned said to the girl who had hurried to pour it out for her. It was her habit to wash in the morning, and she felt the need of it more acutely than ever. Under the robe, she smelled of him. Of them together. But she would wait until she might do it discreetly. "I will wear the velvet gown, the yellow."

The girl went to the inner bedroom to fetch the clothes. Eluned reached for the linen square near the basin, dipped the edge of it into the water over the fire, and wiped her face free of tear stains while his back was still turned. Then she took up the cup and drank honeyed water down in gulps, easing the burning dryness in her throat. She gripped the goblet and stared at the fire.

"My lady." The servant emerged from the bedroom, holding the yellow gown. She wore a troubled look. "I do not find your shift."

The heat had only begun to creep up her neck when Robert turned. His look pinned her, forbidding her to move as he came to stand before her. It was a more commanding look than she had ever seen from him, and it sent an incongruent surge of strongest lust through her belly. She turned her eyes down to hide it from him, and saw that he held something out to her. It was only a ball of fabric clutched in his fist, but she knew it was her shift by the button he held between his thumb and forefinger. The griffin etched into its surface seemed to mock her.

"Leave us." The girls seemed to hesitate at his command, looking to Eluned for confirmation. She opened her mouth, but he spoke before she could, loud and firm. "Go. Now."

The girls hurried out and left them alone, but she did not raise her eyes to his. She could not look away from her shift in his hand. She waited for him to say whatever he would say, fearing her mind was not quick enough to answer him well. But he said nothing, and the silence spun out between them. When she could no longer bear it, she took a deep and bracing breath and spoke.

"You were looking to the sky." She gestured faintly toward the window where he had stood, where last night he had kissed her. "Do you ponder some great question?"

"I was watching Kit depart. He journeys to his home today."

"Oh," was her witless reply.

She had meant to be distant and cool, but he was in command of the moment. She looked at his fingers gripping the linen, curled and motionless, and tried not to think of how different her body must have felt to him. Soft with age, a sagging imitation of the body he would have remembered. His was more solid, harder with muscle, and she should not be thinking of it. His friend – they were speaking of his friend, who went to retrieve his son.

"Fortune is with him," she said, "that the snows have been so light. But it will be a bitter cold journey." Robert stayed silent. She swallowed. "You did not go into the yard to bid him farewell."

"I waited here. For you."

She heard accusation beneath the words, and knew she should choose her response carefully. There were ways to manage men, to placate and cajole and distract – yet she had no wish to manage him. She could not bring herself to maneuver and gently deceive, not with him. Shrewd thinking was well out of her reach in any case, so she could only speak plainly.

"And here I am." She summoned her courage and met his eyes. There were shadows beneath them. "What would you have me say?"

There was a long moment in which he looked at her, considering. She felt a stab of apprehension about what he might see in her, and stiffened her spine, gripped her hands together.

"Why did you end what was between us, those many years ago?"

She blinked. "Why...why I ended it?"

"Why that moment, what prompted it?"

Caught off guard, she only stared at him. It confounded her, that he would demand an explanation of her actions eighteen years ago and not for last night. But she could see he was in earnest, impatient for an answer.

"I told you then, why we -"

"You said only that it was impossible."

"It could not last, we both knew -"

"Damn you, forget what we knew." His hands were on her shoulders now, his breath hot on her face. "Tell me what happened that I must swear never to come near you again, that you would not come away with me, tell me *why*."

There was pain in her shoulders from his hard grip, and tension in her neck from straining away from his vehemence. Everything in her had gone still in reaction to it, even her breath. It woke her from her bewilderment, made it easier to issue a freezing command. "Release me," she said through clenched teeth, "and I will tell you."

He eased away from her. One step back and his hands fell in fists to his sides as he waited for her to answer him. She clung to the little anger that had granted her the icy calm, but it was already slipping away. She had too near an understanding of madness to think him beyond his senses, and too clear a view of his nature to believe he would want to frighten her, or hurt her.

"Walter suspected me," she said shortly. "A servant spoke careless words. He never knew your name, nor did I wish him to learn it and so I knew it must end between us."

His thumb passed over the button – the ugly, lumpy, long-forgotten button from a shoe she had never worn again – and she knew from the way he traced the edge of it with his nail that he had done so over the years a thousand times, a hundred thousand, a million. She turned her face away and looked instead at the gown that the girl had set on a chair. The golden velvet seemed to catch all the morning light. Her eyes ached with the glow of it.

"Did he hurt you, Eluned?"

She did not know how to answer the gentle question, but found she had begun to shake her head in denial nonetheless. She stopped, and frowned. "No. Yes. I…you have heard he was mad?"

"I heard the rumors later."

"That was the beginning of it. The Church did not name him holy, nor did they wish to name him heretic. He did not preach nor seek followers, so they took pity on him." She smiled a little wryly, remembering Brother Dominic's letters. "Aloud, they called it fervent belief, and in whispers they said it was a kind of madness."

She heard Robert draw a breath, and knew what he would ask. She raised a hand to forestall it. "He believed my soul in great danger, and he must watch over me every instant. I knew it must end between us, that it should never have begun. So I banished you from my life." She stroked a finger across the velvet, against the nap, then again to smooth it over. "I tell you, it was not lightly done."

He came toward her, a hesitant step that brought him near enough for her to hear the soft sigh he gave.

"You made the choice for both of us, then," he said with a disapproval she could not miss, "to protect me from him."

She swung around so swiftly that she nearly collided with him. She stepped back a pace to accommodate her outthrust chin. "Gwenllian," she said too loudly. "My daughter, to protect her. Aye, and you – and me, and all my family. Think you that it could have been any different if you had known?"

He looked at her, his dark gaze passing over her face. "Nay. Even had I known, you would have decided it the same. And I would have been even more lovesick and full of vain hope for all these years." He dropped the shift finally, and it came to rest atop the golden gown. He looked at it now, and she could not read his expression. "Yet you might have come away with me, if you did not love your place here so well."

This was too much. "My place here? At Walter's side?" She did not hide her scorn. "You forget I risked it every moment I was with you."

"And you forget that I know you, Eluned. Even then, you wielded what power your marriage gave you with relish. You were born to it. You had great dreams, and no small ambitions." He gave a rueful smile. "I have only ever wanted you, but you wanted all the world."

For a wild moment she looked about for something to smash, so forceful was the anger that swept over her. But it dissolved when she saw in his face that this was not accusation at all. It was only the story he had told himself for so long. It was what he believed of her nature, and his own. She swallowed, grasping at calm reason amidst her indignation.

"Do you say you have only ever wanted me?" she challenged. "Oh, verily. That is why you bought the lands from Aaron and improved them, and why you stayed to the bitter end at Kenilworth. That is why you have toiled for years to increase the value of your French estate, to build your wealth through the vineyards. That is how you preserved the Aquitaine from Spaniards, how you have made yourself a favorite of the king and even now will gain a Marcher lordship. Through your lack of *ambition*."

After a moment his mouth quirked in a familiar half-smile, the one designed to deflect suspicion that he cared for anything at all. "Most of it was done in defiance of my father."

"Then call it your greatest ambition, to displease your father by making a great man of yourself. Only do not say that I am the only one with ambitions that kept us apart."

She turned away, regretting that she had said those last words. It did not matter now, her own vain hopes so long ago. It did not matter that she had grown sick as she waited for him when Walter went off on Crusade. She had indulged foolish dreams for months, knowing he would hear of it – and then more months, sure he had heard of Walter's madness – until she finally understood that Robert would not return to her. He had made a new life for himself, and she had forbidden him to come to her in any case.

That was when she had truly put away the last of her love. She did not fault him for it, then or now. If there had been no kind of respectable life for her with him in France, there had been even less for him as her lover in England. But it had hurt, and she had felt like such a fool for expecting him to run to her side at the first opportunity, so many years later. She had almost forgotten that time, and would be happy never to think of it again. But by Mary, let him not pretend that he had done naught but sit in France pining for her.

"No matter," she said quickly. "It is past. It is all the past, and I will not relive it. Any of it. I will *not*."

Her eyes fell on the psalter, still resting on the seat beneath the window. In the silence she stared at it, and the light that sparked off the jeweled cover seemed to mock her. Even as she declared the past dead, she could hear her uncle telling her that the little ruby on it was plucked from the crown of the Queen of Heaven, and Brother Adda gently chiding him for teasing her.

She put a hand to the bared stone wall between the tapestries to feel the steadying cold against her palm. This was not why she had come here, to lose herself in love, to resurrect all the old feelings and sort through them. She had one purpose only, one duty left to her. She must choose carefully what she dared to desire, and the desire for revenge on Mortimer was sharp, strong, uncomplicated. It did not cause her to weep the night through.

Suddenly Robert's step was behind her, quick and purposeful, and she turned to find he was headed to the door. He opened it, calling to one of his men, a member of his household guard.

"Go you and find the hunting party that leaves this morning," he instructed the man. "Tell them I will join them directly. Then let young Henry prepare my mount and weapons." Robert turned back into the room and, without looking at her, walked into the bedroom.

She watched him open a trunk, pull out a cloth bag, and begin to gather clothes into it. He did it all in silence but not in anger. He only looked weary. When he finished and swept his cloak across his shoulders, he paused at the threshold of the door to look back at her.

"There are wolves near the village, and Edward would have them hunted."

She nodded and searched the silence for something to say. "God grant you will find them soon, in this cold." He did not move, nor speak, and she could not help herself asking, "You will return this evening?"

"I cannot say. It is not likely," he said, and she bit her lips against protesting the danger of it.

She should be relieved. In his absence, she could lay her plans and prepare. With luck he might even be gone until the Epiphany. Her tongue would not move to bid him farewell.

"All night I have lain awake in an empty bed, with only this to dwell upon. Whatever your reasons in the past, I cannot escape the truth that if you wanted me now there is naught to stop you having me. Yet you shun me, and flee our bed, and stand there stiff in every limb. I will live no longer in hope and dread, Eluned."

She opened her mouth, but could say nothing. She

could only hear his words echoing endlessly inside her head. Hope and dread. They were such living things. *How long does love live on*, she had wondered, *if left unfed?* Here was her answer.

It was better this way. For him, for her. She was sure it must be better.

"If I have made a great man of myself, it is because I knew you then." His mouth tried to form that half-smile, but failed. He abandoned his well-worn irony and all his charm, and spoke so plainly that it caused a burning in her throat. "To love you was the making of me. But now it is only my undoing."

He left, and she stood there – stiff in every limb, just as he said – staring at the spot where he had been. She stayed there for so long that when Joan came to find her, the noon bells were tolling.

✠ ✠ ✠

It was easier, when he was gone. There was no distraction, and she could give herself entirely to her purpose. Aside from the first night of his absence, when she had made the mistake of trying to sleep in the bed she had shared with him, she felt only an increased detachment. When the hunting party had been out for five days, Isabella Mortimer came into the hall, brushing snow from her cloak and saying they had sent word of their success and would soon return.

"I would guess from the messenger's words that they could have had it done in three days," mused Isabella as she warmed her hands by the fire. "But it is the season for diversions, and they would prolong their sport."

Roger Mortimer had joined the party, a fact that had threatened Eluned's pleasant detachment when she learned of it. But she had wasted no time in taking advantage of his absence. Isabella spoke freely of his tendencies and habits, giving Eluned a fine idea of the best way to strike at him. She even thought his sister would not mourn him much, so plainly did his debauchery disgust her.

She watched now as Isabella Mortimer's eyes strayed discreetly to the musicians who played a sweet *chanson*. The handsome man whom Kit had named Robert de Hastang stood there looking toward them. Eluned was sure he had the musicians play the song only for Isabella, who had become much better at hiding her feelings over the last weeks. Indeed, had Eluned not seen her blush weeks ago, she would never guess that there was anything between these two.

"The entire party will return tomorrow, then?" she asked Isabella, who nodded.

That would leave four days and nights until the Epiphany. She wondered if Robert would return to their bed or stay away from their rooms altogether. Whatever he might choose, she would contrive to avoid him. The court gossips had little interest in their doings, she had found, being far more entertained by the many Twelvetide diversions. So long as she and Robert gave no other reason for tongues to wag, they need not share their nights together. He plainly wanted the distance between them now. *Now and forever*, she reminded herself.

She steered the conversation with Isabella in such a way that she could confirm Kit Manton's son was undoubtedly released and on course to be home within days. Then she excused herself to seek the serving girl at whom Roger Mortimer had leered for weeks. The girl had done her best to stay in the kitchens, but ventured out more in these last few days because she knew he was gone on the hunt. Eluned had first approached her as she drew water from the well two days ago. The girl had nearly jumped out of her skin when Eluned had come near, only to relax in clear relief when she saw it was not Roger Mortimer sneaking up on her.

Now Eluned found her in the buttery with a few other kitchen servants.

"The men return from the hunt tomorrow and I will have them served a certain mead from my own stores, to congratulate their success," she said with a calculated brusqueness. "I would put it direct into your hand so you may be sure to serve it. Do you understand, girl?"

She was called Nan, and her large blue eyes turned up to look directly into Eluned's for a single swift moment of understanding before she cast down her look and said, "Yes, lady. Will you bring the bottle here?"

Eluned wondered what the young girl's life must have been like already, to be so skilled in necessary deception. No one observing her would guess she had ever spoken to Eluned without fear, or that she had expected this request. Her timid deference made it easy for Eluned to play the great lady.

To that end, she gave a little scoffing sound and smoothed the fur trim of her cuffs with an idle air. "You will come to my rooms after this evening's meal. And if you leave the hour so late as to wake me,

I will find another who will be happy to have the task."

Nan bobbed her head and was still murmuring her promise to be there when Eluned swept out and made her way to her rooms. Once there, she arranged the small table and chair near the fire to keep her fingers warm as she wrote. The letter was already half-written, but she had put aside the task until she could be sure Joan would see her at it. She wrote slowly, saying a silent word of thanks to her uncle for ensuring she had been taught to write as well as read. He was the one who had told her not to disdain the work, for if she learned it then she need not trust a scribe or cleric with her words.

But for Mortimer, our Prince would yet live, she wrote. *I vow on my life I will not let him be rewarded with half of Wales.* She had spent days choosing the words. They must implicate her without being an outright declaration of guilt. They must put others beyond reach of suspicion. *My son is loyal as a hound to Edward,* she was careful to include. *My husband even more so.*

Joan entered in the hour before the evening meal, as she always did, to ask if Eluned would eat in the hall or remain in her rooms.

"In the hall, I think, but I will not stay long. I grow weary of these courtiers." She paused in her writing to look up at Joan. "You will be married to Sir Heward when you are returned to Ruardean in the spring. I have spoken of it to my son and, do your parents give their consent, there is naught to prevent it."

Joan blushed and smiled. "My father has raised no objection, my lady."

Good. That was one more thing done. "Let us hope he likes the marriage contract equally well. I have looked over it and think I could do no better for my own daughter."

She waved off Joan's thanks and reached for the ivory box that she had set on the table. It was a pretty thing, one of her few possessions that came from a mother she had barely known. Inside was a lock of her mother's hair and a little blue flower, pressed and dried, and other small keepsakes that meant nothing to anyone but Eluned. Yet anyone near her for all her life knew that she always kept it close, and it was always locked. She took the key to it, opened it and dropped the letter inside, glad to note that Joan's eyes followed her actions.

"After the Epiphany, there will be many who will leave court. I would send word to my brother's son who is at Holywell, if you find a party who will journey that way. But I would not have it known commonly."

"I will be discreet, lady."

"It is no secret, I only want no tiresome questions. On the king's mercy my nephew is allowed to live with the brothers there, and he is stripped of all title and lands. But he is my brother's son and my family, for all that he fought Edward's rule, and I have been remiss not to send news to him." She locked the ivory box and made a show of putting the key, on its long string, around her neck and tucked away beneath her gown. "My lord husband returns from the hunt tomorrow. See that his bed linen is fresh ere he lays in it."

After that, there was little to do but sup in the hall, where speculation ran high as to how many wolves had been killed. Eluned found herself speculating more about the snow that had begun to fall. It seemed light enough, but came in hard, mean little flakes that rode on bitterly cold winds. She would trade the cutting wind for more snow, if she could. There were many in Wales now who had been displaced by the fighting, and without good shelter the wind was cruel.

She returned to her room early, telling Joan she wished to be left alone. She had pulled the bundle of herbs from her trunk and was just finishing their preparation when Nan arrived.

"Take this," she said, holding the envelope out to the girl. "I have mixed it with spices so that you may easily put it in his wine without suspicion. A fat pinch of this and he will want sleep far more than he will want you."

"There is much here," observed the girl. "You said…I thought I was to give it to him once, and then find you."

"Aye, but you will find me only on the Epiphany, or after. There will be four nights until then, and he may reach for you each one of those nights. What else but this can be your defense against him?"

"Haps he will choose a willing woman instead."

"Nan," she said kindly. "If you thought he might, you would not be here."

Still, the girl plainly had misgivings. Eluned had said only that she would help her to escape his advances if Nan would drug Mortimer and then help Eluned to slip into his room unseen. Probably she worried over what Eluned might do with him while he lay senseless, but Eluned had no intention of telling her.

"Here," she said, putting the bottle of mead and some coins into Nan's hand. At the hesitation on the girl's face, Eluned took one of the rings from her own hand and gave it to her too. Clearly this generosity roused her suspicions, though, and Eluned watched the big blue eyes look back and forth between the coins and the pouch of herbs. Smart girl. Cynical girl. Had she ever been an innocent?

"It is not poison," Eluned said. When Nan did not seem reassured, Eluned took the herbs from her, cast a healthy pinch of them into her own wine, and gave the cup a brief swirl. "There, I will do well to sleep soundly tonight."

She drank it down and watched the girl's expression lighten.

"No sooner than the Epiphany," Nan said with a firm nod. "I will watch him drink it, and find you in the chapel."

"And after," said Eluned, and paused. "If ever you are questioned about it afterwards?"

"I will tell no one, I swear it."

Eluned looked at her. She was a determined little thing, and it was not hard to imagine her refusing to speak. "You will, if they would hurt you. Promise me that. I will not have you on my conscience. Lie at first, however you will, but give the truth if you are threatened. Remember that. The truth is more apt to be believed when it is hidden behind a lie."

Then, whether Nan gave her name or suspicion fell on her for other reasons, they would take Eluned. They would question her ladies, search and find the letter, and all blame would be hers alone. She could only pray she had thought of everything.

The girl ran a finger over the tiny chips of sapphire embedded in the silver ring Eluned have given her, and looked at her with hundred questions in her eyes.

She asked none. Smart girl. When she nodded, Eluned yawned and said, "You see, already I want nothing more than my bed. Go now."

Eluned slept, and woke, and watched from afar the next day as the hunting party returned. She spent the following days avoiding Robert, treating him with a mutual cold courtesy whenever they must speak or be near one another. It was easier now that he did not try to reach her. There were no charming smiles, no sidelong glances, no warmth directed at her at all. At night, they slept apart as they had before, with no comment. He moved past her in their rooms like she was not there, and she did the same.

Sometimes during the night, she would hear his breathing in the next room and feel the threat of tears rising up. Not sadness, but the terrible panicked sobs that threatened to take her. Then she would retreat to the chapel, lamp in hand, and stare hard at the statue of the Madonna until it was under control. It made her laugh a little, knowing that the trick to keeping her head was not to think too much.

On the night of the Epiphany feast she watched Mortimer in the hall, growing steadily more inebriated, reaching ever more determinedly for Nan as she filled his cup. Finally, just as the revelers had reached new heights of merriment, he caught her around the hips. He carried her and her jug of wine out of the hall, laughing. Eluned excused herself from the boisterous hall, pleading a headache, and waited in the empty chapel. Nan came to her within the hour, a quick wave from the door of the chapel.

Eluned followed her at a little distance, down the corridor and up a short stair. Nan gestured at the door left slightly ajar, saying, "He is there, in the chair by the fire, almost asleep when I left him."

"You are well?" Eluned asked in a whisper. "Did he harm you?"

Nan shook her head, but Eluned saw the start of a very large bruise on her wrist. She fought the urge to embrace the girl, and instead dismissed her quickly. "Back to the hall and serve until the celebrations are ended," she instructed Nan.

Then she was alone, staring at the door. She reached beneath her cloak and pulled out Madog's dagger, running her thumb across the crude etching in the otherwise plain square pommel. It was meant to be an eagle, but she only knew that because she had watched him as he had practiced drawing it with a stick in the dirt, trying to perfect it before scratching it into the handle. He must have been about twelve years old. He had been so proud of it.

She looked at the dagger a long time. In her other hand she held the small phial of nightshade. Now that she had come to the moment, she thought it might be poison instead of the blade. But when she set eyes on him, she would know which to use. She put the dagger in her right hand and held it behind her back, in case his eyes were still open when she entered. There was a draft of cold air that flowed from behind a loosely hung tapestry next to her. There must be a window there, behind it. She could hear Robert's voice asking, *do you still look into the sky?*

It was still possible to walk away. The stair was behind her, the door before her, the dagger resting lightly in her palm. But when she imagined walking away, leaving the universe undisturbed, everything in her rebelled. She could only see the bruise that even now spread on Nan's thin arm. She could only remember the laughter on Madog's lips as he died, and she knew she could not bear to be in a world where Roger Mortimer lived and laughed and prospered. The memory of Llewellyn's head swaying above London sent a spike of purest hatred through her heart, shot down her arm to tighten her fingers around the weapon as she stepped forward.

With her arm outstretched to push open the door, she felt a sudden grip on her wrist behind her, one strong hand wrenching the weapon away easily, another coming over her mouth. Her heart hammered. He was tall, looming over her as he dragged her back from the door, down the stair. She had only just gathered her wits enough to draw breath and begin to struggle when he set her down, put her back to the wall, and reached above her to pull a torch from its bracket. He looked down at the dagger and raised his brows in recognition of it before turning his gaze to her.

She did not even try to hide her shock as she looked back at her daughter's husband, Ranulf of Morency.

Chapter 10

The Unseen

Robert had the strong suspicion he was the only entirely sober guest in the hall. Even Edward seemed more jovial than could reasonably be expected of a king. It was loud and crowded, and Robert wanted more than anything to be out of it. But he had seen his wife leave – he was still incapable of ignoring her comings and goings – and planned to wait long enough that he would not interrupt her as she dressed for bed. He did not think he could stand that paralyzing awkwardness atop their frozen courtesy.

"Come, have more." Simon was trying, with limited success, to fill Robert's cup with more of the punch. It splashed to the floor, narrowly missing their feet, but finally enough made it into the cup that Simon grinned in triumph. "To your good health, brother. To your fortune here in England."

They had already toasted both of these things, and

many others, several times. But Simon was celebrating more than the Epiphany. Edward had given the command for the royal ordinance to be drawn up, outlining the new Marcher lordships, and the de Lascaux name would be on it. When it was done and the king set his seal to it, the new order of Wales would be law.

"It's your doing as much as my own," he assured Simon. "And it will be your son's fortune one day."

If Robert were in a better humor, Simon's expression would have made him laugh. He watched his brother choke on his drink in surprised dismay. When he'd finished spluttering he gripped Robert's shoulder and looked with a determined steadiness into his face, eyebrows drawn low.

"You don't mean to go back to France."

"How much have you drunk? I have no mind to return to France." He watched relief, almost comical in its intensity, wash over Simon's face. Becoming better acquainted with his brother was, Robert thought, one of the few pleasurable surprises he'd had at Edward's court. "I meant only that it will be your son's because I am unlikely to have a son myself."

Simon gave an audible sigh of satisfaction and sat back, his grip on Robert's shoulder relaxing. He reached for his wine again, but Robert pulled it away. It was amusing to see his careful and proper brother in his cups, but he didn't like the thought of Simon getting sick all over his warmest cloak.

"Do you mean she's barren?"

The question startled him, not least because there was such genuine concern in Simon's voice. Robert could think of no answer that did not announce his intention to avoid sleeping with his wife, an intimate detail that was more than he cared to share with his brother. If Kit were still here, though, he might speak of it. He could say to his friend that the thought of going to her out of duty, forcing himself to do the act as she lay cold and stiff and indifferent – he could tell his friend how it sickened him even to think it. And if she was not cold, if she melted beneath his hands and kissed him with a greedy passion – if she did that again and *then* turned cold again, it would be even worse.

Even to Kit, he did not know if he could explain why and how it would be so much worse. If he could stop loving her to desperation, it would be easy enough. Maybe one day he would stop. But no. Kit had said she would always have his heart, and it was true. Robert was too old now, to learn another way to be. He should have tried, somewhere along the way, to love someone else.

And now Simon was looking at him expectantly, wondering if she was barren.

"Nay, I have no reason to think it," he said, hoping to move Simon off the topic. "She is not a girl, though, and neither am I young enough that we can expect to be so blessed. Your oldest is how old?"

"Ten, this past summer."

"Send him to us for squire, then. Unless you have other plans for him? He's of an age with Robin, who will come to us and they can learn together." He smiled at the thought, but Simon seemed confused.

"Robin?"

"Kit's son. Christopher Manton, my friend," he explained patiently. "His boy Robin is released from Mortimer's custody and will be fostered with me."

Simon began to look too flushed, and a little too

careful not to look Robert in the eye. Robert wondered if he ever drank this much. It was possible he'd never had so much good news to celebrate. "Walk with me where the air is fresher, Simon," he said, grateful at the chance to be out of the hall.

It was too cold to wander outside, so he steered Simon down the corridor that led to the rooms he shared with Eluned, where even now she had retreated to avoid him. The color in his brother's face was dying down until he paused, leaned against the wall, and startled to see a couple hiding behind the tapestry. Robert laughed to see the red come into Simon's cheeks again as he muttered an apology and fairly ran away. They walked farther down, Robert laughing all the while. It really was too bad he had spent years away from Simon. He was proving to be a diverting companion, as was any brother who was easy to tease. The sounds of the hall began to fade as they walked on, until they were nearly to the queen's small chapel.

Simon frowned in the direction of the isolated little chapel. "We're likely to disturb some other young lovers, if we wander in there."

"Aye, is the place I would choose for it, were I young and daring again." Except that when he was young and daring, he had chosen the chapel only as the place where she would leave the sign to meet him somewhere more remote, more safe. "Down these stairs instead, then. Tell me, will you stay here with Edward's court even now the prize of my lordship is won?"

Simon shrugged, his steps slowing to an easy, lazy pace. "Haps there are more prizes to be gained, do I stay near and listen well. But I will ask our father what he would have me do."

"The French estate," said Robert. He had been thinking of it for days. "I have left it in capable hands, but if you have no plans for your second son I would see him as seneschal there. If he has the wits, it is important work."

"He has such wit that we have thought to give him to the Church."

"It is yours to say which will suit him best. But if you will ask what would please me well, it would be to have you learn the place and the people, the business of the vineyards, so that you may to teach it to your son. It has grown in wealth and consequence, and if I am to be a Marcher lord here then I fear I will neglect _"

"You want me to administer the French estate?" Poor Simon looked as though he were somewhere between dazed and determined, trying to force his unwilling mind to make sense of the conversation.

"For a time, yes. Only if you wish to. And only if you will learn to hold your wine with more grace," Robert answered with a broad smile. "There will be much more of it in France."

Simon had stopped walking and was looking at him in surprise. He shook his head as if to clear it and leaned back against the wall.

"Father said… He worried you would go back there yourself, I think."

Robert had spent the last week and more thinking of just that prospect. So difficult had it proved to imagine living with Eluned – this life where she ignored him and he pretended he did not notice her every breath – that he tried to think of how to compose a life without her at his side. They did not have to live together, and she was well practiced in ruling in an absent husband's stead.

Though it was not like to please the king, Robert could return to France, go back to a place he understood better. It had not always been easy, but compared to this new life in England it was like a sunny dream. There were no dashed hopes there, no complex court politics, no need to establish himself as a new lord. In France there were days of routine work, improving on something he'd already built. There was laughter with old friends and watching little Robin grow into a man, the amusement of frustrating his father from afar and the distant, glowing memory of a woman he had once loved and lost.

He could go back to that comfortable kind of dream. There would be no bosom friend, because Kit would stay here – and no Robin to brighten his days, nor any unspoiled memory of Eluned to soften his most solitary moments. It would never be the same. But even so, it would be easier than the path here. Which was likely why his father had thought he would take it.

"Haps I should go back only to bedevil him." He said it with a smile, but quickly perceived his brother saw nothing humorous in it. "Simon, be easy. I said it in jest."

"Ever has that been your favorite jest. You spend your life at it, and say it is only jest." Simon pushed Robert's hand of his shoulder and stepped back, still a little unsteady from the drink. His voice rose. "But you act on it. The consequence of it matters. You jest, you…laugh. You are the only one who is amused."

"Simon -"

"Father does not laugh, *I* do not laugh." He was well and truly drunk. He looked as if he was close to tears, but Robert could not say if they were tears of rage or sorrow. Maybe it was only the excess of drink that caused such emotion. Or maybe it had been there all along and the drink only uncovered it. "All he wanted was to build something of worth, but you worked against him at every turn."

"Simon, I have made the French estate -"

"I know you have! In spite of his plans you succeed, in the manner of *your* choosing. And he loves you for it. Never will he say it but the pride in him…" Simon looked away, and Robert could see the shadow of a sullen boy in his posture. "Is not enough, you know. God alone knows what would satisfy him. He will be no more happy with you, now you have finally been made to do his bidding. I have done it all along, and willingly. It is not enough."

Robert was not sure if this was meant as complaint or warning. He was not sure what to think at all, except that while he had whiled away the years in France, happily defying his father, he had given no thought at all to his brother. If ever he had thought of Simon in all those years, it had been as his father's creature, the good son. He barely remembered him as a boy. Younger by almost a decade, eager to please and anxious at every harsh word, Simon had been easy to disregard.

"It pains you," he said now, beginning to understand a little. "You only want there to be peace between us, between father and me."

Simon shrugged. "Mayhap I did want it, but I see it is too late now. It is too much a habit between you, the strife. He will not live much longer, anyway."

Poor wretched Simon, who had spent his life in obedience and love for their sour old father. When he was sober, Robert resolved to tell him what he had understood long, long ago: that when you will be found wanting no matter your course, it is better to do as you please.

But for now, he put an arm across his brother's shoulders and leaned against the wall beside him. "Take comfort in knowing that in the end, there is no strife between us. I have done as he wished. For once, it was what I wanted too."

"You wanted to leave France?"

"I wanted to marry Eluned," he said.

After a long silence, Simon spoke.

"But it was not the marriage and the promise of a lordship that lured you away. It never would have. He knew that."

Robert watched as Simon dragged a hand over his face, a sudden sense of foreboding growing in him. It was true. His father could never have known that only saying Eluned's name would be enough. No, he would have asked Robert to return to take a wife and gain a title, and would have reasonably expect to be refused.

It was the news of Kit's son that had brought Robert to England, and had kept him here in the hopes of finding a resolution.

He recognized it now, the feeling that was coming in waves off of Simon. It was guilt. *Look you to learn who would whisper poison against your friend*, young William had said. And: *Your brother is the kind of man who might know.*

Robert stared at his brother's downturned face. His limbs felt heavy, his whole body wooden. He told himself it should not cut so deep, yet it did. Pain welled up, a dark and terrible hurt bubbling up beneath a frozen surface, and his mind improbably served him a vision of Eluned. Cold as the frozen sea.

His arm would not obey his command, and stayed around his brother's shoulders. Finally Simon, overwhelmed by conscience or dizzy with wine, sank to the floor and sat there with his back braced against the wall. He said nothing, and so Robert roused himself to speak.

"What did you tell Mortimer?"

"I'm sorry," said Simon, who sounded as miserable as Robert felt.

"What lies did you give Mortimer about Kit?"

"Not lies. I only..." He raised his head and looked around the deserted corridor. He seemed to have sobered up rapidly. "I played on their doubts. They were fighting the campaign in Wales. They worried their lands would be threatened while their attention was turned. Old Mortimer was vigilant, you know? Jealous and greedy. He said once that there was a corner of his land much disputed."

"What luck that his dispute was with my friend."

Robert took a step away from his brother. He felt like sinking to the floor himself, but had no wish to be near Simon, who waved a hand in dismissal.

"Mortimer has disputes with half the men who own land in England. A thousand suspicions, and I fed one of them."

"So you were sure to make them wary of Kit. And when he crossed into Mortimer land -"

"That was the luck, for me. I did not have to push your friend into the trap, so eagerly did he rush into it. Then Mortimer demanded the son as surety. It might have been resolved in a week, but that was not time enough. Not enough time to get you here. So I advised them to hold the boy. Indefinitely."

Robert almost asked what other reward there was for all this effort, for surely luring him to England was not enough reason to go to so much trouble. But as he looked down at his brother, he remembered where they were. This court where Simon had operated for so long was held together by alliances, favors, whispers. The trust and esteem of a Mortimer was reward enough. And, of course, it would please their father. Simon did love to please their father.

Robert leaned on the wall opposite Simon, as happy now to put a little distance between them as he had been to embrace his brother minutes ago. Perhaps he should not be surprised that his father would manipulate him in this way. But he was surprised, and aggrieved. Under it all, he had always thought his father cared for him. There was anger and frustration and disappointment – always that. But he had not thought there was malice.

"He knew how well I love Kit's son."

Simon nodded. "He thought… He said you only needed one more reason, a good one, to leave France. The fighting done, and the king ready to give a reward – Father said you only needed to be asked to come. If he asked it, you would refuse, so he…" Simon stopped and pushed his hands through his hair. He looked as though he wished he had brought the wine on this little walk. "I called it a poor plan. But then you came. At first word from your friend, you came. You stayed in France and refused marriage for years. And then when you thought it might help the boy -"

"Of course. Kit is like a brother to me."

"Yet if your true brother had asked you, would you have come?"

Simon looked fixedly at the floor as he asked it, and Robert was glad he did. All the times over the years that Simon had hinted at it, without ever saying it, came to him now. Every message he had sent, and in his brief visit to France years ago, Simon had hoped his brother would come to England. He never asked it outright, but he never failed to express the wish. Yet Robert had barely even heard it. He had paid it no mind at all.

His father knew him all too well. If the plea had come from anyone but Kit, Robert would have refused. He would have refused only because his father wanted it, and Robert loved to spite his father.

"See how much of yourself you have given for this friend you call brother. And for his son who you say is like your own." Now Simon looked up at him. "Do you even know my son's name? Any of them?" He dropped his hands to the floor and pushed himself up, leaning against the wall for support. There seemed to be no anger in him, only resignation. "I am not proud of it. But you need not wonder why it was so easy for me to agree to the scheme."

They stood for a very long time in silence as Robert considered. He looked at the fur that trimmed Simon's tunic and remembered what Kit had said – that Simon, too, would benefit from Robert's advancement. That he craved Robert's approval at least as much as that advancement.

"Do you hate me, brother?"

A sound like a laugh came from Simon. He shook his head in denial. "Were there true hatred in me, I would not have spent these many weeks in persuading

Mortimer to release the boy." He actually grinned a little. "But I have said you gave your word that he has nothing to fear of Kit Manton, and to mistrust Kit is to mistrust you, and he should be wary of giving such offense to someone so favored by the king. Roger Mortimer envies you, you know."

"Me? Why would Roger Mortimer envy me?"

"There are few enough men to whom Edward would give a Marcher lordship. And even fewer whose worth as battle commander is as valued as Roger Mortimer."

Now it was Robert who laughed. "Had I known protecting the Aquitaine would gain me so great a reputation, I might not have done it."

Simon gave an assenting grunt. He looked and sounded exactly like their father as he said, "God forbid you knowingly do something worthy with your life." He pushed away from the wall. "My room is not far from here, and I would take myself there while I can still stand."

Robert watched him take a few careful steps down the corridor, and wondered if it was wise to trust his brother. Plotting and planning, two years at least of maneuvering and lying. What kind of man did that, and to his own blood? Yet it was the same man who had confessed it, unprompted.

"Your oldest boy," he called to Simon, who paused in his step but did not turn. "His name is Adam."

He knew it, remembered it, because it had been the name of his twin.

Simon nodded. "The younger is John, and David the youngest," he said, and walked on.

✠ ✠ ✠

Outside the door to his chambers, Robert paused. The hour was late yet if he strained to hear it, there was faint music still drifting from the hall where the revels continued. It lent a dream-like air, the perfect accompaniment to his mood.

Too long had he lived enslaved to a memory. That was what Kit, best of friends, had told him only weeks ago. Robert had thought it only meant he had held too long to his love for Eluned. Now he saw how much more was in it. Now he saw that he had lived so much in memory that he had failed to see the present. For years and years he had looked steadfastly at the past, as if that one moment in time, that one summer with her, was the only thing in his life that deserved such attention and devotion.

He leaned his head against the doorframe, his hand on the hasp. She might be there, on the other side of this door. For the first time since she had fled his bed, he wanted her to be there. These past few days had seen them avoiding and ignoring each other, and every night he had stood at this door and hoped she was asleep so he would not have to pretend indifference to her presence. But tonight he wished she was there, and awake, sitting at her place before the window. Because he was a great fool who, even as he recognized that his devotion to a memory was weakness and folly, still needed her.

If she was now who she had been before... But no. There was the sticking point, the thing he could not make himself disbelieve. That was the hell of it, his absolute certainty that she was still the woman he had known and loved. If she would let herself be again what she was – that was it. If she would let herself be the Eluned of old, then he could sit next to her and confide it all. Then he would enter this room and take her hand. She would listen with furrowed brow as he described what his father had done, and he would ask her why it still had the power to wound him. He would tell her about Simon, the look in his face when he had confessed it and the terrible sinking feeling it had caused in him. He would wonder aloud how he could have closed his eyes to so much for so long, and she would say…something. The right thing. The memory of her always said the right thing.

He opened the door on darkness and knew she was not within. He crossed to the fire, bent to the glowing embers and rose with a dim rushlight that carried him in fading hope to the place she had made her bed. She was not there. There was only the neatly folded blanket in the corner and her ivory box on the cushion.

How fitting, that he should hope for her and find instead a locked box, cool and hard and beautiful.

In his own bed, their half-empty marriage bed, he pulled the blankets tight around him. It was cold, the present world. No wonder he had resisted it so long.

Chapter 11

The Choosing

Eluned stood frozen in disbelief before Ranulf Ombrier, lord of Morency, devoted servant of the king, renowned murderer, and her barely tolerated son-in-law. The first coherent thought that broke through her amazement was that he could only be here at King Edward's bidding. Which would mean that Edward knew her plans, or suspected her, and that made so little sense that she cast about for some other explanation. She could think of no other reason for Ranulf to come to court except that the king had summoned him.

Unless he had come to bring news of Gwenllian.

The sound she made must have been terrible, for he looked up so swiftly and so sharply that she was forced to focus on his face. His eyes were clear of grief, no madness or rage or despair in them. After a long and panicked moment, relief crashed through her. If any evil had befallen her daughter, she would see it in his face. And it was not there.

"Gwenllian is well," she said, and found she was breathing hard, her fists gripping his tunic. He had dropped the torch to the bare stone floor, but made no move to retrieve it. "The child came? They are both in good health?"

He nodded, and for a brief and dazzling moment she loved him like a son, would happily have embraced him – only because he told her Gwenllian was well. His hand came up to cover hers, a gesture of reassurance so unlikely that she could only stare at his fingers on hers.

"And if I said they were not?" he asked.

If her daughter were not well, then she would beg him to plunge the knife into her breast. But Gwenllian lived. Eluned uncurled her fists and, as she pulled her hands away from him, felt the forgotten phial of poison falling from her fingers. She caught it, closed her hand around it again and held it against her skirt as she sagged against the wall.

"You would not be here if they were not," she answered.

He picked up the torch again. His eyes, dark blue and assessing, moved over her face. "Nor would I be here had she given me any other choice."

She waited for him to explain his words, but he did not elaborate. Instead, he took two long strides away from her and through an open chamber door that she had not seen until now. Before she had gathered her wits to wonder what he was about, he stepped back into the corridor to grasp her arm and jerk her inside the little room.

Still he said nothing. He only pulled the wooden door closed behind her and returned his attention to the dagger in his hand, tilting it so the light slid along the blade. The torch now sat in the little bracket on the wall, lighting the tiny room which held only two small beds piled with blankets, some well-worn baggage in a corner, and clothes hanging on wall hooks. Some minor lords lodged here, likely. She wondered vaguely if he knew whose room it was, then returned to wondering why he was here.

"How did you know to find me here?" she asked at last.

"I followed you from the hall. I had barely arrived and seen you there when you slipped out." He kept his eyes on the blade in his hands, passing a thumb lightly over the quillon. "It was a boy, if you care to know it. Another son," he said, his expression unreadable. "We named him Madog."

The name flooded her chest with emotion. She wanted to snatch the weapon back from him, and would have done it if she had not known it for a foolish impulse. He was Ranulf of Morency and he held a blade in his hand. If he wished it, the steel would be at her throat before she had moved an inch. She stared at the etching on the dagger's pommel instead. *We were true friends*, Madog had said. And longer ago, solemnly, on his knees: *I swear fealty to Gwenllian ferch Eluned.* Long before Morency had entered their lives, there had been Madog's protection and loyalty and love. His blade did not belong in this man's hand.

"In truth, *she* named the boy." Ranulf smiled faintly to himself before his expression turned grim. "I could not spare a thought for his naming, so busy was I in persuading her she must not rise from childbed the instant he was born to travel the winter road. Naught would do but that she must come to her lady mother, and force you to break your silence."

She held his hard gaze, gritting her teeth and feeling her lips pinch together. Twice had Gwenllian sent letters to her since Madog's death, and Eluned had answered only once, briefly and formally. Her replies were impersonal, dictated to the scribe and ignoring nearly every question posed to her. Her daughter asked how the men of Ruardean fared in the face of Madog's death, asked why Eluned had agreed to marriage to a stranger, invited her to come to Morency, wondered if she grieved Walter's passing or the loss of Ruardean's rule – all things that Eluned could not bring herself to answer. She could not even bring herself to think of those things, or of Gwenllian's concern.

And now it was Gwenllian's husband she must deal with, standing over her with narrowed eyes, dagger in hand.

"Come, lady mother," he said, taking a step closer until he towered over her. "Surely there is something you would say for yourself."

She kept her eyes level with his chest, felt her breath grow thinner and quicker as he seemed to grow impossibly taller. She bore it for a moment, and then something in her snapped. Her hands came up and pushed him away, a peevish gesture as she stepped back from him and said, exasperated, "Oh, stop *looming*."

There was a smirk on his lips, of course, but it did not provoke her as it should. There was something comfortable about it, the natural response to a woman's harmless scold. God save her, that she must count this man as family now.

"I confess I never thought to find you on the threshold of murder. Tell me," he said with a thoughtful little flip of the dagger in his palm. "Why Roger Mortimer?"

She did not bother pretending he was wrong about her intention or her target. It was dawning on her now, the truth of it sinking like a stone thrown into her spirit, that she would not realize her goal. There was no use dissembling, not with what he had seen. She looked down at the poison in her hand briefly before opening the purse on her belt and dropping it in. He watched her closely. At his politely questioning look, she said, "Nightshade."

He acknowledged this with an appreciative expression, then seemed to consider it for the barest moment.

"But you would use poison only if you must. You prefer the blade, and the blood it brings." It was matter of fact, offhanded in a way that only a murderer could be about such a thing. "The maidservant who helps you, what is her part in it?"

"She has no part. I only promised her a coin if she told me when he was alone and asleep."

His brows lifted with skepticism. "What good fortune, that he should fall asleep alone by his fire while the rest of the court is gathered in celebration."

She took a breath, waiting for more. But he did not accuse, or mock, or demand answers. "The girl is innocent entirely." She looked at the dagger gripped comfortably in his hand and felt the bitterness of defeat rise to the back of her throat. It welled up under her tongue. Thwarted. Again. And by him, again. "When you tell your king, you may say in honesty that none knew of my plans this night. I have laid them well, and all in secret and alone."

"Nor do I doubt there will be hints and proofs of it, exactly such bits as will paint the very picture you wish the king to see. Well do I know your skill in that art." He shifted his weight, leaning his shoulder to the wall and crossing his ankles – a casual, conversational pose. "But you do not answer me. Why Roger Mortimer?"

All the reasons tumbled through her mind, a blur of anger and hate that reached beyond one man. She gave him the simple answer.

"He set the trap for Llewellyn. He carried his head as trophy to the king."

She felt Ranulf's eyes on her, and kept her own blank and staring into nothing. So close. She had been so close. Mortimer should be dead, right now. She pictured it and felt a pang that was like hunger or sorrow, and knew it showed in her face. It occurred to her that of anyone she had ever known, Ranulf of Morency might recognize it.

Even as the idea came to her, he said, "So sweet is the thought of his death that you ache with wanting it." He spoke like one reminiscing about a pleasant dream, nostalgia for something lost. "You think...the blade slides into flesh and there will be relief. Satisfaction. You think the ache will stop with his heart."

She met his eyes, calm and deep blue. She knew, even before the small shake of his head, what he would say.

"It never stops," he said, utterly still, utterly certain.

He had been only seventeen when he killed his father. *Foster father*, she reminded herself reflexively, but it was a distinction that was almost meaningless. The man who had raised him, loved him as a son. A cruel man who was dreaded and loathed, from everything she had learned. She had made it her business to learn about that brute because he had been betrothed to her daughter. Eluned had done everything she could to delay the marriage and keep Gwenllian safe, ensuring her child learned every necessary defense against the day she must be given to him. And then he was dead, suddenly and most fortuitously, by Ranulf's hand.

She should thank him for it. But he hadn't done it for her, or for Gwenllian. He had done it to gain the king's favor. Murder in cold blood, the unsuspecting victim asleep and alone, a knife in the night as he lay helpless in sleep. It was not a comfortable thought, to know how nearly her actions mirrored his own.

"Never tell me you have come here to save me from the disappointment of success." She pressed her palms, suddenly damp and shaking, to her skirt. Would he take her to the king now, or would he give her time first to go to Robert and explain? She did not know what to hope. She could not imagine what to say to her husband, how he would react. *Robin*, she thought, and a pang worse than hunger or sorrow bit into her.

Ranulf's face changed subtly, a tightening of his mouth that said he was no happier than she, to find himself here.

"I have told you true – I come for the sake of my lady wife, who is troubled by your silence." There was the faintest trace of disgust in his expression. "And what can I tell her on my return, but that you have spared no thought for her grief, sent no word of comfort, because you cared more for bloody vengeance than for her?"

There was a delay between his uttering the words and her comprehension. There was no mistaking the accusation and it caused a cold rage to shoot through her, to her very fingertips. "Do you dare to say I have abandoned her?"

"I say you are here with dagger in hand, while she mourns alone."

"Alone!" she fairly shouted at him. Her anger, so long and deeply hidden beneath the cold, burst into riotous bloom. "*I* watched him die. I held his hand and heard him speak of her with his last *breath*. I mourned alone as they lowered him into the ground, him and his father, my uncle who I loved with my whole heart. *I* watched alone and helpless as Wales was vanquished, and I could give no aid, I must watch it happen, I must bear all of it alone because she chose *you*." She was breathing hard now, heedless words tumbling out. But she did not care. Let him see, let anyone see what she felt, what did it matter anymore? "The sword that might have defended him, the sword that I put in her hand, she yielded it to *you*."

She could still see it, the image burned into her mind: Gwenllian striding away, offering up her weapon to this man. The sight of it had touched off something in Eluned, something like a mortal terror so overwhelming that she remembered nothing of what she had done or said in that moment. The memory of it must show on her face now, for Ranulf looked at her warily, too obviously unsure of what to say.

His uncertainty brought her up short, calmed her with its very humanness. He was only a man. Not a monster, not a thief who had set out to rob her of her hopes and her daughter. Just a man in love who, like any other, could not see beyond that love. The resentment drained from her, leaving only an honest appeal in her eyes as she looked to him.

"Do you know what it cost me, to put that sword in her hands? Can you fathom the price?" She turned her gaze on the flame from the torch. She stared at the brightness until her eyes burned, until it blinded her. Still she could see Robin, young and smiling, summer sun on his hair.

"Would you change it, if you could?" Ranulf asked. "Knowing she would never use the sword as you wished, would you keep it from her and spare yourself the cost?"

She knew the answer. She had always known the answer, but she waited a long time before telling him. "No. I would not."

"I am glad to hear it," he said, "for she still wields it, sometimes. She would not have the women of Morency as weak creatures, and so she teaches them such defenses as they may need against lecherous men. And she would not have her husband grow soft." He quirked a sudden smile at her. "She trains with me in secret. There is none can match her skill."

Eluned felt her heart burst back to life at the picture his words painted. What a wonder was her daughter: strength like hope, stubbornly growing in places it was never meant to thrive. What a scene it must have been, if she was determined to seek out Eluned and her husband was equally determined to prevent it. It almost made her smile.

In the silence, she turned her back to Ranulf and rubbed her hands over her face. She let herself imagine Gwenllian grieving at the news of Madog, bewildered at her mother's hasty marriage. "Did she fear I would grow mad?"

"Nay, she feared your spirit would wither, and you

become like a ghost. It was I who thought madness, or something like. Nor did I tell her so, for I would not add to her distress." She turned back to find him looking down again at the dagger, turning it over in his hand. "Did you think to slit his throat or put it in his heart?" There was a note of professional interest in his voice. "I think you would not put it in his back."

"The neck," she said, through lips grown suddenly numb. "To sink it at the base of his throat."

"And leave it there?" He raised his brows in appreciation. "So to stop the blood from rushing over you, and the dagger left planted in his corpse as message." He shrugged. "A fitting symbol of vengeance, even if only you would understand it fully. And your daughter, and me."

She could not say how she knew it, but she was suddenly certain that he would not tell the king, or warn Mortimer. He would stop her tonight, and then depend on her to abandon her plot for the sake of her daughter. Or maybe he meant to menace her, she thought, as he leveled a speculative look at her.

"You would do it on the Epiphany. In truth I had little time to remark who was in the hall before you quit it, but I can think of no one who was absent from the revelries that you might easily blame."

"Because there is no one." He stared hard at her and she lifted her chin abruptly, a jab at him and his presumptions. "What is left of my life is little value to anyone. I will not have an innocent hang for my sins."

The look he gave her was supremely skeptical.

"Little value? It was a short time I spent observing in the hall, but it wanted only an instant to recognize Robert de Lascaux by the way he looks at you." She blinked, but gave him no more than that. "I know naught of him and would say it marked him a fool, did not one so worthy as Gwenllian look on you also with love. Would you have her lose her mother to the noose, then, even as she has lost her friend to your war?"

"Not my war," she said. "You saw to that, as did she."

He inclined his head in acknowledgement. "And if you sought to entangle Gwenllian in this scheme, be assured we would not stand here in peace. It does seem as you will harm only yourself, by design. I would wager you have labored to keep your new husband safe from this plot, and your son. You even try to protect the serving girl."

He looked at her a long moment, the dark eyes considering her closely, as she thought how different was this man from any other she had known. He was dangerous without the edge of lechery or madness. Like Kit Manton, he was quietly observant – but with none of Kit's kindness. She knew he saw her, what she was, in a way no one else had ever done. No one except Robert. But Robert saw her true nature and loved her. Ranulf of Morency saw and understood her, a cold recognition with no room for anything like love in it.

"Do you know why I killed my foster father?" he asked, as idly as though he were inquiring after the dinner menu. Still it made her heart stop, so strange and sudden was the question. "The true reason, that lay beneath the furious hunger for revenge – what there was in the clearheaded moment of choosing? I have not even told Gwenllian, but I will tell you."

His eyes were still fixed on hers, demanding

attention, but he seemed to see more than just her face before him. He was looking too at the memory of that moment, the memory of the decision that had changed the course of his life.

"I chose to be a villain," he said simply, and his mouth curled up gently at the corner. "The one who would be feared, and respected. Who they would whisper about, and dread to see. I knew well what I chose. And yet I did not know. Villainy outlasts the vengeance, you see." He looked her up and down, a brief assessment, curious. "What will outlast your moment of revenge, my lady? What do you think to accomplish this night?"

She watched the play of torchlight on the wall. How strange, to speak of such things so easily. She said, "His death. That he will not be allowed to claim a slice of my homeland as his own."

"So Roger Mortimer is dead, and then what?"

"Then his brother Edmund, if I am granted the opportunity."

"And then their sons? Their sisters, their nephews? Yet when every one of them is slain and buried, some other lord who is just as cruel and brutish as Mortimer will take his place, and Wales will still be under Edward's rule." He shifted, leaning both shoulders against the wall, looking down at her with faint but unmistakable contempt. "Such wit as you possess, and you find no better use for it than the work of a butcher."

She did not even feel the insult of it. She knew he was right. Some rational part of her had known it from the first and she had paid it no heed. It was easy to bury the sound of that small voice of reason when all of her cried out for a reckoning.

"I want…" *Revenge for Wales*, she thought. An impossible thing. Wales was lost. No amount of blood could ever serve as payment for so huge a loss. "It is no matter."

"Oh it matters, else we would not be here now. What do you want?"

She closed her eyes and saw Robert, moonlight falling on his face as he called her *cariad* and reached for her. And with it, she heard the sad finality in his voice when he declared that loving her now would be the ruin of him. These crucial lessons she had forced herself to learn: she could not have Robert; she could not save Wales.

"Impossible things," she said, opening her eyes again. "It is my fate to want impossible things."

He shrugged. "Verily, how impossible for the wife of a new marcher lord to care for the Welsh who will fall under her protection. To allow them the exercise of their own laws, to preserve their customs and help them to prosper under an English king. To accomplish something lasting."

There was irony in his voice, but it spoke volumes that he did not mock her, or sneer. She let the import of his words sink in, allowed the voice of reason to be heard over the voice that cried out for blood. How singular, that he of all men would make her see this.

"To build instead of kill?" she asked lightly, assessing him in her turn. He had stayed away from court and king for three years. Three years at least, then, that he had played at being not villain but noble lord. "Was it a fine harvest at Morency this year?"

His mouth twitched in suppressed laughter, a sign that he would not belabor the point. "Very fine." He straightened from the wall and let his arms drop to his sides, the dagger still in one hand. "Come, it grows late and Sir Ademar will want his bed soon enough," he said with a nod toward one of the mattresses.

He reached up and took the torch from the bracket, then stood watching the light play off the blade of the dagger again. His thumb rubbed across the crude etching on the pommel, the markings that identified it as Madog's weapon.

He held it out to her, hilt first, for a long and silent moment. The air between them was heavy, crowded with countless unvoiced thoughts, the blade shining at the center of it all.

"If you will do it," he said, "do it far from court. And it is worth the time and forethought to make it look like an accident."

The torch lit his face from beneath, shadowing his eyes. She stretched out a hand to the dagger, felt its heft again and saw all the gleaming possibilities in the sharp point. Then she set it back in his waiting palm.

"Take it to Gwenllian," she said. She swallowed hard around a sudden swelling in her throat. "It should never have left her side."

✠ ✠ ✠

Drunken revelers were beginning to drift from the hall as she reached her chambers. She walked slowly, feeling no need for haste. Robert may be within, and she was unsure if she was yet ready to speak to him after her encounter.

But when she entered and found the outer room empty, a sudden and terrible loneliness swept over her. She stood with it, breathless and cold in the face of her longing for him. What would she not give to lean on him in moments like these, to come home to his embrace? She looked at the glowing embers in the hearth and remembered him on the night they were wed, all openness and hope and affection. And she, cold and unhesitating, had pushed him away. It was as much a sin as any the priests taught, she was sure, though they were like to call it venial while she thought it more unforgivable than most she had committed.

She lit the small lamp and took careful, quiet steps across the floor until she reached the threshold of the inner room. His bed curtains were drawn shut, but she pulled them gently aside, to be sure he was there. The sound of his breath reached her first, and then the soft light fell on his sleeping form. His back was to her, or she might have watched him longer. Instead, she stepped back and let the curtain fall closed again.

With the sound of his occasional sleeping sighs to interrupt her thoughts, she stood in the cold beside his bed. The conversation with her daughter's husband echoed through her mind. What did she want? *Choose carefully what you dare to desire*, she had told herself, time and again. And Robert had spoken true: she had no small ambitions.

She could still choose villainy. It was plain as the dagger he had held forth that Ranulf would not stop her. Her mind was churning without her prompting, as it so often did, calculating details and possibilities – but not for revenge. No, now she was thinking of the manor house at Dinwen, which the king would grant to Robert, and how it should be better fortified to serve as refuge for the nearby town. She was thinking of how the Welsh priests had complained of interference from the English archbishop, and of a cousin who would lose her right of inheritance under English law, and of what could be done for them. She was thinking that she wished Robert was awake so that she could tell him all these things, and hear his thoughts.

She could have revenge, or she could have him.

There was a faint sound in the outer room, and she went to find one of the servants entering. Eluned whispered instructions to the girl, then bade her leave. When she was alone again, she uncoiled her braid to let it hang down her back, then removed her belt and the phial from inside the purse. She wrapped her heavy cloak around her shoulders and walked to the makeshift bed where she had slept these many nights. Her ivory box rested there amid the cushions. Taking the key from around her neck, she opened it and saw the letter she had so carefully written, neat and easy evidence. She put the phial in the box and lifted the letter out, sparing a long moment to look at the keepsakes that lay beneath it.

She walked to the hearth and held the parchment to the embers until it began to smoke and caught fire. When it was nothing but ash she extinguished the lamp she held.

There was a chair in the room where Robert slept, hard and uncomfortable even with the thick pillow that was on its seat. She sat there, in the dark, hands folded in her lap. The sounds of the castle drifted in for an hour or so, drunken stumblings past the door, faint strains of music fading in and out. It grew quiet as she sat unmoving, all the world asleep as she looked back at the path that had led her here.

She thought of Gwenllian as a child, her grubby

face by candlelight and her sweet sleeping breath as Eluned decided she must let Robert go. But Gwenllian was grown now, and fierce, and feared no man – just as Eluned had wanted. She thought of Walter's fervent praying, the strength in his hands and the wildness in his eyes. But Walter was dead. Her fate was no longer bound to him.

Tentatively, by slow and timid degrees, as though something in her expected disaster if it was done too freely, she let herself remember the feel of Robert. First, his hand in hers, fingers entwined as he swore he still saw the girl he had loved. Then his kiss. His arms around her. His mouth on her. A tangle of vivid memories undimmed by time: he sorted her hair into a braid as she hummed a Welsh melody, her heart soaring at the sight of him returning from his meeting with Aaron, the feel of her face stretched wide in a helpless smile while he admired the elusive dimple in her cheek.

A dream. It was all a beautiful dream. And so she had told herself for years. Now she looked at the bed curtains as they were gradually lit with the breaking dawn, and allowed herself to believe it was possible. The dream could be made real. There was no unbearable price, no delicate balance to consider. She could have what she wanted. She truly could.

If he still wanted her.

Eluned gathered her arms around herself under the cloak. She wanted more than anything to enter the warmth of his bed, slip behind the curtains and burrow beneath the covers, wrap herself around him until no part of her was cold. But she had no right. She could only wait for his waking as she carefully examined a lifetime of choices and desires and defenses.

When the sun was fully up, she heard him stirring. Before she was ready, he was there, pushing aside the bed curtains and grimacing against the light as his feet dropped to the floor. He stopped, the smooth flow of his movements suspended when he saw her, the simple shirt he had worn to sleep in pulled crookedly across his chest, gaping at the throat. He blinked in surprise. Her heart beat out of control as his glance flicked over her, no doubt wondering why she was here after so many days of their cordially ignoring one another.

He was drawing a breath now, opening his mouth to say something. He would admonish her to leave him in peace, or say something cutting, and she must speak first to stop him.

"I was not a girl," she said, nonsensically, her mind serving up an obscure insight that had moments ago floated through her thoughts. It was the wrong place to start; he could not be expected to understand, but she persevered. "All these years, I have remembered myself as a girl who foolishly fell into love, reckless and rash. I told myself…that we must all leave youth behind, and childish impulses, and girlish infatuations. But it was a lie." Beneath the cloak she pressed her hands hard against her chest, willing her breath to slow. "I was not a girl. I was a woman grown, and I loved you with a woman's heart."

He looked at her, faintly perplexed but silent as she searched for more words. She had known, once, how to speak the truth of her heart – unvarnished, with no art and no caution. Had she lost that, too? As she hesitated, he began to move. He was going to stand and walk away and dismiss her, and the thought of it brought her to her feet. She held her hand out, a staying motion.

"Robin. Please."

At the sound of his name he stopped his movement. He looked at her outstretched hand as though transfixed, and lowered himself again to sit on the bed. She looked down at his hair, tousled from sleep, and wanted to smooth it with her fingers. It seemed to her that she must explain herself, every moment that she had lived and how she had lived it, since she had parted from him in the dark with unseen bruises on her jaw and the taste of her tears mingled with the smell of rosemary. But there was so much, and she was so weary, and she only wanted to put herself in his arms.

She feared he still preferred to hunt wolves in the snow than to be in her presence. She stepped forward, close enough that she could touch him if she dared. She did not, yet.

"You said that loving me was the making of you. But it was losing you that was the making of me." She breathed the next words, the bare truth of it too awful for anything but a whisper. "I do not like what it has made me. Nor can I be what I once was. Not without you."

He turned his face up, a wary look. "What do you ask me?" His voice was hoarse with sleep. The wintry light picked out the lines around his eyes, just as she was sure it highlighted the years in her face. There could be no illusion that she was very far, in every way, from the young love whose image he had cherished for so long.

"I ask..." It felt wrong, standing above him like this, so she lowered herself slowly to her knees. Her hands folded over his where it rested on the bed. "I ask if you will trust me with your heart again, cariad. I ask you will not forget the woman who loved you with abandon, lest I forget her too. I ask…" Her breath caught as she looked at him and saw the careful reserve on his face. "I ask too much, because you are right when you say I dream no small dreams. I am greedy beyond reason, that I should ask to be your lover as well as your wife."

He looked away. His hand moved under hers, flexing into a fist that pressed into the bed as he spoke. "I have been blind to so much. A willful blindness, and it is only now that I begin to see it as my own failing." Still he did not look at her. "Yet though I may blame myself for it in the end, I am certain sure I cannot forgive you if you will embrace me again only to flee from me in the night and turn cold in the morn."

She tightened her hand around his. "I swear by my hope of heaven, Robert, if you will have me in your bed again all the armies of the king could not drag me out of it."

She felt the skin of his wrist gather into goosebumps, heard his exhalation of breath that might be a laugh. But when she looked in his face there was only wariness and caution.

What would she become, if he would not have her? It raised a dread and a desolation in her breast, an icy clutch at her heart, and her words tumbled out. "There is much to tell you, I know. In faith I cannot be unchanged by so many years and haps you will not want me as before, is in our nature to -"

But now his hands were moving, seizing her face with a sweeping motion to bring his lips to hers and he was kissing her, paying no heed to her babble of words. The threatening panic in her breast burst instead into warmth and color, a chaos of feeling that she recognized. It was of a piece with the sunlight on her back, the feel of his hair between her fingers, this old familiar craving that had never left her.

When she reached to remove her belt, he found the clasp of her cloak. Their hands moved in concert to peel off her surcoat, he pulling her undertunic over her head while she rid herself of her shoes, only breaking the kiss when they could not help it – practiced movements, learned together and never forgotten. He leaned back into the bed and took her with him, until she was braced on her forearms above him.

Oh, let him not regret it. Let him not see all of her in the daylight again, and regret how different she was from their youth. There would be time enough, when she told him of her many sins, for him to reckon the distance from that summer. But for now let her look at him stretched beneath her as she sat up, straddled across him, the ache between her legs pressed against his hardness as she unraveled her braid. Let her have this moment, little though she deserved it, when he watched her with something like reverence in his eyes and raked his fingers through her hair until it spread free across her shoulders.

"I dreamed of this," he said. He curled a handful of her hair around his fist, looking at it transfixed. "For so long, I dreamed of it."

She smiled a little wistfully. "Too long. In your dreams there was no silver in my hair, or yours."

"There was," he said, pressing his lips to it, pulling her gently down to him. "That was the dream even then, that we would grow old together."

She hid her face against his neck, too overcome to do anything but stay there, her arms wrapped around him. The heat of him soaked into every part of her, banished the cold that had been her nearest companion for so long. His hands smoothed down her back, his hips lifting a little under her, stoking the hunger in her. She kissed him then, as they shifted and moved to bring him into her. Their breaths mingled and she held him there, deep inside.

It felt new and miraculous – and comfortable and familiar and true. She could not fathom that she had ever been so foolish that she had wanted anything else, ever in her life, but to have this.

She pulled her head back so she could see his face. "I love you, Robert," she said into his eyes. "I love you." She said it again, between kisses on his lips and across his face until she reached his ear, where she whispered it again and again until she was breathless and gasping.

Years and years to make up for, she told herself as he moved in her. And she would fill the days left to them with loving him freely – declaring it, gasping it – in daylight and in darkness. However it pleased them, so long as he would have her, she would love him with her last breath.

Chapter 12

The Bright

Robert moved his mouth up the furrow of her spine, taking his time to kiss every inch of it. He had meant it to tease her gently awake so that she might kiss him back and take him in her arms again. But if it did not cause her to wake and respond, then it allowed him to savor the taste of her naked skin at his leisure. By the time his lips reached the nape of her neck, he decided he was not sure which he wanted more. They were equally delightful prospects and he really only cared that she was here in his bed.

In spite of the cold, he'd pulled the bed curtains open just enough to let in the sun. It was too irresistible, to make love to her in the daylight and to watch it touch her nakedness while she slept next to him. It was in daylight that he had always known her, had always pictured her during their years apart.

She came awake with a soft little sigh and pushed herself against him, comfortable and inviting, her bottom pressed against his erection. It banished all the idle thoughts from his mind and set off an animal hunger. His teeth against her neck, her hand coming up to the back of his head to hold him there, the wetness that was between her legs when his fingers parted her flesh – it was feeling and not thought, nothing but raw sensation. He took her from behind, her gasps and moans fueling his movements until they both collapsed together, limp and sweaty limbs entwined in the sunlight. All of him ached with the familiarity of it, the delicious delight.

Eventually she turned over beneath him, sighed, and declared herself desperately thirsty.

"Is strange the servants have not come," he noted, eyeing the window where the light streamed through. "It is well past the hour to break fast."

"I have told them they must not disturb us unless we call them. Last night, I thought if…" Her smile dimmed a little, as though she was loathe to introduce even the idea of uncertainty. "But first I told them to leave drink and some small refreshment. There will be that, at least, in the outer room."

"Then it is for me to bring it here, for you have sworn that you will not leave my bed," was his happy reply as he pulled himself up on his elbows to hover over her. "And I shall hold you to it, cariad." He kissed her deeply.

"You may hold me any way you like," she answered, smiling against his lips.

He indulged in one more kiss before dashing out to find the tray. The air was cold so he was quick, but still there was something lost when he returned to her. It was the first bit of awareness, the first recognition that they could not go on as though the world had fallen away. She was looking at the little window of opaque glass, an echo of sadness in those great gray eyes. Daylight had its drawbacks.

"If we must reckon with reality, let it not be on an

empty stomach," he said, and set the tray on the small table beside the bed. He poured sweet water from the jug into a cup and as he handed it to her, she held out one of the stuffed wastel breads from the platter. She tucked her feet under her and drank. He sat in front of her in the same pose, their knees touching, and broke the bread in half. There were bits of apple in it, and he held out half to her.

She took it, but did not eat. Instead she pulled a blanket across her shoulders, another across her bare legs, then drank and watched him eat. Finally she set the cup aside and looked down at the bread.

"It shames me that I have thought little, and spoken even less, of the lordship that will be yours, what best to do with the lands and for the people…" Her fingers were now pinching off bits of the bread, rolling it between her fingers restlessly. "And verily, they will be your lands and your people – yours to rule as you see fit and as your king commands it. Nor would I want ever to dictate or interfere."

He tried and failed to suppress his grin. "But?"

She looked up, those heavy lashes sweeping in a way that drew all his attention, the answering quirk of her lips unmistakable before she pressed them together. "But I have considered such improvements to Dinwen as I think are not amiss, which will make it a fit place to live until the castle that Edward commands is built. I would…if you will not object, I would know where towns will be chartered, so to have some say in their placement if it is possible."

"I am not such a vain fool that I must pretend a superior wisdom in this matter," he said easily. "They will be our lands, and our people. Not mine alone."

He was gratified to see her relax at this, and take a

bite of the bread before laying out her thoughts. Indeed it seemed to release a floodgate of words and ideas, her speech gathering momentum so that she often forgot her mouth was full as she detailed her plans. She seemed to be thinking it through for the first time, ideas sprouting forth and feeding off each other, her brow furrowed in thoughtfulness as she flicked a look up to him from time to time, asking, "Would that not be too soon?" or "Unless you would prefer to invest elsewhere?" or "Is that right? Is there aught I have forgotten to consider in my haste?"

It was a joy to watch her come alive with it. For the first time since their shared youth, she did not carefully choose her words. He thought he might like to stay here and listen to her unguarded talk and eat bread until he became fat and old. And happy. Terribly, terribly happy.

When she began to ask about the vineyards and the money to be made from the wine – how much he expected and what must go back into the French estate to best increase its yield – he dragged himself out of his happy stupor to answer her. He estimated barrels of wine, the cost of transport, and at her suggestion the price he might pay for his own ships. "I will have my steward send copies of the ledgers," he said finally, knowing she had an itch that would only go away when she could see every fact laid before her.

"I will satisfy myself that your steward is honest," she said, straightening her spine a little. "But though I would learn enough that I am not entirely ignorant, I would not take the management of it from you. It is the Welsh lands that are to be made England that I would concern myself with, as much as you think it good and proper."

"I will gladly heed your counsel in the matter of those lands and those people." He would not have thought it needed saying, but she had the air of someone who was determined to stake a claim. "Already have I said that I am not such a vain fool, Eluned. You understand these matters more deeply, just as I better understand the French lands."

A smile spread across her face, a lively delight that she buried in the cup from which she drank. She swallowed and looked up at him with a more sober expression. How like her, to forgo the use of her smile, her eyes – all the feminine wiles that might easily dazzle a man, make him agree to anything. She never used them, at least not with him. She never had, and he wondered if she even knew the power she possessed.

"The towns, I think," she was saying. "If we can but influence their number and where they are placed...Know you yet how far west it will reach?"

"Simon will know," he said, busying himself with pouring more drink for them both. "He can say what boundaries are considered, and where Edward is thinking to build castles and towns."

Something must have shown in his face at the mention of Simon. As he pulled his blanket up further to cover his shoulders, he felt her touch on his knee, gentle and uncertain.

"Have you argued with your brother?" She said it almost teasingly, but when he met her eyes she took her hand from his knee. "You need not confide in me, Robert. Only please do not say that all is well when your disquiet is plain to me."

To think she believed he would not tell her of it,

when he had longed for it from the moment it had happened.

"Never have I had a hope of deceiving you, nor even the desire. I am only reluctant to tell you of my own witlessness and pride." He curled his fingers around his cup, to have something solid to hold on to. "I have an uncommon talent for deceiving myself, I think."

He told her, then, of everything his brother had said and all that his father had done. He could not banish the near memory of Simon's unhappy face as he confessed the ruse, nor the specter of Kit's concern these many months and his wife's worry, their son's unjust treatment. All because he could not let go the habit of spiting his father. He did not try to put it into words, but trusted her to understand the breadth of his failings. He only said that he had not thought his father would strike so low a blow. "Beneath the bitterness, I believed there was some love between us. Nor did I even know I believed that, until I saw there was not."

"I do not defend your father," she said, and he knew she was choosing her words carefully, stepping lightly. "But do you not think he called it love for you that forced his hand? He wanted you here."

"He wanted the lands and titles, the rewards that a king might bestow on a de Lascaux. Advancement of the family name and fortunes, not love, was his concern."

"It is cold," she acknowledged, "and calculated, that he would search a way to make you reach for a power you would otherwise shun. But I know well what it is to wish a thing for a beloved child, and when that child refuses it – how easily reason is lost.

It does not mean there is no love there."

"Would you do it?" he challenged. "For your son or your daughter, would you lie and deceive and imperil those they love best, only for a chance to force them to become what you want them to be?"

It almost alarmed him, the arrested look she gave him, the long, long pause before she answered. There seemed a thousand things that passed through her eyes, yet they were still and calm, looking steady in his. "No," she said at last. "No. I would do that and more to protect them, if I must, but never to change their desires. I might plead and cajole, and beg they will not forget how well I love them."

"And if you pleaded for years and still they never heeded you, haps you would not care so much for them." He shook his head, dismissing that. It made him feel like a sulky child to complain of it, and it did not distress him as much as his brother's part in it. "It is Simon who deserved better of me."

The telltale pinch appeared in her lip. "It is Simon who will profit most from this scheme. Is no wonder he agreed to it."

"Nay, Eluned." He reached out a finger to touch her tight mouth. "In faith I had only to open my eyes to him even once, to see that he…well, to see him at all. But I saw only what I wanted to see, and paid him too little regard."

She pressed his hand against her face, turned her lips to kiss his palm and said, "It is my failing too, husband. I have dwelled overlong on my own troubles when I had only to observe him, and consider the matter, to guess a little of their scheming. I am well practiced at finding deceit, when I care to watch for it."

A faint sound came from the outer room, so tentative that he would have dismissed it as imagination if Eluned did not turn her attention there. She called out and, with a quick glance to him for approval, told the girl to enter the bedroom.

It was one of her ladies who carried in a fresh jug of water and asked if they would have wine or ale, and if my lady would dress now and which gown she preferred. He watched in delight as Eluned lifted her chin and waved her hand in a gesture that transformed the blanket she wore into a robe befitting a queen.

"I would stay abed, Joan, and when you have brought enough refreshment for us to make our meal here, you may leave us until the morrow. If we have need of anything, I will find the servants."

The girl was trying her best not to gape in amazement. She nodded finally, and said as though it might change Eluned's mind, "Lord Morency has arrived at court, my lady, deep in the dark of night."

But Eluned showed no surprise at this. "Pray you will discover for me when he returns to Morency. He may carry such messages as I have to send, but I would know if he will remain here at Edward's side or if he stays only the night."

"Three days, my lady. I heard him tell Lord de Bohun, who did answer that the snow may keep many here longer when it comes."

"Does it snow?" Eluned asked, suppressing a yawn. She could not have slept more than an hour this morning.

Robert stirred. "I will study the sky a moment," he said, dropping a kiss on Eluned's head and reaching for his tunic.

Eluned's broad yawn followed him as he walked behind Joan to the outer room, where servants were bringing plates of food. Robert pulled the tapestry away from the window. There was only a dusting of snow on the ground and the air felt too icy cold for there to be snow today. In the sky he saw only sun and no gray clouds on the horizon.

When the servants withdrew, he filled a plate with bits of meat and cheese and bread and fruit, unsure of what she might want and so taking a bit of everything. He carried it into the bedroom, burning with curiosity to know why Ranulf of Morency had arrived in the dead of night – and why Eluned seemed already to know all about it.

But when he came to the bed he found that she had fallen asleep, curled on her side and burrowed into the covers. He held the plate under her nose and poked hopefully at her shoulder, but she did not wake. Thus thwarted from hearing whatever she might know, he stretched out beside her and smiled to think of her declaration that even the king's army would not drag her from his bed. They would be left undisturbed, by her orders, all this day and night.

It was enough to watch her sleep, the light of day shifting slowly with the hours over her face. Day and night, awake and asleep, she was his – just as he had longed for through all that glorious summer, and just as he had secretly imagined every day since. No longer was she but a cherished memory, nor a ghost he conjured, but a woman real and whole. With secrets in her heart and sorrow in her past. With lines in her forehead and glints of silver in her hair – and a birthmark on the right of her throat, not the left.

He did not love the memory any less. But he loved

this more.

✣ ✣ ✣

He ate, and she slept. He hummed what he could remember of the Welsh air she had taught him when they were young, and she slept. He combed her hair through his fingers and braided it loosely, and still she slept. Finally in the late afternoon as the light was dwindling, after she had turned over and wrapped her arms around him and issued a deep sigh – and continued sleeping – he closed his eyes too.

When he woke it was full night and he found himself alone in the bed. There was only an instant of alarm before he realized she was there, in a circle of lamplight near the window. As the wild beating of his heart slowed, he saw that she had ink and pen. She was bent over the small table in deep concentration, her ink-splattered fingers carefully scratching words onto the parchment. She seemed to pause often, considering every new word before setting another down.

She noticed his wakefulness after a while, and her eyes lifted up to him. Such a simple thing, but it was filled with a sudden and breathtaking beauty. She had such lovely eyes, large and gray under heavy lashes that swept a graceful arc in the soft lamplight.

"It is for Gwenllian," she said, lifting the page. "I shall send it with her husband."

It seemed remarkably short, but he did not say so. Instead, he grinned and stretched and said, "Have you finished it? Then come back to bed, my love."

He could not say what was in her face as she looked back at him, for the briefest of moments, before lowering her eyes and saying, "I must wash the ink from my hands."

She set aside the parchment and reached for a small jar of oil that she spread over her fingertips, rubbing it in to loosen the ink before she wiped it off with a wet cloth. It was only because he watched so closely that he saw she spent too long at the task. Her hands did not shake, but they moved restlessly. He thought back to what her son William had said to him: there was something between herself, her daughter, and the king. And that things had changed between Eluned and her daughter, in a way that made Gwenllian uneasy and fearful.

Robert waited to see what Eluned would tell him freely, those restless hands of hers worrying at the ink under her fingernails. But her silence went on too long, so he broke it.

"You were not surprised to learn Morency is come." He watched as she twisted the cloth in her hands. "You left the hall in the midst of the revelries. Did you meet him?"

Her hands stopped. "Not by design," she said, and now he could not mistake the misgiving in her face. She dropped the cloth into a bowl that sat on the table next to her letter.

Robert sat up in the bed. She had put the lamp near the clouded window-glass, so that the light was reflected a little, and now she looked at the glow of light as she had looked at the stars. Like she could read the story of the world and all its workings there.

"William told me," he murmured, ignoring the almost imperceptible flinch at the mention of her son, "that so long as your secrets do not risk his rule of Ruardean, he need not know them. And so I will say to you now, Eluned: I care not what schemes and secrets you may hide, so long as they do not stand between us."

"And if it is the telling of it that will stand between us?" She pressed a finger to the surface of the table, and they both watched her fingertip turn white.

"You need not fear it," he said. "Eluned. Cariad." She did not look up. "There is naught you can say will kill my love for you."

She looked at him then and her face seemed younger than he had ever seen it, but with eyes older than he could imagine. He could see she wanted contradict him, and also saw her decide that it was futile. There was a sudden and absolute stillness in the room. The faintest wisp of dread began to rise in him, like smoke.

"Last night I left the hall and went to Roger Mortimer's room with the intent to kill him."

He felt the words fall with a thud inside him, and knew she said it plain and blunt only so he could not claim to mishear her. It left him too stunned and bewildered to do anything more than wait for further explanation. The color was high in her cheeks, a flush that had no place in a room that had seemed to him to become impossibly cold. When moments had passed and he did not reply or look away, she stood.

Her movement freed him from the dumb astonishment and set his mind to work. He knew her passion well, had savored the lingering taste of it on his tongue for eighteen long years. This was not passion, not a sudden and uncontrollable rage. All her distance for these many months, the careful watchfulness, the ice in her veins – she had been planning this.

"Why?" he finally asked, and it felt as though he

had not used his voice in days.

"Why." Her eyes grew bright, the flush in her cheeks deepening. Here was the feeling that had lurked, hidden for all these months. "Because he betrayed Llewellyn, a foul trick that felled a kingdom. Because Wales is lost, Wales is no more, and *he* will be rewarded with the spoils." A look of bitterest disgust showed in her face as she looked down at the lamplight, fists tight at her sides. "Because the blood of my countrymen is on his hands, because he lusts after helpless servant girls, because he killed those Welsh boy princes, because I could not bear to think of him alive and well while my uncle is cold in the ground and everything I fought for, everything I loved -"

She pressed a hand hard to her mouth to stop her rising voice. Her breathing was ragged, her eyes wide, avoiding his. Finally she lowered her hand from her mouth, pulled the heavy robe tight around her, and spoke more calmly. "There is such a hate has lived in me, Robert. Of late I perceive it was but a seed planted many years ago, in that same moment I knew I could not have you. It has grown like a weed in a corner of my heart until it has overgrown all my spirit. Until I am become nothing but anger and despair."

He looked at her hands clutching the robe about her, the knuckles white. How different they were, that even in the first moment of their parting he had never thought to hate anyone except, perhaps a little, her husband. "I only drank too much, and fought at Kenilworth, and ran to France."

"How lucky for you," she said, "that you could choose whither you may come and go."

The thread of bitterness ran through her voice like

a silver sparkling of river far at the bottom of a deep and empty gorge. It froze the tongue in his mouth, warned him off judging a lifetime of circumstance he could not even conceive. It would be easier by far to say nothing more about this.

But no, he must not be deterred. He had no illusions about the limitations of his own wit. There was more here than he would ever be able to guess. He could only force his benumbed mind to the most important things.

"Does Mortimer live still?"

"He does."

"Will Morency..." He had heard the rumors, the whispers about her daughter's husband. "Will your son-in-law kill him in your stead?"

She gave a choked laugh. "Nay, it was he who stopped me."

He put aside the crop of questions that sprang up at this remark. Mortimer's sins were only part of what drove her, he was sure. He thought and thought, made himself do what he should have done with his brother. He pulled his knees up, wrapped his arms about them and considered. He thought over everything William had said to him. The image of her on her knees before the king was burned into his memory.

"What was there between you and your daughter, and the king? More than just the marriage the king made and you did not approve?" She seemed frozen, staring without seeing at the outer edge of the circle of light, where it gleamed against the window. "Tell me, Eluned."

It was something in her quiet breathing that told him she had not expected this, and something in the way she would not look at him that said she was fighting against tears. He wished she would come to him, sit next to him on the bed, but she looked rooted to the spot. She took a long, slow, deep breath and wrapped her arms around herself.

"The king suspected my Welsh sympathies, and feared I would join the force of Ruardean with Llewellyn's army. He thought I meant to be a part of the rebellion. And so he married my daughter to his favorite, that it might constrain me from acting and that Ranulf might learn if I plotted against the English crown. It was clever, but I…" She pressed her lips together a moment, judging her words. "I had spent years in making plans for my daughter that had naught to do with marriage. She was betrothed to old Morency, did you know?"

He shook his head, at a loss for what other plans she might have had for the girl if not marriage, but content to know she would tell him.

"Old Morency – Aymer was his name. He was cruel to all, but especially to his wives. He had already outlived three, each younger and healthier than the last. I objected to the match, not least because Gwenllian was only a girl of ten. But Walter said an angel had visited his dreams to tell him she must be married to this man without delay. I could convince him only to marry her by proxy, to keep her from him as long as possible, until she was older." She looked up at him briefly, a quick and searching glance that asked him to remember how little she herself had liked being married young. "So he was her husband when he was murdered in his bed, and I made the claim that the lands which were her marriage portion should not go to Ranulf, who had killed him and who was named heir to Morency. There were details enough to keep the lawyers and clerics debating all those years and so long as it was in dispute, it was easy to claim she could not marry."

"And Walter?" he asked.

"He was in the Holy Land then, and cared for nothing but his visions. Already had I arranged that Gwenllian might be made to learn such defenses as may protect her." Now she lifted her chin in that old gesture, thrusting it out to dare the world to tell her she was wrong. "She learned the sword, and studied battle tactics, and in secret led the best men of Ruardean."

He could feel his mouth fall open slightly, his amazement too great to hide entirely. He only stared and held his breath to suppress the astonished laughter that threatened. If he laughed, she would think he mocked her. But it was only that it was so like Eluned, to come up with a scheme so bold and unexpected.

"Have I not said you dreamed you no small dreams?" He put a hand through his hair, and let himself smile a little in wonder. "Had she any skill at the sword?" he finally asked.

"More than even I dreamed possible," she answered with an unsuppressed pride.

He tried to imagine it, that little girl from his memories grown into such an improbable woman. And her mother, who fought to keep her unmarried, educate her as a man, all of it certainly in secrecy – what had it cost Eluned, to arrange and sustain it all? He would ask her, one day. But not today.

"What were these plans for her, then," he asked instead, "that were interrupted when the king insisted she marry? You ensured she had defenses enough against any man, even one as villainous as Ranulf."

She looked at him a long time, and he could not decide if her eyes asked for pity, or pitied him a little. "Edward was right, cariad," she said at last. "I planned a war against him, for the freedom of Wales. Llewellyn was to lead the country, and Gwenllian was to lead the army."

When Robert said nothing in response to this extraordinary statement, she turned her eyes back to the reflection of light in the window. "She used to dream of it, you know. There was another Gwenllian long ago, a legend who led an army against the Norman invasion. *My* Gwenllian wanted to be that. There was a time she spoke of little else. I had only meant her to learn defense, but then it became so much more. I should have seen…"

"Seen what?"

She shook her head a little, and a barely discernable crease appeared between her brows. "It was a youthful passion. There were other things too she wanted to learn, just as eagerly, but I did not let myself see it. It was my own misjudgment to think she would always want to lead the rebellion. When the moment came to act, she refused it. Though the king had her married by that time, still she might have declared for Wales. And so did I say it to her. Yet she refused."

He could hear, clear and distinct, the sting of betrayal in her words. It surprised him, after what she had seen in the last twelvemonth.

"You watched as the last Welsh rebel leader was torn to pieces," he said quietly. "Surely you must thank God that neither of you were part of such a plot."

"Never did I dream such a fate would meet those who fought against Edward. In my worst imaginings, she only died in battle."

She said it so simply. As her words settled in the room, his blood chilled by degrees.

"You have no illusions what war is," he said in disbelief, unable to hide how it appalled him. "You remember the carnage of Evesham, what they did to Montfort. Yet you would give your daughter to war?"

She turned her eyes to him in a hard stare. She looked him up and down, unclenched her jaw at last, and spoke in a thoughtful tone. "You condemn it."

"I do."

"Because I am a woman, or because she is?" Her head tilted a little to the side, her brows lifting in inquiry. "If I send my son to fight for his lands and his people, am I an abomination? For how many fathers have survived battle, only to throw their sons into the jaws of war?" She turned her face again to the window, and the lines in her forehead were etched in high relief. "Valor and honor. Unnatural and heartless. Choose which you call it and I will tell you the sex you describe."

If he had been capable of finding words, he did not know what he might have flung at her. But he was speechless, his mind grasping for a way to articulate his outrage, and that saved him. In his silence there was only what she had said – *valor and honor* – and the resignation in her face as she seemed to wait for his protest.

But he could not protest. She was right. He was angry only because she was not wrong. He loved Kit's son dearly, could not think of the boy without a gentle pang in his heart, but when one day little Robin would ride off to fight in battle – and he would, of course – Robert would not condemn the father who sent him, or the king who ordered it. He would not even question it. Duty, honor, and glory. He could say to her that such was reserved for men alone and that women should be protected from it at all costs, but that would only invite disdain. She was Eluned, who scorned what the world expected of her and of her daughter, and who would say only a fool thought anyone could truly be protected from anything.

"It was doomed," he said, the only honest objection to be made. "You would send her to fight a war that could only end in defeat, and put her neck in a noose."

Nothing in her expression changed, but the blood drained from her face. She did not look at him.

"She said that very thing." A long moment of silence, a faint lift of her shoulder. "I say she doomed all hope by refusing to fight. We will never agree. But hear me: only two years before, Llewellyn moved against Edward and I did not aid him, nor commit Gwenllian to the fight. The time was not ripe, and it failed. There was only one perfect moment to strike, and it passed us by. That is what I see. My daughter will ever see it differently."

His eyes fell to the parchment where she had written her message to be carried to Gwenllian. "What message do you send to her?"

Eluned turned her face up to the ceiling, a deep breath and her eyes blinking back the tears he knew she did not wish to shed. "Only that she was right to send her husband to me. That her best-loved cousin spoke of his devotion to her in the hour of his death.

That I will come to her soon, and hold her children in my arms. That I love her more than my own breath."

She did not move, blinking up at the ceiling, her swallow traveling the graceful length of her neck. Robert thought again as he watched her of what William had said, of everything she had told him. He had known she was bold, had loved her for it from the first. But he had never imagined her plotting rebellion, giving her daughter to war, planning to murder a man with her own hands for revenge. He remembered a pretty picture of a young lover lost. It was every bit as foolish as how he had thought of his brother all these years, and his father: as though they did not exist except as he remembered them, as though they did not live outside his imagination at all. What a blind fool, to think they remained unchanged and waiting, like puppets put in a box between performances.

Eluned looked again at the window, the reflection of light in the glass. She put a hand to it and watched the thin sheen of frost melt under her palm.

"I have told you that losing you was the making of me," she said. "And you see now, who I am become." She turned to face him, her hand falling to her side. "It was not only the lack of you at my side. It was the losing of you – the way I was made to choose and the way I have been made to live. It is not like water that is made ice, and can thaw to be what it was. It is like iron made into steel, and beaten into a new shape. It cannot be unmade."

Something stopped him from rising, going forward to embrace her. It rattled at the back of his head, the sort of troubling thought he had always disregarded in favor of his own more agreeable version of things. Now he let himself think it, and say it.

"It was only in service to your plans that you did consent to marry me."

She hesitated only a moment before she nodded, a slow and silent assent. "To bring me to court, where Mortimer was like to be. I thought you would be changed as I was, after so much time." She bit her lips together to still their trembling. "But I knew you would still be a good man. I knew that could never change."

It did not cut as deep as he expected, to know she had not married him out of affection. It was far more difficult to accept how far was this woman from the girl he had loved so long. All these things that had changed her… No, she could not be unmade.

No more could he stop loving her.

He held his hand out to her. When she stepped forward and took it, he said, "Only lately have I watched you sleep and thought how the memory of you is nothing to having you here, warm and living and real, in my bed."

She tightened her fingers around his. "She is not completely lost, the girl you loved. But I cannot promise, cariad, that I will ever be who I once was. I will try." Her smile was slight and sad and heartbreaking. "I miss her too."

He brought her hand to his lips and warmed her fingers with his breath. She stood before him as she was, with no apologies, no promises. She gave him the truth of herself, and he could only give her the same.

"The first thing ever you said to me was that it mattered less which belief I held, than that I believed in a thing enough to die for it. And I chose then, in the moment you said it, what I believed." He put his hand to her face, the same way he had touched her in the dark when he thought it would be the last time. "It is you I believe in, Eluned. Even when you do not. From that day to this one, and for all the days left to me, I believe in you."

Chapter 13

The Terrible

Eluned was relieved to know that Robert too wanted to be away from court as soon as was possible. At his urging, she came with him to meet with his brother and Burnell, the king's right hand, and learned everything there was to know about the lands that would be granted to him. The division of Wales would be set forth by law in weeks and instead of feeling only fury and bitterness to see how it would be doled out to English lords, she had as well the satisfaction that one piece of it would fall into her hands. And she could not deny her pride in knowing that Robert would become the first Baron de Lascaux, lord of the new principality of Darian.

She squeezed his hand when she heard the name. "Darian is a Welsh word. It means shield. Protection."

There would be access to the sea, which would facilitate the wine imports. Even better, they were formally granted Eluned's childhood home of Dinwen, and they could easily go there now. Though other visitors to the court would wait a bit longer to scatter, she and Robert prepared to leave only a week behind Ranulf's departure. While Robert drank and dined with her son-in-law, Eluned searched out Nan to tell the girl she would have a place in their household and need no longer suffer Mortimer's advances. The girl blushed and stammered her thanks, but said there was a stable boy who wanted nothing more than to marry her, and he was not like to want to move deeper into Wales.

Eluned did not press the matter. She only said that Nan and her stable boy were welcome if ever they wanted a new home. Then she went to find Robert's brother and talked with him throughout the evening meal about his father, Simon's hopes for his sons, and his own ambitions. It surprised her, how willing she was to believe the good in him. That was Robert's influence. Without it, she would not have seen the genuine eagerness in Simon, the way he so clearly wished to know his brother better, the surprisingly little greediness in any of his desires.

"If we go to Dinwen now, we will be there for the spring planting," she said to Robert as they lay in bed that night. "Haps I will ask Gwenllian if she will come to us there, to visit. Your brother has said he will come in summer with his sons, so that their education may begin."

"His education, or his son's?" asked Robert, looking up from where he rested his head against her breast.

She smiled. "Both, though God willing it is only his son will ever rule there, should we have none of our own. Tonight he assured me that the succession has been approved by the king and written into – why do you laugh?"

"Nay, not for that," protested Robert, pulling

himself up to the pillow. "I only thought that while you spoke of grave matters of succession with my brother, I watched your daughter's husband threaten Sir Hawse's future generations. Hawse drank too much and said something unkind about…"

A dark red flush came to his neck. "About me?" she asked, but then remembered it was Ranulf who had threatened the man. "Ah no, he insulted Gwenllian?"

Robert nodded. "I think he did not realize Ranulf sat so near to him. Barely had he declared that she would make a better carthorse than a wife – your pardon, my love, they are his vile words and not mine – than Ranulf had slipped a dagger beneath his ballocks. I have never seen a man sip his ale so calm while his companion sweated and stuttered and dared not move a hair. And Ranulf said only that Hawse must never speak of the lady of Morency again in his life, unless he cared to lose first his manhood, and then his life at the point of Ranulf's sword."

Eluned absorbed this description, relishing the picture he painted and furious at the insult to her daughter. Mostly, though, she grappled with a new and wholly unexpected emotion that accompanied the image of Ranulf of Morency defending her daughter with his famed blade.

"God preserve me," she said, as startled by the thought as by the giggle that suddenly escaped her. "I may actually come to like the man."

Robert's look of mild disbelief caused her burbling of delight to gradually become shouts of laughter. His growing smile only made her laugh harder, until she was gasping and tears sparkled at the corners of her eyes. His rumble of laughter joined hers, and she thought there was no sweeter music in all the world.

Oh, she remembered this kind of incautious joy. She remembered now what it was to be naked and carefree and happy. To be warm in winter, to know that spring would come again.

✠ ✠ ✠

She had expected to be overwhelmed to return to Dinwen after so many years but it only felt comfortable, and right, and good. The people greeted her warmly, though only a few of the oldest servants remembered her from her girlhood. When she spoke to them in Welsh – and more, when Robert greeted them with the few words of it he had learned – they breathed easy. When they were assured that until King Edward proclaimed otherwise, their grievances would be heard and judged according to Welsh and not English law, they gave their hearts completely to their new lord and lady.

April brought with it the little blue flowers, wood bells that spread like a carpet across the ground in every direction. She took him to a place where they bloomed as far as the eye could see, an isolated clearing with trees all around, and there she laid back among the flowers and made love to him in the sunlight. Every day, more and more, there was hope in her breast and dreams in her head – and none of it felt new and different, but old and comfortable. She was meant to be thus, and if she ever worried that it could not be so easy to slip back into a skin she had shed so long ago, she reminded herself that he believed in her. He believed in her.

When the message came, she and Robert were in

deep discussion, trying to recall what Aaron of Lincoln had ever said about the methods used in England to persecute his people. "Be assured they will employ similar laws against the Welsh to prevent them having equal power to the English," she said with a sigh. "Except they cannot say the Welsh are not Christian. We can hope that is some protection."

They had only got as far as determining which of the nearby churchmen were more likely to be unsympathetic to the Welsh when the messenger was announced. He brought word from Simon, who was leaving the king's court sooner than he had planned. He was traveling to see their father, who was ailing unto death.

"You think I should go to him, too," said Robert when they were alone.

She heard the question in it, how he wanted her to tell him why he should or should not go. But her only thought was the selfish one, that she did not want him to leave her side. There lived in her an irrational terror that he would not return. She forced herself to dismiss it as superstition, saying, "And you think he lies and says he is near to death, in hopes you will come."

Robert shrugged, the wry smile curling his lip as he looked away. "Haps."

"But it is Simon who has said it," she pointed out. "And if your father were to deceive you into coming to him, he would not think his own poor health would be the best way to bring you to him."

He gave a huff of a laugh. "Now in your wisdom you will ask me which I would regret more – to go to him, or not to go? But I have no answer to that."

She put her arms around him. "Then I shall be

very old and wise and tell you that the answer will come in the morning, do you sleep well on the question."

So he did, and in the morning he said he would go. When she replied that she would come with him, he stopped her words with a deep kiss, pressing her into the pillows and leaving her breathless. "Cariad," he said. "Never would I forgive myself if I took you away from here when every day brings a hundred new decisions that will affect these people who are all your concern. Stay."

She stayed. It was nearly three weeks until she had word from him that his father had had last rites, and Robert would soon return to her. *I have not spoken to him of his deceit, for I do not want to speak also of my many years of defiance,* he wrote. *A lifetime of strife cannot be reversed in an hour, even if it be the last hour, and no more can he or I be made different from what we have always been. But I am glad I have come.*

William had brought her this message in the last leg of its journey to Dinwen. Her son had come here after leaving court, on his way to Ruardean. She sat with him in the small solar one morning, distracted by how much he looked like his father and answering his queries about the management of the Ruardean estate, when a mud-covered man burst into the room.

"Where is Robert?" she asked, her voice absurdly polite and calm while her heart stopped dead in her chest. For she recognized this man as one of Robert's, who had ridden off with him a month ago and who should not be here without his lord. He was panting and covered in mud, and she could not rightly hear what he said for the panic rising in her.

He was saying *Mortimer* and something about

murder and hostages and retaliation. She could understand nothing at all in the world, except that Robert was not here. Finally she forced air into her chest and leaned forward to grasp the man by the ears, to hold him steady and silence his babbling. She spoke her words like a curse. "You must tell me plain if my husband has died."

His eyes went wide and he shook his head. "Nay, lady, not dead."

Blood seemed to flow into her heart again, all in a rush. Only when William touched her shoulder did she release the man, who sat back and rubbed his ears as he looked at her in astonishment. She stood, fighting the weakness in her legs, turning from them and demanding composure from herself. *Oh Mary make me brave*, she prayed. *Let me not be undone.*

"Tell me," she turned and said when she had command of herself, "and waste no words."

"Barely more than a day's ride from here, we were overtaken by Roger Mortimer's men. They accuse my lord of a plot to murder Mortimer. They claim he employed a servant who tampered with the saddle on Mortimer's horse and when that failed, put poison in his wine. The servant was caught in the attempt."

She could feel her son's bewildered look on the side of her face, like heat from a nearby fire. She did not take her eyes from the muddy man who spoke.

"Why does Mortimer believe it was my lord husband? What proof has he?"

"Lady," he said in a strained voice, "the servant was betrothed to a girl who was known to be in possession of a ring that Mortimer himself saw on your hand. Mortimer believed it was given to the servant as payment for the deed, and the girl was questioned. When asked on pain of death who plotted against Mortimer, she gave the name of de Lascaux."

The blood pounded in her ears, beating the name through her brain: *Nan, Nan, Nan.* For an instant, Eluned thought she might be ill. But it was only an instant. There was no time for blame, for this fury at herself. Later. She would indulge those thoughts later. Now there was only room for action.

William was asking questions about where they had captured Robert, how many men – so many unimportant words flowing forth. She held up her hand in a silencing gesture to cut him off. "You tell me Roger Mortimer holds my husband captive, but you have not told me his demands. What ransom would he have?"

The answer was unlikely, but she expected it all the same. "His life, lady." The man spared a glance at William, but spoke only to her. "They hold him at a nearby manor called Rowland, to await Mortimer who is three day's travel from there. They have said Mortimer himself will…" He seemed unwilling to put words to it. "With his own hands, they said."

"The king will never allow it," said William.

"The king will not know until it is done," she said through numb lips.

The man who delivered the news – what was his name? She must remember to ask – held worn leather gloves in his hands. She stared at the cracks and creases in them, her eyes following the lines that intersected like rivers, like lives. She could see it all there – how Mortimer would call it defense of his own life, how he would twist the facts and bide his time and somehow be forgiven. Likely he would arrange it so that someday, somehow, he would be granted these lands that had no natural heir. Why not? He had the advantage, so long as he did not hesitate to strike. She had three days.

She went to the window. The fields were all upturned earth, the sky was endless blue. There were hidden stars behind the daylight sky, just as there were hidden advantages to being a woman whose heart could be made stone.

"Mother, only think." William was speaking urgently at her ear now. "If we can reach Edward quickly, we can use this circumstance well to -"

She held her hand up again, and knew by the look on him that it was the force of her anger more than the gesture that silenced him. Her son who she so little knew, who was so like her. Opportunity in strife, always finding a way to turn adversity to advantage – had she passed nothing else on to him? A forlorn regret swelled in her at the thought.

She touched her fingertips lightly to the side of his face. She had not touched him so since he was a child, and he looked down at her, rapt. Whatever she said now, he would remember it.

"The things we do out of hate, and those we do for love," she told him. "They come back to us. One by one, they return to us in some form, some time."

She turned back to the window and breathed the cool spring air. She gathered together everything she knew of the Mortimers, every last scrap she had hoarded while at court. She looked deep inside her heart, to assess its worth to her if Robert was not in it.

Around the blazing fire at her center, she let the cold seep into every part of her. Into the waiting silence, looking out dry-eyed across the lands she had so lately claimed, she spoke her command.

"I will have the twelve finest of our knights with me, mounted and armed. Send the marshal to me now, and make all haste," she said as she swept past them, already halfway to the door. "I ride within the hour."

✠ ✠ ✠

It was easy enough to find the place when she asked the Welsh villagers in their own language about the woman with hair like sunset, whose sons were little lordlings. She had not thought to find both boys there, but took it as a stroke of luck. It would have been better luck still if the woman had been a little more stupid, but Eluned overcame her reticence by saying, "Come closer, and I will whisper a secret from your beloved."

Instead she whispered that her knights could easily take the boys by force, and was it not easier to give them over peaceably? Then she turned to the boys and bent to say to them in a gentle voice, "There now, your mother will have your bags packed in a moment and then it will be only a day of travel. Just a short visit. Won't that be a lovely surprise?"

They were intrepid little souls, who thrilled at the speed of the ride and thought it great fun to sleep under the open sky. When their party met up with the small host that waited among the trees a mile from Rowland, they were filled with questions about the longbows but did not ask why so many were assembled here to meet them. Eluned sent her chosen envoy with a message to the manor at Rowland, then dismounted and spoke to Sir Lucas, who held the command of these men.

"We stand ready, lady. Our scout saw Mortimer's arrival only an hour ago. He came with a woman, who is described in every particular as his lady sister, and six men-at-arms."

He told her about the low wall that ran across a field to the west of the manor house, and they made their way toward it as they waited for the envoy to return. All the while, he described the meager defenses here, how many more armed men made their way on foot from Dinwen, and the reported state of the roads between here and Ruardean.

"If I signal," she told him when the envoy rode into view, "it is meant for Sir Alan, who has my instruction. When there is aught the greater host must do, you will hear it from my own lips. Heed me well and do not dare to defy me, for it is my lord husband's life in the balance. And you see plainly what I am prepared to do in defense of that life."

He bowed his head in agreement, and the envoy approached. It was Father Morgan, a Franciscan who was more than eager to play peacemaker, and pleased to tell her that Mortimer had agreed to a meeting. The strain in the priest's smile told her that Mortimer had only agreed to it when he learned she came with a host of armed men. "I have seen your lord husband with my own eyes, Lady Eluned," the priest assured her. "He is treated as an honored guest by this house and is very well, though his patience is sorely tested. He has sworn to me that he knows nothing of a plot to kill Lord Mortimer, of course."

"Because he is entirely innocent," she said, and watched the priest recoil from her vehemence.

She chose one knight to accompany her to the meeting place, and told him he would wait outside and only enter if she called for him. It was a little stone building not far from the trees, just barely within sight of the manor but in plain view of the wall where her soldiers waited. It was used by hunters, the priest babbled as they made their way, and the master of this manor was happy to offer it and wished for a quick and peaceful solution to the troubles that had landed at his door only because he called Roger Mortimer his liege lord.

She strode past the horses that were tied outside, past the man who had already collected an assortment of blades and demanded that her knight disarm if he was to enter, and into the room where Roger Mortimer stood with hands on hips and a thunderous expression. She did not hesitate or pause, but walked straight on, fury compelling her, feeling the drag and billow of her cloak behind her as she rounded the corner of a long table until she was inches from him. The fabric swirled at her ankles with the suddenness of her stop. She locked eyes with him and spoke with iron in her voice.

"Give me my husband."

He opened his mouth a fraction, taking in air as preparation to a mocking laugh, but she had the satisfaction of watching the intention die in the face of her unwavering stare. There was a rustle beside her, a familiar voice saying her name, but she did not turn.

"Your husband is unharmed, as your priest has seen," said Isabella, her voice taut.

"Give him to me," repeated Eluned, never taking her eyes from Roger Mortimer, "or it will be war."

Mortimer raised his brows. Now he was mocking. "War? A fine war you will wage with barely more than seventy men."

"Against your six, and the two dozen that defend this manor," she replied.

"They can hold this place against your force for the few days it will require to bring a hundred mounted knights. My men are well trained in dodging the arrows of Welsh longbows, I promise you, and even more experienced in killing ragged Welsh soldiers."

She bit her tongue as the memory of her uncle's blood-spattered face rose up in her, his lifeless hand in hers. She willed herself not to look away, not to rage at him and lunge at his smug face.

"The men of Ruardean are a fine match for them," she said evenly. "My son rides to there now in preparation. I have only to say the word. And though their march is longer, the forces of Morency are not to be dismissed as ragged soldiers. Or did you forget that I am not alone?" She allowed herself the barest hint of a smile. "Our Welshmen from the north and west, Ruardean from the south, Morency from the east – and if it come to that, there are the de Lascaux men who will set sail from France when they hear their lord is threatened. You have heard how well they defended the Aquitaine against all the forces of Castile, yes? And how well my husband is loved by the king for that service?"

His eyes narrowed. She could almost hear him recalculating.

"The king loves me no less. He will not like to hear how nearly I was murdered by your husband's design."

"Fool." With that one scathing word, she turned from him and addressed his sister. "You are not vain or empty-headed, Isabella. Tell me, then, why Robert would want your brother dead?"

Isabella sat and smoothed her hands over her knees, as though determined to discuss the matter civilly. "There are reasons aplenty to be guessed at, but we are little concerned with them. It is the evidence that has brought us to this."

"Evidence? The word of a servant girl, no doubt given at knifepoint, and who had the name of de Lascaux at her lips only because of the ring *I* gave her, not my husband. It was a token in thanks because she served me well, no more than that, with my wishes for a happy marriage. And this you turn into a payment for murder." She curled her lip in scorn. "Such weak reasoning is not worthy of you."

Eluned turned back to Roger Mortimer, who did not seem in the least to be reconsidering his stance. Indeed he seemed only to grow angrier as she stared her hatred at him. She had forgotten Father Morgan, who now decided his intervention was called for.

"Surely with reflection and prayer, a compromise can be found that will prevent bloodshed," he began in a soothing tone, but Eluned did not care to hear more.

"There is no compromise. You will release my husband. Today."

"Do you think to command me?" Mortimer thundered, blood rising in his face, incensed by her imperious tone. "I am not ruled by shrewish women!"

"You are ruled by vile passions and greed and you will not imprison my husband for the wild fantasies in your head!" She heard Isabella leap to her feet in alarm. "I tell you it will come to war if you hold him one more *hour*, I swear it on my soul."

"War! What know you of war? I have led the king's army and won Wales. Think you that you can win against me?"

He was like a bull, a great wall of muscle staring her down and snorting his rage. She lifted her chin and considered him calmly.

"Haps not," she said, and allowed the honest uncertainty to be heard in her voice. "I am not a soldier and I have fought in no wars. I am but a woman, with a woman's weapons." She walked to the window that was behind Isabella, which faced west. Far across a broad field there was the stone wall, her men ranged out behind it. She turned her head over her shoulder and beckoned. "Come you and see the weapon I have mastered."

It was the priest who came first, standing at her shoulder and looking out across the field with her. He gestured to the others, who came closer. She could feel them at her back, the heat and bulk of the brother, the cool caution of the sister.

"What am I meant to see but these men you have brought?" Mortimer asked. "They are so far even their longbows cannot reach us."

Eluned swallowed against the dryness in her throat, raised her hand, and waved it out the window. An answering wave came in return. A moment later, two boys were hoisted up to stand along the distant stone wall. The younger had strawberry blond hair that caught the afternoon sun and caused his aunt to gasp. It took Mortimer a fraction of a moment longer to realize.

"My sons."

He whispered it as he stepped closer to the window, and she knew she had not miscalculated. He

stood too close to her or else he would have struck
her, she was sure. Instead he gripped her shoulders
and pressed her to the wall. He had only begun to
shake her, looking to smash her head against the
stones, no doubt, when Isabella managed to wedge an
arm between them. He roared, and his sister shouted
frantically at him to stop.

"Listen to her!" Eluned spat the words at him. She
smiled and thrust her chin upwards, not caring that
she must seem mad, only knowing that she would not
shrink before him, that she would die before she
surrendered her will to brute strength again. She
smiled a cold smile and pointed out the window. His
eyes followed. The boys still stood on the wall,
waving now, and one of the archers stood behind
them with arrow poised.

"Release me, and the danger is removed." His
hands fell away from her and he stepped back. She
raised a hand in signal, and the archer lowered his
bow. "Release my husband and no harm will come to
them."

Mortimer stared out at the distant gleam of his
son's hair. She watched his jaw work, his fists clench.
It was pride that kept him silent, the disbelief that he
must concede defeat. It was a very fine thing, to
watch him struggle to swallow it.

"You would not." Isabella stood tall and cool and
almost certain, blinking down at Eluned. "It is too
cruel. You would not kill them."

Eluned kept her eyes on Roger, who swung
around at his sister's words. He looked at Isabella,
then back to Eluned. He studied her closely through
narrowed eyes.

"In faith, haps my sister has the right of it." He

glanced out the window again, then back at her, trying to see whether she dissembled. "It is a hard heart that would murder innocents."

Eluned tilted her head quizzically. "How hard was the second King Henry's heart when he plucked the eyes from twenty-two Welshmen he held hostage? My grandmother's grandfather was one of those he blinded. We remember."

"The second King Henry!" he scoffed. "A hundred years ago at the least -"

"And then there was your King John," she continued, her voice rising, "who murdered twenty-eight Welsh boys, hostages whose safety he claimed to hold sacred until he hanged them from the walls of Nottingham castle. Boys as young as your sons, all of them. One was my father's uncle. We remember."

"What has this to -"

"And the Welsh princes in your care, sons of Powys, last of their line." She was shouting now, the blood rushing in her ears. "They were kin to my mother, did you know it? Two innocent little boys and they were drowned and we *remember*." She took a ragged breath, listening to the echo of her voice ringing off the stones in the small room. "Do not think me incapable of cruelty toward innocents. I have learned it from masters of the art."

"And do you kill my sons, lady, then I shall kill your husband and that is the end of it!"

"Think you I will stop there? Nay, my lord, for I prefer the flavor of a wound well salted. War, I have said, and also…" She looked to Isabella and said, "There is a place called Northop, and a man named Robert de Hastang there. Three men who are loyal to me lie in wait. At my word he will be captured." The

275

blood drained from Isabella's face. "What think you I will do to him, if I am made mad with grief for my husband?"

There was no pleasure in it for Eluned. There was only the mirror of the fear and helplessness that lived in her own breast. Certainty came over the other woman's face as Eluned watched. She did not have to ask Isabella what she would do to protect the man she loved. They both already knew.

"She will do it, Roger," Isabella said tonelessly. She was looking at Eluned, her eyes clear. "If you would have your sons safe, end this now."

A long, silent moment, and then the air in the room changed, and she knew she had won. Roger Mortimer nodded. Eluned turned and swept past the priest she had utterly forgotten, until she reached the door. She turned back in afterthought.

"Two boys are fairly exchanged for two hostages in kind. Does the serving girl who confessed live?"

"Aye," said Mortimer with a shrug. "Is only her betrothed I killed, then I brought her here to give evidence."

As though he had planned a fair trial. But at least Nan was here, and it was easy enough to guess why her betrothed – or anyone who cared for her – would want Mortimer dead. She was Eluned's responsibility now.

"I will have her from you too, with my husband. You shall have your sons. And then let this business between us be over."

✠✠✠

The priest walked between the hostages as they

came out of the manor, and Eluned allowed herself to look away from the distant figure of Roger Mortimer to rake her eyes over Robert. He was perfectly well – unhurt, slightly rumpled, a bemused look on his face – and then she spared a glance for Nan, who was not well at all. But she did not let her gaze linger, preferring instead to keep Mortimer in her sights until they were well away.

To the boys, she said, "Your father is anxious to see you, and your auntie too. Go now to Father Morgan and he will bring you to them." She took Nan onto her own mount while Robert was given a horse, and they rode off immediately, with no time for any words, before even the boys had reached the doors of the manor house where their father waited.

They traveled until night fell and were half way to home when they stopped and made camp for the night. Eluned had little experience with comforting overwrought women, and little patience for them, but she did not want to push Nan away. The girl cringed and shook, but only wept if she tried to speak. Her face was purple with a large bruise, but when Eluned asked if she was otherwise hurt, she shook her head.

"Nan," she whispered as the men lit a cook fire. "You need not fear my anger. There is no blame to you. You did well. You did exactly as I told you." Only the certainty that her own tears would distress the girl more kept Eluned from weeping. She felt Robert's presence at her shoulder and looked up to see him there.

"Nor do I blame you," he said to the girl. He did not look at Eluned, and she felt the force of the words he did not speak. All his attention was on the shivering servant girl. "Rest easy, Nan. You are safe now." His eyes turned to Eluned and his look softened. "You are under my wife's protection, and she will let no evil befall any who are in her care."

Nan clung to her all night, and he kept his distance. Only once, as the men sat around the fire talking, did he look to her. The man who had wielded the bow that threatened the captive boys was asked by one of his fellows if he suffered pangs of conscience for the act. "Nay," scoffed the bowman, "for I did not even nock the arrow. My lady gave only the signal for a show, not action."

Robert's face was unreadable in the little firelight, his eyes shadowed but fixed on her. She held his gaze and wondered what he thought until he turned away.

They reached Dinwen the next day, just as the sky turned to twilight. After giving instruction for messages to be sent to Ruardean and Morency, she took the time to give Nan over to the keeping of an old Welsh woman who worked in the kitchens and possessed a practical sort of kindness. The woman wrapped a length of wool around the girl, thrust a hot drink into her hands, and then went about her work, narrating her every action in an unbroken murmur of Welsh that seemed to soothe Nan.

Outside the door to their bedchamber, Eluned paused and leaned against the stone wall. He was here. He was safe. That was what mattered, above all else. There should be no reason for her to fear facing him, for her to shrink away from it like a girl caught out. She was too old for such childish worries, but still she wanted to weep at the thought that perhaps he did not like her very much.

When she entered he was looking with a frown at the psalter that had belonged to her uncle, where it sat on a little table near the bed. His finger was on it, tracing the jewels set in the cover, but he turned away when he heard her. He busied himself by sitting on the only chair, taking off his boots, and knocking the clumps of mud off them.

"You were not hurt when they captured you?" she asked in a voice that seemed impossibly small.

"Nay."

"They did treat you with honor?"

"Aye, it was a very civilized abduction."

The dry irony was in his voice again. He reached for a square of cloth that hung beside the hearth and began to wipe the mud that clung to the boot in his hand. She wanted to laugh and be easy, to tell him to leave this work for a servant, to join her in the bed. Instead she sat on the edge of the bed, watched his hands working across the leather, and said, "I am sorry." His hands stopped. "It was my sin, and almost did you pay the price of it."

He looked at her, and she saw it was not this that troubled him. "Would you have killed them?"

She took a breath and returned his look. "They were never in the least danger. I knew Mortimer loved them too well to risk them. That is why I took them, because I was sure of it."

"And if he had refused to let me go, kept me imprisoned? Or injured me? Or slain me?"

"That is why I wasted no time in getting to you."

"You do not answer my question."

Her lips pinched together, and his gaze went there to her mouth. He knew her too well, and knew when she bit back words. She knew him, too, and knew he was thinking of his friend's son who had been Mortimer's prisoner for more than a year and who had never been threatened with a weapon in all that time.

"What would I do if he had killed you? I know not, Robert. That is the truth of it."

"You would have killed his children in revenge?"

"I cannot say what I would do, for I cannot contemplate a world without you." The truth was unnerving, terrible to see. But she would not turn away from it, or pretend she was something she was not. "You are my heart, Robert. If they kill you, they make me heartless."

She could hear men below their window in the yard, talking loudly and laughing. They seemed a thousand miles from this room where the only man she had ever loved sat across from her in an endless silence.

"Eighteen – no, nineteen years ago now," she said finally, "I risked my soul to eternal hellfire to be with you. Did you not know even then the kind of woman I am? If you would love me, you cannot love only the woman who lies with you among the flowers and laughs and sings. You must love also the woman who will bring the whole world to wrack and ruin if she loses you again, and who will scorch the earth to save you."

He did not look away. He only said, "You will not do evil in my name or for my sake. If it comes to that, remember this moment, and that I made you swear it."

She nodded solemnly. "And so I do swear it."

A strange and unexpected relief flowed through her, and something in his expression relaxed. He dropped the forgotten boot to the floor.

"Think you I do not know the fire in you, that I

have loved the memory of some sweet and guileless girl? Such a one could never burn so bright and hot that I am kept warm by the memory for eighteen long years."

He leaned forward to catch her hand, and pulled her toward him until she was close enough to kiss soundly. "I only ask you do not make such a tangle that you must threaten to scorch the earth again."

She gave a choked laugh into the side of his neck, settling into his lap. Now, with his arms strong around her, she began to tremble a little. "I am sorry," she said again. "He suspected you because of me. Whatever might have befallen you, it would have been my doing."

"Well," he said with his mouth against her temple, a smile in his voice, "You might have confessed it to Mortimer and spared him that scene yesterday."

"I thought of it," she told him, and felt him stiffen in surprise. "I would have, but I feared he would only accuse us both of acting as one."

She kissed him again, to stop the shaking that had taken root deep inside, reaction to the threat of losing him. He was warm and alive and in her arms, and eventually his hands were pushing off her headdress, his mouth on her neck. She found the ties to his jerkin and pulled at them until it was loose, then answered the low rumble of desire in his throat by keeping her mouth on his as she stood and pulled him to the bed.

He was only a little taller, and their eyes were level when they stood like this. It struck her again, how good and gentle he was, how there was nothing menacing or intimidating in his person or manner, and never had been. "In faith, you meant it," she asked, still a little disbelieving, "that you love even the ruthless part of me?"

He held her face in his hands. "I will tell you true, Eluned, that there has been only one thing in you that has ever given me pause. It is no failing of yours, but my own vanity." He hesitated, and she saw resentment in the set of his mouth for the barest instant. "You stopped loving me, when we were parted. You put it away, like a deck of playing cards, when I could not. It is an easy thing to forgive, for we were so certain never to meet again, and now I can see that I should not have held on so tight to it for so long."

"You think…" She blinked at him. "You think I stopped loving you in truth, for all those years?" She shook her head. "I will love you until I die, Robin. I said that once, and meant it. It was as true then as it is true now."

But she could see he did not fully believe her, that he thought she spoke pretty words only to soothe him. Her hands covered his, where they rested at the sides of her face. She tried to conjure the words to make him understand, but knew there were none. "Cariad," she whispered, and pulled away from him.

The ivory box was on the mantel shelf, and the key was on a long ribbon in the purse that hung from her belt. She took it out, pausing a moment to stroke a finger over the silver button that hung with the key. How small and how important, these sentimental tokens of young love. She reached into the ivory box, then turned back and walked the few steps to where he stood. He had dreamed of this, he said – of loving her as they grew old together. How could he think she would not dream as far and as long as he?

She kissed him as she had used to do in a secret clearing, in a time and a place that was theirs alone. And just as he had done every time they met, she slipped the little stone into his palm. He raised his hand between them, looking at it in amazement, its rosy sheen undiminished by the years.

"It hurt too much to want you, when I knew I could not have you." She lifted his other hand and kissed his fingers. "But never did I stop loving you."

"You kept it," he breathed, still staring in wonder at the humble pink stone. "All those years, you kept it."

She waited for him to raise his eyes to hers again. "I knew I could not call you to me. But I wanted to, my Robin. I always wanted to."

They followed the ritual, begun when they were young and interrupted for too many years: their mouths joined, the stone passed between their hands, their clothes falling away as they reached for one another. He kissed her, made her all his own again, and she called up the best parts of herself to give to him in unreserved joy.

Epilogue

The Fair

There were many more expedient ways to get her out of bed than this, but he could not resist the rare chance to kiss her awake. She always rose up from the warmth of the bed like a flower out of the ground, unfolding herself to the sun.

"Cariad, you must rise," he said between kisses, with a laughable attempt at admonishment, because she seemed more interested in him than in waking. "Come, the day awaits and you will be loath to waste these morning hours."

"Waste?" She laughed, her head tilted back, the teardrop mark on her throat tempting him. Her hands stayed at his waist, smoothing over his skin, pushing up his tunic until she could lean forward and touch her mouth to the plane of his stomach.

"You were my first kiss, Robin," she murmured, "and the only man who has ever kissed me." Now she rested her chin on his belly and turned her sleepy gray eyes up to him. "I am owed eighteen full years of kisses. I mean to collect on my debt."

She returned to kissing his stomach, her fingers pulling at the ties of his braies. He could not quite find it in himself to push her away but before he lost all control of himself, he summoned up every ounce of gallantry he possessed to say, "Aye, and God help the man who withholds what is rightfully yours, but they are arriving today."

She pulled back, startled. "Today?"

He nodded. "They sent a rider ahead, who says they will be here by mid-morning."

She was already out of bed even before he had finished speaking, running to the door to call for her servant.

"I must dress, have you informed the kitchens? No, I should do it, I must tell them to put some of the goose fat aside, but has the wine arrived? Where is that girl Catrin, she knows she should await outside my door, and have you seen Nan this morning?"

He stopped the whirlwind of words and motion by putting his arms around her waist from behind while her hands were raised in the task of raking the tousled braid out of her hair. "Cariad," he said soothingly into her ear, and felt her go still under her hands. "The chamberlain greeted the messenger and even now prepares everything. The wine was delivered this morning. I sent Catrin to fetch Nan and some bread, and now I will have your promise that you won't forget to eat in all the excitement."

It was always the first task she forgot on any day where there was much to do. That described most days since they had come to Dinwen, and he did not doubt their future days would be even busier, as the castle Darian had only begun to be built. Even when his own day was so full that he could barely remember to breathe, he never forgot to eat. Therefore he had made it his private little concern that she was properly nourished, just as she was forever reminding him to wear thicker hose and boots, so often did he misjudge the cold.

"I will eat." Her hands covered his and gave them a gentle squeeze. She pulled away and turned to him, a smile bursting forth on her face. "They are coming," she said, and her chin lifted high in that way she'd had in her youth and that had been lost for so long – as though the world were hanging before her, and she would take a bite of it.

He would have kissed her again, but she was in motion already. Instead he went to see that enough of the new wine was brought up to the buttery, and opened a bottle of the finer vintage to sample. It was better than last year's attempt, and he was glad to have something so impressive to serve. He would be sure to send some bottles of this to Simon, with suggestions on how next year's batch might be even more improved. His brother would go to France in the spring, and was eager for as much instruction as Robert could give.

When the party arrived, he stood in the yard with Eluned to greet them. But when Eluned rushed forward, he stayed where he was and observed from a few paces away. So did the others. Only when she pushed back her hood did he realize it was a woman on horseback. She was uncommonly tall and broad, and she leapt from the mount without any assistance at all – more like a man than a woman. She only stood, looking down at her mother until Eluned embraced her.

Robert waited, not wanting to interrupt their reunion. When Eluned had determined that they could not leave to visit Morency until next summer,

Gwenllian had said she would not wait for another year to go by. She and her family were to stay here for the whole of the Christmas season, but he scanned the small number of riders with her and did not see Ranulf.

"You look well." Gwenllian's eyes were sweeping over Eluned's face. They were exactly like her mother's – wide and gray, framed by a thick fringe of long, black lashes. "You look so well."

"As do you." Though Robert could not see her face, he could hear that Eluned was near to tears. "But where are your children?"

"They come with their nurse, who is too slow for me, and my lord husband. Half an hour behind me, no more." Gwenllian wrapped her arms around her mother. "You look so *well*."

Robert turned to the chamberlain, who hovered at his elbow, and distracted himself with talk about the wine stores until he felt the two women approaching him and heard Eluned say, "My lord husband is curious to meet you."

Gwenllian was responding with something about how she too was curious because everyone but herself had already met him, when she broke off, looking at him. Robert found himself as arrested as she was when he met her gaze. She looked nothing like her mother except for her eyes, and at first glance he saw that the look in them was different in essence from Eluned. There were no shifting secrets or hidden depths there, no banked fire. Instead there was a kind of serenity and clarity, a centeredness that was disconcerting when it should not be. It matched the way she held herself and moved, with a balance and grace that was wholly unexpected in someone her size. She was frowning in confusion and then, as he watched, she recognized him.

"I remember you!" she gasped. She stared at him in wonder, her mouth slowly dropping open as she looked to her mother and then back him. "You danced -" She stopped herself from saying more, suddenly conscious, and dropped into a very brief and awkward courtesy that allowed her to drop her eyes.

He looked to Eluned, whose lips were pinched shut, her cheeks turning pink. He gave her the crooked smile that never failed to soften her, and she covered a startled laugh with a small cough followed by a query about the roads. Gwenllian looked at her in shock, and then back to him in unabated amazement.

They talked of the journey here and a wide variety of mutual acquaintances as they waited for the rest of the party to arrive. They spoke of William's plans to visit France next year, of a Welsh cousin named Davydd who lived at Morency and hoped to wed in the spring, and of Kit, with whom Ranulf had stayed on his journey from court last year and become great friends. Kit would come too, with his wife and other children, to pass the Christmas season.

At the mention of his friend, Robert looked around the yard in search of little Robin. He found the boy standing very near to Nan, whose virtual absolute silence Robin seemed to value greatly. The boy had grown shy during his time as a hostage, and had been so tongue-tied during Ranulf's stay in his household that he'd never said a word to the man, even in greeting. But Robin had confided that he wanted more than anything to see Ranulf of Morency's skill with a sword.

Robert said so to Gwenllian, who replied, "Nor do I doubt he will be glad to give the boys a show, and if it is done today when he is weary from travel, there is yet the chance that he might be bested."

"He is never bested," came the sudden response from Robin, who retreated a half-step behind Nan as though surprised by his own boldness.

"So do all men tell me," she answered mildly, then turned to the sound of her husband arriving.

Gwenllian reached up and took a child from the nurse's arms, while Ranulf lowered their older boy down from the saddle they shared. She brought them forward and said, "Henry, this is your grandmother."

The boy looked between Eluned and Gwenllian for an anxious moment before taking a breath and giving an almost lengthy speech in Welsh. Robert recognized some of it – *well-loved*, and *may God bless this household*, and *honor, memory* – and knew that the boy was not parroting words in a language unknown to him.

Eluned covered her mouth briefly, to stop the trembling of her lips, before she stooped down to the boy and put a hand on his shoulder. She spoke in Welsh, and Robert understood enough to know she said, "*Wales lives on in you, beloved.*"

Then she rose onto her toes to press a kiss to Gwenllian's cheek, and took the baby from her. Little Madog was beginning to cry, but Eluned soothed him easily and continued to speak to Henry in Welsh, telling him to follow her as she led him on a meandering path around the yard. In the meantime, Ranulf had seen Robin and began to draw him out. The boy had a look of hero-worship on his face, and Robert thought he might actually have begun to drool when Ranulf pulled his sword from his scabbard to show it.

Gwenllian stood next to Robert, watching her mother with her sons. Her expression was unreadable, but he thought she saw what he did when he looked at Eluned now – that she was quicker to smile, less impatient, and that she moved differently, as if all her muscles and joints had been loosened a little.

"She is teaching Henry all the words to do with horses which are different in the dialect she grew up speaking. How could she know how well he will love that?" Gwenllian wondered. She turned those disconcerting eyes to Robert for a long moment of assessment before returning her gaze to her mother. "My husband has said you love my mother very well."

Robert nodded. "In faith, he was surprised to know it. He was inclined to amazement that any man could love her." He watched her eyes flick to Ranulf, and sensed her tension. He grinned. "His amazement died when I asked him if he thought you could come from a woman any less remarkable than you are."

She had a serious air about her, so he knew the slight twitch at the corner of her lip was a rare and wonderful thing. "Haps that is why he has taken to saying that our sons will grow to be as fierce as lions, and we must guard against their pride. Their inheritance will be my ferocity and his arrogance."

He laughed and said low, "I have heard his arrogance was bested by your ferocity, despite what all men say."

She looked sharply at him, and he knew she had not expected that Eluned had told him about her studies with the sword. Gwenllian looked at him a long time, her brow slightly furrowed. Her thoughtful frown created the same pattern of lines across her forehead as Eluned's.

"She trusts you." She seemed hardly to believe it. "She loves you, then. With all her heart."

"It is as much a marvel to me as it is to you," he assured her.

He looked to Eluned, whose smile was so wide that the dimple had appeared in her cheek. He had forgotten many things over the years, and remembered other things wrong, but it seemed to him that it little mattered anymore. Now he lived for today and tomorrow, not yesterday. And so did Eluned.

THE END

✠

Author's Note

Readers unfamiliar with 13th century England can be assured that the author researched like mad and yet certainly still managed to get a lot wrong. Here are a few things you might not have known:

One perhaps surprising fact about the time is that hostage-taking (including of young children) was an extremely common custom that was well-entrenched for hundreds of years. It was not considered cruel or a punishment; it was simply a transaction.

Less surprisingly, the prevalence of rich speculators grabbing up the estates of those indebted to moneylenders is not at all a modern phenomenon and, in fact, the Statute of the Jewry (1275) came about in part because it had become such a problem. The statute was a response to the increasing virulence of anti-Semitism (which is not at all either a modern *or* outdated phenomenon, but seems to be depressingly timeless) which eventually led to the expulsion of all Jews from England in 1290.

Dafydd really was the first English noble to be hanged, drawn, and quartered, and it really did appall people. Nevertheless it became the standard punishment for treason in England.

The Statute of Rhuddlan was promulgated in March 1284, and created four new Marcher lordships out of the conquered Welsh territory. Robert's lordship of Darian is a fictional invention of a fifth lordship.

Roger Mortimer became the first Baron of Chirk and had a long and storied life which ended in the Tower of London, where he was imprisoned for revolting against King Edward II.

Isabella Mortimer married Robert de Hastang in 1285. Failing to find any other advantage for her in the marriage, and noting that the historical record shows it was done without the king's permission, the author has chosen to believe it was love.

Readers may be interested to know that Ranulf and Gwenllian's story is the subject of *The King's Man*.

For more information and to sign up for the Elizabeth Kingston mailing list, please visit
ElizabethKingstonBooks.com

Acknowledgements

As ever, Susanna Malcolm is the best beta-reader, editor, writing buddy, and DFF a girl could ever ask for, and none of this would be possible without her all-around magnificence. Instrumental to my understanding of and fascination with medieval England and Wales are the following fantastic resources: Sharon Kay Penman's Welsh Princes trilogy, Mark Morris' *A Great and Terrible King*, virtually everything Frances and Joseph Gies ever wrote, and all of Medievalists.net. Thanks also to the incomparable Amanda Dewees for the help and cheerleading, Dr. Dawn Zapinski for the psych consult, Charles R. Rutledge for the murder advice, Laura Kinsale for the usual stellar friendship and fairy godmothership, and my friends and fellow regulars at Just Write Chicago for their support.

66986508R00184

Made in the USA
Charleston, SC
01 February 2017